That Was Then

That Was Then

a novel

MICHAEL QUADLAND

RED HEN PRESS | Los Angeles, California

That Was Then
Copyright © 2008 by Michael Quadland

Cover design: Mark E. Cull
Cover photo by Michael Quadland
Book design: Richard O. Niño

ISBN: 978-1-59709-088-9
Library of Congress Catalog Card Number: 2007926586

The City of Los Angeles Department of Cultural Affairs, Los Angeles County Arts Commission, California Arts Council and the National Endowement for the Arts partially support Red Hen Press.

Published by Red Hen Press
www.redhen.org

First Edition

I am especially grateful to Lynette Brasfield,
also to Joseph Montebello and to Eric Meyers.

In Memory of My Father

. . . the companions of our childhood always possess a certain power over our minds which hardly any later friend can obtain.
—Mary Shelley, *Frankenstein*

Chapter One
1985

I sleep hunched on my stomach, fists to my chest like I'm about to be hit. Gina sleeps looking up at the world, facing it. Incompatibility or a perfect match, it's hard to say.

We met the year our fathers—both confirmed Democrats—became partners in a Ford dealership in western Massachusetts. It was also the year John Kennedy was shot. You could say that our relationship was born in that mix of real optimism and enormous disappointment, as if we'd been branded by the events around us, imprinted with feelings we could never quite shed, or even understand. We went to movies and dances that fall of 1963, pals with nothing better to do. Then, one thing led to another, as it can for teenagers, though no one would ever have accused Gina of lacking direction. Her attraction to me was more likely part of a general instinct for rebellion. Tall, determined, attractive, she could have had any number of boys at Williston High School. We grabbed onto one another, two marooned tourists in the land of early adolescence, until, three years later, Gina suddenly let go.

Deserted, I grew my hair and went off to become a geek at Yale, where hiding in a library carrel was acceptable if not admired behavior. After that, I made my way to New York University to study psychology. Books and papers were always right there where you left them the day before.

Twenty years later, remarkably, Gina and I run into one another just four blocks north of Washington Square Park, where elegant, 1920s apartment buildings line Fifth Avenue and uniformed doormen stand like sentries outside their marble entrances. New York's First Presbyterian Church, smaller in scale and surrounded by flowering shrubs, graces the corner of Eleventh Street, where Gina stands, waiting to cross. Her impatient, splayed-leg stance is utterly familiar from ninth grade, as if the rush of traffic down Fifth Avenue were a challenge set deliberately and specifically for her.

Or maybe it isn't so remarkable, our meeting this afternoon. We both live south of Fourteenth Street in Manhattan, which is not as big a place as people think. In fact, I have imagined just such an encounter plenty of times, having heard regular updates about Gina from my parents—her successful acting career, her marriage and divorce, twice. Still, actually seeing her sends a fearful tingle up my spine, and I start to turn away. But that feels silly, and cowardly, and so I continue down Fifth Avenue, smack into the distressing yet exhilarating pull she's always had on me.

"Corey, Corey Moore," she says, a statement, not a question.

A passing taxi douses the sidewalk between us. Strands of hair cling to Gina's rain-soaked cheeks; her eyes betray a fleeting moment of insecurity, I think, or maybe hope. I have an umbrella, she doesn't, which says a lot. She smiles and steps next to me, and we begin talking as if we can just pick up where we left off so long ago. I walk her to her apartment at Ninth Street and First Avenue, while she tells me how she's been attempting to steer her career toward directing and is currently assisting in an Off-Broadway production of Our Town. She's still poised and confident, but seasoned now, the attractive woman she'd been destined to become.

Neither of us mentions what drove us apart twenty years ago.

"Would you like to see the play this evening?" she asks me in front of her building, a walk-up with a beveled glass door and an array of drenched Chinese take-out menus strewn across the stoop.

Being with her feels like slipping into a favorite old jacket. Her ambition, her courage and colossal resilience, her slightly breathless demeanor, are dollar bills unearthed in the frayed lining of a pocket. She says she's intrigued by my choice of psychology as a career, wondering, I suppose, if I took up the profession in order to figure myself out. A lot of people think that about psychologists. There are worse motivations.

Her hand feels small and cool. "Tonight, then," I say.

We spend most evenings together after that, and she invites me into her world of rehearsals, opening nights and after-theater parties. Four months later we get married at City Hall, the way a body in interrupted motion tends to regain its initial momentum. That sounds flippant, and my decision to marry Gina is anything but that. I'm thirty-four years old, a loner lured a second time by feelings I've never been able to decipher. I label them love, though more than anything, what I feel, marrying Gina, is gratitude.

But why does she want to marry me? Her life is filled with the passion that has ruled her since childhood—the theater. Even now, she doesn't seem to need people, much less a mate. But that's only the part of Gina that shows. Underneath lie the fears and longings only I know about, from when we were thirteen. This quirky Gina isn't as confident as she appears. She has a conventional side, not unlike those of the women she disdains. She is forever questioning whether she should have kids, though outwardly, she scorns parenthood as selfish and wasteful of the world's resources. Her blithe spirit belies a penchant to worry about money, about how people see her, about whether her mark on the world will be indelible or guaranteed-to-bleed.

Though she would never admit it, marriage for Gina is a hedge, in case the road less traveled leads nowhere. I'm the insurance policy not offered by Actor's Equity. Do I mind? Not really. At thirty-four, I am beyond illusions, or so I like to think.

We move into a larger apartment on West Sixteenth Street in Chelsea, advance professionally over the next three years, buy a Volvo and visit friends in the Hamptons. Sex is good, as it was when we were teenagers. Couples who can't quite reach one another verbally find other ways. What I never realized was how fragile sex is; how it can't carry the weight of a relationship. It's like asking a two-by-four to do the work of a joist. It buckles. Maybe not right away, but eventually. The frequency of our love-making begins to dwindle after a while, and I can feel myself slowly steeling against Gina. I dread the smug partnerships of convenience and habit that I observe in some of our friends, cogs in a wheel that, fast as it might spin, isn't really going anywhere.

Three years into our marriage, I get the idea to buy a house. It's ironic that I want to work on something physical when it's my bewildering feelings that need attention. So much for psychologists figuring themselves out!

"Why not East Hampton?" Gina asks when I mention rural Connecticut.

"I want a home, not a scene."

"But that's where our friends are."

"Your friends."

"Yours, too. What about Jim, and Robert?"

Among our men friends, Jim and Robert are my favorites. Jim is married to a successful Broadway dancer and is the stay-at-home dad to their two boys. Robert, an actor, is gay and suffers a series of lovers, none of whom ever last more than a few weeks. Gina sometimes jokes that I have a crush on Robert. At dinner parties in East Hampton, he and I occasionally stay up talking long after the others have gone to bed. Sometimes we drive to the beach and walk along the high-tide line until the horizon turns pale. We never touch, not even the occasional hug that is common among men in our group.

"I need a project," I tell Gina one bitter cold Saturday, as we drive out of the city into northern Fairfield County. "I want to get my hands dirty."

"You're always searching," she says. "Why can't you just settle down and focus?"

"Like you?"

"Well, if you put it that way, yes. I have my career, and I have you. That's plenty for me."

We spend the afternoon jumping in and out of a real estate agent's bulbous SUV. "You can't just shake your head," Gina whines when we pull up to some sad aluminum-sided ranch, a skeletal ficus tree on the front step.

"It's not what I want."

"You haven't even seen inside."

"I can tell."

"Now, all of a sudden, you know."

She's right—it isn't like me to be so clear about something. Yet I know one old farmhouse is right the minute we turn into its rutted driveway—the dignified lines, the graceful red barn, the frozen pond with its rushing spillway.

"Men are like that," the agent says, winking at Gina. "Not like us women who have to look in the cupboards and count the closets."

The agent's comment irritates Gina. She is definitely not the closet-counting type. Her hair has come loose, and the Hermés scarf I gave her hangs off her shoulder and smells of the coffee she spilled on it this morning. I have the urge to console her, but hold back, afraid I might surrender my vulnerable house plan to the comfort of her good will. Hell, it's a risk for me too, blowing most of my savings on a down-payment. For some time, I've felt guilty, wondering if whatever is missing from our relationship is missing in me. I hope that Gina and I, as if adopting some forsaken child, can nurture this place back to life and shore up our own sagging connection in the process.

We haul and hammer and clean every weekend that spring, and the house begins to regain some of the proud features it had lost to neglect. We have the cedar clapboards scraped and the old window panes re-glazed. Inside, we plaster and paint, wax the wide-board floors and grout the fireplace stones. I can't wait to arrive here on Thursday nights, reviewing my mental list of tasks as we unload the Volvo, inhaling the closed-in smell of the house as we step inside.

Then one June weekend, Gina brings an acting friend from New York to the house. During our three years together, I have met most of Gina's friends from the theater, but I have only heard about Jack, and I suspect she has kept him under wraps because he is so important to her. Gina has always held the things she values most closest to her chest, as if in sharing them, she risks losing them. I read this departure as a deepening of trust in our relationship, and of course I'm eager to meet this man Gina holds so dear.

Jack's defiant blue eyes reveal a lost quality that tugs at me right from the start—some sort of reflection of myself, no doubt. His body is strong, yet adolescent, as if he still plays sand-lot football. There's a stern set to his mouth, at odds with a face younger than its thirty or so years.

I regard my own body that first evening, reflected in the kitchen window. Fairer than Jack, I see my mother's thin torso and unruly blond-ish hair. I want to believe that my eyes, like hers, are alert to the re-deeming qualities in people. But more likely, they reveal a propensity for distrust. I know that I've always tended to occupy a space slightly outside my body, regarding myself with critical side glances. And there's a nervous quality to the way I move, not fluid or graceful like Jack.

He comes several weekends that June, until working without him alongside feels unnatural. I watch him as we cut brush or rebuild a collapsed stone wall, and I wonder what makes him so aloof. Is he brooding or simply quiet? He comes alive, though, when he and Gina argue about acting.

"The business is for shit," he says one evening after dinner, while I sponge off the counters. "It's all about who you know or who you sleep with."

"Real talent gets recognized, eventually," Gina insists. Hers had. Her directing career fizzled, but she still lands substantial roles Off-Broadway, and the occasional part in a film, which takes her off to Toronto or some other city for a couple of months at a time. Yet, like most successful people in the theater, she believes she is only as good as her last performance, and she never knows for sure if or when her next gig will materialize.

"You're saying I don't have that?" Jack asks her.

"Just the opposite." Gina gets up and runs water into the kettle. "You have a great gift. It's just that the right people haven't seen it, yet. Don't give up is all I'm saying." She takes tea bags from the cupboard and sets out three mugs. The idea of giving up is a foreign concept to Gina, even in a friend.

"When, then? When do you say you've had enough rejection? Enough bullshit?"

"You're so angry, Jack. Maybe it comes through. Maybe people are put off."

Another thing about Gina—she's an ace at diagnosing other people's problems, and like the rest of us, I suppose, far less perceptive about herself. She won't admit to weakness, particularly if it means she has to let up in any way.

"Cookies, anyone?" I say, opening a pack of Pepperidge Farm Milanos. I admire the way Jack and Gina can argue vociferously one minute and hug the next, something Gina and I have never been able to do. In fact, there has never been a whole lot of arguing or hugging between us. Sometimes it seems that Gina flaunts her closeness to Jack, that she wants to make me jealous or at least wants to demonstrate what she's capable of in the intimacy department. But that may all be in my head.

"Who?" Jack asks Gina. "Has anyone said they were put off?"

"I'm just guessing it might come across in auditions. You need to apply the anger—inside. Make it work for you."

Something I don't trust about actors is this casual use of the anger or sadness of their real lives to bolster their craft. On occasion, when Gina and I do fight, or even when we make love, I wonder if she might be storing emotions she can use later on the stage, where they really count.

"Maybe you're just more willing than I am," Jack says. "You'll do whatever you have to, right? The rejections don't seem to get to you."

"You're bitter, Jack."

"How could he not be?" I put in. "Maybe some people just aren't cut out for it. They're too sensitive." I bite into a cookie and brush crumbs from my lap.

Gina shrugs and looks away. Jack's expression suggests he doesn't like the insinuation that he's weak, which isn't at all what I mean. I often feel awkward and inarticulate around him in a way I don't with other friends. I can see why he's so important to Gina. There's something compelling about him—formidable yet gentle, with plenty of mystery thrown in. The truth is, I feel more in sync with Jack's argument than with Gina's.

I love our routine these summer Saturdays, the three of us stumbling sleepily out the back door into the dawn chill, coffee in hand. Mist curls off the pond. The barn door creaks on its ancient strap hinges. Inside, the scent of old hay vies for prominence with a whiff of parched dirt floor. All day, we mend and refurbish and touch up, lunching in the shade of the oaks by the barn—for me, an unprecedented, reliable bliss. Afterward, we swim naked in the pond as the sun begins its brilliant withdrawal. I notice that Jack's back is a long perfect V, from his shoulders to his waist. The same with his thighs and calves, his biceps and forearms, an accord of V's descending into one another, elegant and simple as dovetail joints.

One Saturday afternoon, he returns from a trip to the hardware store in the old pickup that, to our mutual delight, I had bought at a farm auction two weeks before. In the back sits a fifty-pound bag of wild-flower seed. He calls me over, grinning, pointing to the huge burlap sack.

"Jesus, Jack, this must have cost you a fortune," I say, examining the label.

He shrugs, proud, yet tentative as a boy harboring a stray dog. "I thought that field beyond the pond would be a good place. The blossoms would get reflected in the surface of the water next spring." He hoists the bag onto his shoulder. "You don't have to prepare the soil or anything. We can just spread it."

I follow him into the field, where he drops the bag and yanks it open. A dusty, clean odor rises between us. Jack plunges his hand into the seed, raises it to his face and blows on it. He grins. I take a handful and fling it, like sparkling shards of glass, into the waning sun. A breeze sprinkles it back across my shirt. Jack chuckles and brushes it away. "Maybe we should try working upwind," he says. Like medieval farmers, we traverse the field, tossing handfuls of the feathery seed in graceful arcs and watching it ride the wind to the ground. I wonder if Jack will come around in the spring to see the colorful fruits of our labor.

Then something happens that tarnishes the glow of that blissful time, one of those rare dizzying moments when reality shifts, and try as you might, you can't get back to where you'd just been, minutes before.

Gina joins us from the house, running at her usual breakneck pace. She's had a call from the city about an audition she thought would be perfect for Jack. I leave them there in the newly-seeded field, pick up the empty burlap sack, and drop it off in the barn. After putting some tools away, I circle back up to the house, where I wash up at the kitchen sink and pull a chicken out of the refrigerator for dinner. Then I remember there are a couple of bottles of Chardonnay that Gina and I stored in the cellar when we bought the place back in February. I'm down there, wiping dust off the bottles, when I hear Gina and Jack enter the kitchen directly above my head. They're laughing. "That was such a crazy time," I think I hear Jack say, and then I can't make out Gina's response. As I step toward the stairs, I hear the clang of the roasting pan being set in the oven and the bang of the oven door closing. "Does Corey know?" I hear Jack ask. Again, I can't hear Gina's response "I suppose you're right," Jack says. Their tone, if you can read tone without much content, is conspiratorial, maybe even flirtatious.

Then I hear Jack step across the kitchen floor and into the ell. The whole incident is over in less than a minute.

A painful constriction invades my chest as I stand at the foot of the cellar stairs. I turn to the dim, musty space behind me, taking in the outcropping of ledge that comprises half the foundation and probably accounts for why the house has remained so square all these years. Suddenly, my foundation with Gina feels far less solid. Are she and Jack withholding something from me? The bottles of wine in each hand sink to my sides, my celebratory mood replaced by a gnawing dread as I climb the stairs to the kitchen. Gina sits at the table, going through the mail. I set the wine on the counter. "I'm going to change," I say, turning to the stairs to our room.

Weeks pass, and our cheerful, productive weekends help me put the incident out of my mind. With time, what I overheard becomes less clear—barely audible fragments of a playful conversation, probably nothing more. I even wonder if I manufactured the whole episode in some anhedonic impulse to dilute the joy of our time together.

On a Saturday evening late in July, the three of us eat supper outside, our conversation drowned out by a cacophony of tree frogs in the oaks around the barn. Shooting stars breach the horizon, pause and vanish, leaving us to wonder at our own insignificance. My hare-brained scheme has worked. The property is taking on the renewed life I'd envisioned for it. More important, I have acquired the focus I had sought for so long, and it isn't cerebral for a change, it's physical. And I have a new friend. Gina seems happier, too.

Jack turns in early, and Gina and I linger at the pond, finishing the wine from dinner. "I don't know how to tell you this," she starts. "Jim, the director. . . . We. . . ."

A tremor grips my shoulders and runs down my arms, disturbing the wine in my glass. I notice a trout, or maybe it's a box turtle, stir beneath the surface of the pond, spreading murmuring ripples to the shoreline in front of us. The leaning barn seems to shift precariously, and the sky grow darker. Is this what I had overheard Gina and Jack talking about weeks ago? Should I have perceived some telltale signs of withdrawal in Gina? She's wanted to return to the city early the last several Sundays. Our sex is infrequent, but it has been for the last year.

How foolish I've been to think that our life here at the house would be enough for her. Or perhaps it was too much, too cozy, too—I don't know—tender. I know Gina loves me, but I also know she has never really been committed to anything other than her career.

She starts to explain. "When you spend this much time together. . . . I never intended. . . ."

"Spare me the rationalizations, okay?"

Gina pulls a blade of grass from the ground beside her chair and twists it around her finger. "You're different, since we bought this place," she says.

"So this director is my fault?" She winds and unwinds the narrow stalk until a dark green bruise begins to bleed toward its center vein. "I like my life more right now than I have since I can remember, Gina. I'm not sure I want to change anything."

"That doesn't leave much room for discussion, does it?"

"What am I supposed to say? You're the one who. . . ." I flick the last of my wine into the shallows at the edge of the pond and get up from my chair. "Just let me know what you decide, okay?"

I feel her eyes on my back as I make my way to the house, thinking she's probably measuring me against this director, an unfair comparison, given that she's known me since I was thirteen and he's fresh off the lot.

The light is on in Jack's room in the ell. Has he known about the affair? I envy Jack his simple life, one day of hard physical work following the last, reading at night, writing the occasional letter that he walks down to the mailbox at the end of the driveway. Jack Krakouski. Can I trust him?

In the kitchen, I set my empty glass in the sink and head upstairs. Gina comes in later, slips into her side of the bed and turns her back to me. It takes me a good while to fall asleep.

The next morning, I help her load her things into the Volvo. For three years, the idea that she might leave me, the way she did when we were sixteen, has occupied a dark, remote fissure of my consciousness. Our lack of passion makes us vulnerable, and closeness binds Gina like a pair of expensive shoes she couldn't resist though they're a size too small. She can't quite squeeze into them and yet she can't get herself to throw them out either. Still, I suspect, as I lower her suitcase into the trunk, that she isn't leaving for good. More likely she'll return to me after a while, guilty and solicitous until all is forgotten. I watch her ease the Volvo away from the barn and down the driveway, watch the glow of brake lights as she pauses before pulling onto the highway.

Jack has coffee ready when I come into the kitchen. He pours two cups and sets one on the counter next to me. "That looked serious," he says, sitting at the table and pulling on his work boots. He bends over to lace them, his tee shirt rising out of his jeans in back. "I didn't get my usual goodbye hug."

My hand jostles the coffee as I lift my cup. "We're going to take a little break, Gina and me."

"Jesus," he says, sitting up. "What happened?"

"I'm not sure. She met some director." It occurs to me that Jack might even know the guy. "Things have been tense between us for a while, as you probably know. I was hoping, maybe, working on this house together. . . ."

Jack sits back into the wooden slats of the chair. "Are you okay?"

"Did you know about this, Jack?"

"No, I didn't." He holds my eyes. I remind myself that Jack is an actor, too. And yet, I believe him. "How much has Gina told you about us?" I ask him.

"I know she relies on you—emotionally, I mean."

"So, I'm good for something."

Jack runs his finger up and down the side of his cup. "I'm sure Gina loves you. She just . . . She eats and breathes theater. There's maybe not the room for other stuff that most people have."

By stuff, presumably, Jack means marriage. He's right. Gina juggles commitments like a circus performer, but it's all illusion. There's really only one torch in the air—acting, and she never takes her eye off it. "You weren't like that," I say, though what do I know, really? It's just a sense I have that Jack wouldn't let his work come first.

"Which is probably why she gets work and I don't."

I think I hear a car door slam—Gina coming back. I step to the window, but it's nothing.

"Is there anything I can do?" Jack asks.

A tightness rises in my throat. The only person I have relied on for the last twenty years is myself. I have no idea what to ask for now. What could I need from Jack? "I don't think so," I say. "But thanks for asking."

He stands and lifts his denim jacket off the clothes rack. "I thought I would re-hang that loft door in the barn so it closes tight," he says. "The rain's going to rot the floor up there." He slaps on his New York Yankees cap and reaches for the door, then turns back and leans against the wall. "I was thinking I might like to stay on," he says.

Something gives way inside me, some tautness. I feel dizzy without it, as if that tension has been holding me upright.

"Sorry," he says, pushing his cap back. "This is probably not a good time."

"No, it's okay."

"It's just. . . . My acting career is pretty stalled, or maybe over for good. I'm not sure. I was thinking I could help you here, while I figure out what to do next. That is, if you want me to."

I look down at my scuffed boots. They're the same as Jack's. We bought them together at Kmart two months ago. "Do you have any ideas about that?" I ask, looking back up at him. "What you might do next?"

"Ideas or dreams?"

"I don't know, either."

"I guess I always dreamed I would be an actor. It's the only thing I was really good at—taking on another identity, being someone else. I loved that. I never cared much for who I was, myself, you know? Acting let me change all that, at least temporarily. I never thought I'd be a movie star or anything." He shifts his jacket from one hand to the other. "Maybe a good solid stage actor. Someone theater regulars recognize. The actor other actors respect. And then maybe I would teach after a while, at some college. Be some venerable old stage rat." He chuckles, suddenly embarrassed, as if he has revealed too much. "I don't think I ever told anybody that." Jack is less guarded without Gina around. "How about you?" he asks.

"Me? I don't know. I always thought I'd be some hot-shot New York shrink with a teaching appointment at Columbia, a lucrative practice and a long list of publications." Like Jack, I'm a little unrehearsed when it comes to goals, and this one sounds uninspired. "I don't think I ever really considered what I wanted to do. Not in the sense of a whole world of opportunity out there, not in the sense of real choices. I always did well in school, and then I did what everybody expected—became a professional, made a respectable living."

Jack has a concerned expression when he listens—a creased tightening around the eyes, a slight frown of concentration. I'm so used to Gina's half-attention whenever I talk about my work. "I played the piano when I was a kid. For a while, in high school, I thought I might have a concert career. But that didn't work out." I pause, thinking how long it's been since Gina and I talked about our dreams. Since we were teenagers— that other life we'd had back in Williston.

Jack waits for me to go on.

"You know what I would really like to do?" I say, setting my empty coffee cup on the counter. "Buy old houses like this one and restore them. The old relics you see falling down on themselves around here. I'd buy them all and give them a new life."

Jack grins.

"What? You don't think I could do it?"

"I know you could. I was just thinking how neither of us is doing what he wants. It doesn't make much sense, does it?"

I'm happier with Jack's offer to stay on here than seems warranted, as if someone has extended a hand to me just as I'm about to slip over the edge. "Sure, you can stay if you want," I say. "There's plenty to keep us busy, right?" A tepid response, considering the urgency I feel, but I'm weeks away from being able to really talk to Jack, or even to know what I need to say.

For some reason, the first weekend Jack visited, back in June, comes to mind as we stand there, waiting to start our day. I'd been rummaging through a stack of dusty beams in the barn, looking for a good eight-by-ten to replace a rotted portion of sill under the kitchen. He'd been out walking, heard me banging around in there and appeared at the far end of a warped beam, which he helped me throw out of the way. Without saying anything to each other, we threw one beam after another aside until we found a sound one, which Jack helped me carry up to the house. It's hard to describe what I felt then—being understood without having to explain myself, the sort of connection that makes words, which I had always considered essential, unnecessary.

"Are you sure I wouldn't be in the way?" Jack says now. "I have enough money to stake me. I wouldn't be a burden that way."

"I'm sure."

He reaches out and shakes my hand, locking those amazing blue eyes onto mine once more. "Great," he says. We have a deal, apparently. But he just stands there, as if there's something more. "You know I'm gay, right?"

I feel that same dizziness from before. "I guess I knew that. Yeah."

"Is that cool with you?"

"Of course. Why wouldn't it be?" I turn to the sink and run water into my empty cup.

"I just want everything to be out in the open. No surprises."

"We're friends, right? What difference should it make whether you're gay or not?"

"Good," Jack says. "I'll go get started on the loft." He hunches into his jacket. "I really am sorry about Gina, Corey. But if I know her, she'll be back. She's not one to give up easily."

Then it seems we stand for an instant too long, just looking at each other. Is it really okay that Jack is gay and we'll be living here, just the two of us? "Are you hungry?" I ask him, turning away and opening the refrigerator door.

"I'm always hungry."

I close the door, empty-handed. "Do you want to go into town and grab some breakfast?"

"I'll get my wallet," he says, heading into the ell. "I see a stack of pancakes, dripping with real maple syrup."

Waiting for Jack, I stare out the kitchen window to the barn and the field beyond the pond where we tossed the wildflower seed. I wonder what Gina will think about Jack staying on. This is her house, too. But she's left it, and she's seeing some guy.

I think I can decide this one myself.

Chapter Two
1961

The first day of seventh grade, I was alone, back from the boy's room, where I'd been checking my lip for signs of a five-o'clock shadow. Younger than most seventh graders—not quite twelve—I was massively impatient for the growth spurt of my confidently hirsute classmates. And that's understating it. The sprouting of my first pubic hairs concerned me as much as poverty and discrimination concerned my mother and quarterly sales figures plagued my father. Puberty, just the sound of it, pubescence, so inviting, so mysterious, so intimidating. And once your hormones plunged you in, once your voice cracked and your nipples darkened, once you put that razor to your chin, forget it. There would be no turning back, no being the wimpy, forgivable brat you'd always been before.

I was about to pull open the door to Miss Mason's classroom, the curved bronze handle a solid, cool question mark in my hand, when the sudden clack of a man's heels made me turn. A tall frame approached, reflected in one long sun-drenched squiggle of polished floor tiles. He was over six feet, gray flannel pants, white shirt, madras tie, penny loafers, the overall impression a little stiff even for 1961. He'd clearly acquired his secondary sexual characteristics years ago, maybe even before I was born, and never gave them a second thought now. Pushing back hair the color of sand, he grinned—one sided, conspiratorial—as if we shared some outrageous secret I would understand, if only I were cooler.

Then he thrust his hand out to me. "I'm Mr. Dean," he said, his voice—deep, of course—ricocheting around the empty hallway.

He was the new music teacher. Just that morning, I'd heard some girls giggling about how cute he was. "Corey Moore," I said, gripping his hand hard the way my father had taught me.

"Neat name."

"My mother's idea. The Corey part. Wouldn't have been my choice."

"A lot of things aren't up to us in life." He smiled, apparently satisfied with the comment. Probably majored in philosophy in college. Then he turned, his blond stubble catching the light. "They just happen."

The whole idea of fate was a tough one for me. Were you supposed to accept things as they were, because that was your fate, or try to change them, because that was your fate? My mother believed just about anything in life could be changed, particularly anything unfair. In fact, she believed it was our responsibility, as members of a free society, to amend the status quo when it needed it. But she'd never suggested I could change my name if I wanted to.

"What grade are you in, Corey?"

"Seventh. Miss Mason's." I gestured toward her door.

"I'll be teaching music. How are you in music?"

"I play piano."

"Really? That's great! You'll have to play for me sometime."

There was something "unteacherly" about Mr. Dean. But for the gray flannels and the tie, he might have been a sophomore in high school. I looked down at my sneakers, which pointed slightly inward. My jeans were new and too long. I was self-conscious of just about everything then, my clothes, my random thoughts, most of all, my body. My voice had the range of a mezzo and my dick spent a good half the day throbbing painfully against my stomach. Everybody my age wanted to change, but no one seemed to know what to do with the new person they were becoming.

"I'll send for you, Corey."

I managed a stiff smile.

His fingers pulled at his chin, as if he were trying to figure something out. His watchband caught the rebounding light from the windows at the end of the hallway and made a silver slash across his throat. I reached for Miss Mason's door.

For the rest of class, I couldn't concentrate, thinking about Mr. Dean and our peculiar encounter in the hallway. He was strange, but I liked him. Or maybe I liked the sense that he liked me. Talking with him, watching his nervous flitting eyes, I had felt as if the safety net I'd always taken for granted—my parents, my teachers, that tidy little New England town—was being cut. The crazy thing was that I pictured myself standing right there alongside Mr. Dean, smiling as we sliced through the ropes.

The following afternoon, he sent for me.

The music room was all angles of dusty yellow light from a high wall of windows along one side. Rain-stained shades, like ancient parchment maps, hung at odd levels, their cords knotted and jammed. Rows of folding chairs and music stands were set around a grand piano, its blackness swallowing the light. The door closed behind me with an efficient click.

"You're looking chipper," he said, resting his hand on my shoulder as he led me to the piano.

Chipper? Had I actually found someone less cool than myself? I slid onto the piano bench. A damp heaviness lingered on my shoulder where his hand had been. I'd been pleased when he sent for me, but there in his presence, I felt as if I could actually slip between the piano's taut strings, through the paper-thin soundboard and into its coffin-like interior.

"What key has four sharps?" he asked me, standing at the windows.

"E major."

"Or?"

"D sharp minor."

"Four flats?"

"A flat major, or F minor."

"The relative major of C minor?"

"E flat."

"The dominant of A?"

"E."

"Good," he said. "Now, play me something." That grin again, that private wordless message I needed to decipher.

My right thumb suspended over the E above Middle C, the middle finger of my left hand over the G below, I had the sense that something amazing was about to happen, like during the hush before the curtain goes up at an opera, only more so. You may think this is just hindsight—one hundred percent—but it's true.

"Go ahead, Corey."

My fingers dropped and the broken chords of the first Bach prelude filled the room, modulating from major to minor, deceptively simple. Like Mr. Dean maybe, who had pulled me out of class just to play for him. I'd been taking piano lessons since I was five. For as long as I could remember, I loved the sound of those felt hammers striking the strings, reverberating around inside the case like some crazed animal trying to escape. I used to lie on the floor in front or my parents' stereo, listening to Rubenstein, Van Cliburn, even Liberace, who was amazing at the keyboard, despite being a flaming homo.

I knew that the trick with this prelude was to give each note exactly the same emphasis so that the listener is lulled by the monotony of the melody, drawn in by it. But I also knew that the skilled player actually does give certain notes a barely perceptible stress, an accent by way of a slight hesitation, which deceives the listener, seduces him, you could say. That's the way I played it for Mr. Dean, my eyes shifting from the keys to the windows and the slate roofs of the Victorian houses lined up across South Street.

Mr. Dean circled the piano as I played, running his hand along the bent side and up over the lid. After several revolutions, he stopped behind me. His fingers, with their scant spicy smell of soap, settled against my neck. I jumped.

"That's okay, Corey," he said. "Don't be nervous. You play very well."

Playing was the least of my worries right then. I was weeks away from decoding the message in his grin, yet some sort of danger seemed to float aboard those millions of dusty specks that flashed in and out of the music room's tall angles of sunlight. I might have twisted away, thanked him and left. He wouldn't have stopped me. He never forced me to do anything, the whole time I knew him. But I didn't want him to think I was afraid, or that I didn't like him touching me that way. Because I did.

He sat onto the bench. "No, stay," he said, taking my arm as I moved to get up.

He played the same prelude, his fingers obscuring the ivory keys and traveling easily among the ebonies. Those hands were dizzying to me, the blond hair spilling from under his shirtsleeves, the man-ness of them. Mr. Dean was how I wanted to be someday.

"This is where you got into trouble," he said, as he repeated a passage where I had run out of fingers. "Why don't you try one and three here, then two on the F sharp and you're home free."

"Right," I said. "Thanks." I jumped up.

"Come here," he said, grabbing the top of my jeans and pulling me against the bench. "I think we're going to be a team, you and me. What do you think?"

His fingers made a hot impression against my stomach. Outside the windows, chickadees darted nervously among brittle yellow leaves. "Good," I said.

In the months that followed, he smiled at me in assembly, mussed my hair with one of those remarkable hands as he passed me in the hall, or winked as I stepped off the school bus. I played piano for the school orchestra he started, and practiced on the Steinway after school. One October day, he drove me home after rehearsal, a slow, roundabout route on the hilly, leaf-strewn back roads of Williston.

"You're doing well with that Mozart," he said. "It's almost there, I think."

"Thanks. It needs more work, though."

"You're a perfectionist. I like that."

Our talk those first weeks was cropped by the tension I felt when I was alone with him, a sense of dread accompanying excitement, like climbing higher and higher into a tree.

His old Plymouth idled a while in our driveway before I pushed open my door. Moving away from him was like breaking out of some luminous elastic bubble we shared. I slid off the seat and pushed the door closed. His car turned with a throaty rumble of exhaust and disappeared back onto the road to town.

In the kitchen, my mother leaned over the sink, holding back the curtain. "Isn't that the new music teacher, Mr . . . ."

"Dean," I said, pulling off my jacket and heading for the stairs.

My mother was not your standard 1960s mom. She didn't wear the high heels other women in Williston still wore every day, or dresses that tapered to the waist and billowed out over nylon-enhanced calves. Tall and square-shouldered, with ample breasts, she wore caftans, "muumuus," she called them. And sometimes no bra. At home, she wrapped her hair in a towel after showering and worked at her desk until the towel gave way and her hair tumbled around her face without destroying her concentration. One day she might be a bright, obvious blond, another a ruthlessly cropped red-head with eyebrows to match. Her jewelry was large and colorful, not the heirloom variety that women in that town favored back then.

She had been the oldest of six children. One of the first family stories I ever heard was how her mother had died at the age of forty, carrying number seven. My mother had been denied college, forced to take a job and help raise her five younger brothers and sisters. Her point wasn't lost on me. She'd done all this parenting business before, under duress, and the second time around—even with only one child—was anticlimatic or, worse, a burden. She'd been robbed of her youth.

While other women vacuumed their wall-to-wall carpets, my mother worked her various projects, besieged by a desperate need to make her life count. She painted and sculpted in the basement, she dragged my father to Broadway shows in New York, she joined other women in Pittsfield to develop what became the area's first Planned Parenthood agency, she collected money for the Freedom marchers in Birmingham, Alabama and Jackson, Mississippi. She'd arrive home exhausted at seven in the evening with cartons of Chinese food from Pittsfield. No one in our town had heard of Chinese take-out in 1961. My mother was running some grueling catch-up marathon which she could never win because it was against her own sense of lost time.

When she left home at nineteen to marry my father, she had changed her name from Julia to Joy. Over the refrigerator in our kitchen she tacked a chapter heading from some self-help book that read in large block letters, "Don't Postpone Joy." My mother had inserted a substantial comma after Postpone.

She drove a red Ford Galaxy convertible, her unkempt hair flying around her face. The back seat was stacked with boxes containing the spoils of her day—canned goods for poor families, four new pairs of shoes for herself. Her self-indulgence and her altruism were all part of the same impulse—to right the wrongs of the world. At home, my father hung on her every word, his eyes taking in her gestures in meaningful ways. They had one of the first water beds, and the occasional condom appeared among matchbook covers and loose change on my father's nightstand. My mother's attitude with him was indulgent, as if he were the financial officer and she the creative director of their busy enterprise. But she eschewed the role of businessman's wife. Women needed contraception and abortions, blacks needed education and jobs. All else paled by comparison, and she simply didn't have time.

On weekends, exhausted, she collapsed with a stack of books by the pool they had installed in our back yard. Not many families had pools in 1961. We were not wealthy, but my mother pursued pleasure as relentlessly as she did doing good. Self-involved and embarrassingly unconventional, she was also intensely loyal and protective. She was not the sort of parent who humiliated you for not standing up to the playground bully. She'd be more likely to go down there and take him on herself. This may seem inconsistent in a woman who openly admitted she had more pressing issues to contend with than raising another child. But she knew first-hand that a young person's life could change on a dime. She knew how frightening and disappointing childhood could be. She gave people a wide berth, generally, but if you threatened her son in any way, she could be fierce.

I practiced on the Steinway that fall—a Beethoven sonata, Bach inventions, Mozart, Schubert. The dry chalky smell of the music room, the occasional sound of voices passing in the hallway, the solid heft of the huge instrument itself, were all part of a new confidence growing in me, derived in large part from Mr. Dean's encouragement and obvious affection. I eased up around him as a new sense of potential filled the empty space I had inhabited for so long. His name, Mr. Dean, even slipped from my lips on occasion when he was nowhere around, as if we were comrades in some remarkable adventure and there was something crucial I had to say to him right then. I affected his athletic walk and switched the part in my hair to the other side. And my body finally got around to sprouting tufts of hair where I had wanted them. Whereas, so recently, the changes I had yearned for had also blinked a neon DANGER, I welcomed them now because they would make me more like Mr. Dean.

One Indian summer afternoon, when he was driving me home after orchestra rehearsal, he slammed on the brakes. His rusted-out Plymouth screeched to a halt. On the used car lot of the Esso station sat a 1959 Chevrolet Impala convertible, pale blue with a white top and fins for days. "Would you look at that," he said.

"What?"

"That convertible."

"It's a Chevrolet."

"So?"

"My dad likes Fords."

"It's beautiful."

"It's two years old."

He backed up and pulled into the station. "Wait here," he said, slamming the door.

Soon, he appeared by the convertible with the Esso mechanic, who wiped his hands over and over on a stained rag. They gestured toward the convertible—Mr. Dean actually kicked the tires—and then back toward the Plymouth. They shook hands after a while and walked back to the station, Mr. Dean reaching to wipe his soiled hand on his trousers, then thinking better of it. A few minutes later, he showed up at my side of the Plymouth.

"Let's go," he said, pulling open the door. We gathered up the music scores from the back seat, and I followed him to the convertible. He started the engine and unhitched the canvas top. He pressed a button and we watched the top retract. He flashed his grin.

"Are you going to buy it?" I asked him.

"Already did. Get in."

"Nothing ventured, nothing gained, my mother always says."

Soon we were careening down the back roads of Williston, the wind flapping the music scores in the back seat and slapping Mr. Dean's unruly forelock across his eyes. He sang an old Elvis Presley song from the year I turned six. "You ain't nothin' but a hound dog, rockin' all the time." We laughed. He sang louder. "Come on," he said, "sing along." And I did.

Mr. Dean was the craziest teacher I had ever known, and he had become my best friend.

"I've been thinking about the piano competition in Pittsfield next spring," he said to me late one November afternoon as he stared out the window at the Victorian houses across South Street. His fingers pulled at his chin, as they always did when he was developing a plan. The janitor had just dusted his desk, swept under my feet where I sat at the piano, and left the music room. "What would you think of entering?"

"Me?" I said running my fingers silently up the ebony keys of the Steinway—C sharp, D sharp, F, G and A sharp, or D flat, E flat, G flat, A flat, and B flat. The very same sound could be this note or that note. It was up to you to know the difference.

He turned from the window. "As far as I know, you're the only other person here. What's the matter with you today?"

The competition would mean spending even more time alone with Mr. Dean. Increasingly, it seemed that he wanted something from me, though it's difficult to say now how specific my sense of that was. The way I felt around him was similar to the way my mother seemed to be around my dad, powerful in some way I couldn't define exactly. I had much greater freedom with Mr. Dean than any of the other kids did. I came to the music room to practice after school, but often we just talked or took a drive in the Impala. He continued to pull me out of class during the school day for no real reason other than to be together. And no one ever objected. What had the other teachers been thinking?

I was pretty sure by then that whatever my hold on Mr. Dean was, it was physical, and that it lay in staying just a little bit out of his reach. More than that, the specifics, were obscured by that blurred blend of excitement and fear I always felt around him.

"Yes," I said.

"Yes?"

"The competition."

"But do you want to, Corey? It would mean a lot of work. You shouldn't do it unless you really want to."

"I really want to."

"Good." He was by the piano bench then. He squeezed my shoulder. "Let's go see what we've got for music scores. I think there's a book of Chopin Mazurkas. Chopin's a crowd-pleaser."

I followed him to the storage closet, which extended all the way across one side of the music room. He unlocked the padlock and dropped it into his pants pocket, where it clanked against his keys. He flicked on the dim overhead bulb, as his hand directed me inside. Brass tubas and horns, in half-zippered bags, were piled hit-or-miss; the round shocked faces of snare drums stared out at us. Band uniforms lined the far wall like soldiers at attention. The whole windowless space smelled metallic and wooly, closed in.

I heard a car pass on South Street as he shut the door behind us.

"Which one?" I asked, turning to the file cabinets.

"Let's see. This one, I think." He pulled open the top drawer. The smell of long-stored paper wafted up at us. "You look," he said, stepping aside.

I pulled out a book of Chopin Nocturnes and began thumbing through them. Mr. Dean looked over my shoulder. "How about this one?" I said.

He glanced at it. "Too tricky. Never take on more than you can handle. Reasonable goals, that's the secret."

Reason. There was nothing reasonable about Mr. Dean, as far as I could see.

His fingers settled onto my hair, and I knew right away that we had not come into the storage closet to find a music score. The elastic bubble we inhabited had shrunk, suddenly, and I couldn't catch my breath.

His fingers dropped to my neck, and then to my waist. An aching weakness invaded my legs. I set the book of Nocturnes on top of the filing cabinet and stared at it, not knowing where else to look or what to do with my hands or whether to run.

"You've grown, Corey, just in the two months I've known you."

I watched pages of nocturnes turn themselves over, slowly, one at a time, falling flat, closing up. "We should go, Mr. Dean."

He crouched before me and lifted my shirt. I felt the file cabinet shift, sensed the bagged instruments adjusting themselves like dozing bodies. His breath was damp on my stomach, his lips dry. I knew I could stop him. I could say no, push him away, leave. I could sabotage the perilous course he was charting for us. It's possible—that whole fate argument—to alter the future with a single word, a single movement. But I didn't. I let him be in charge.

A tingling chill spread up my neck. I was amazed to be the one he had chosen. Whatever it was he was doing to me, I wanted it, because I wanted him. I couldn't help him, though. I could only let him.

He tugged at my belt and unzipped my fly. He pulled my jeans down to my knees, exposing the thin whiteness of my legs, their fine blond hairs standing straight. The stubble of his beard scratched my thighs. The sound of sucking both thrilled and shamed me.

Beads of sweat, fine as melting snowflakes, dotted the back of Mr. Dean's neck, where his hair met the downy surface of his skin. The angle of his collar gaped, revealing a gentle protruding knoll of bone, a prelude to the long straight line of his spine, the tantalizing juncture of his shoulders. I imagined those same beads of sweat accumulating in the soaked curly spikes of his underarms and forming a tiny rivulet down his ribcage, dampening the soft cotton of his shirt. I was riveted by these details of Mr. Dean's body, my own sensations erased, my emptiness filled to overflowing with this meticulous, detached scrutiny of his every sensation, the dazzling proof of his pleasure in me. No doubt I will never understand fully the effect of those first furtive moments with Mr. Dean, except to know that I exploded out of myself, out of my body, like a pilot abandoning his wounded and blazing aircraft. I chose free fall over the sure thing of incineration. Time speeded up, severing me from my own life in an exhilarating rush. I chose him over me. Of course, it wasn't a choice—his body over mine, his pleasure over my fear. More that I didn't know how to refuse. Or that I didn't matter. That was really it. I didn't much matter at all.

A cry worked its way into my throat, but came out as a sigh. He unzipped his own pants and stuck his hand inside. I was struck by the size of him—his hunched shoulders, his elegant fingers, his erect penis. After a short time, he groaned. Then he was quiet.

"I should go," I said, pulling up my pants and buckling my belt.

I stepped from where he crouched on the floor, leaving the book of Nocturnes on top of the file cabinet, the heavy drawer gaping above Mr. Dean's head. He didn't look up. I told myself I was different now, as I opened the storage closet door and slipped out. How could I change so fast? Yet, I was certain I would never be the same boy I'd been.

I ran past the Steinway, out into the hallway, down the empty stairs and along the corridor to the Boys Room. The door hissed closed behind me. I checked to be sure the stalls were empty and stood in front of one of the toilets, waiting to throw up. But nothing came. I spit several times into the bowl, wiping my mouth with my sleeve. I flushed the toilet and stepped to the sink where I splashed cold water on my face. I opened my pants and splashed there. I dried with paper towels and ran out of school, up South Street toward home.

"Fairy," I muttered to myself as I ran. "Fucking fairy."

Chapter Three
1985

For weeks, I wake up reaching to Gina's side of the bed. Finding it empty, I pull the sheet to my neck and burrow deeper into the pillow. Turning over only sparks an hour or two of fruitless accusations and self-reproaches—you should have been less focused on the house, you're just a disappointment when it comes to love, you'll never get anything right. And then I start in on her—you never cared about anyone but yourself, go for it if you think this guy can give you more than me. Positive, constructive stuff like that.

Gina. How could I account for our marriage? Ever the psychologist, I crank up my recollections of traditional personality theories based on early childhood experience—the absent father-domineering mother sort of explanations of human behavior. Gina had both—a mother who ranted and used religious and corporal threats to control her, and a reserved father more intimidated than Gina was by her mother. My own parents were both domineering, in their way, and emotionally absent, I suppose, though my mother tried. Neither couple had been well matched. Were Gina and I so shaped by these people that we were compelled to repeat their odd and frustrated couplings? They had been our models, our first impressions of adults and their relationships. We might have done better, but we could have done a lot worse, too.

Sometimes it seems that the more thorough an observer you are as a kid, the more stunted you are by the terrifying antics of your parents, and that the rest of your life is taken up with trying to work out from under the weight of the damage. Sharing our adolescent fears had provided Gina and me a poignant sort of devotion to one another that we'd never

27

been able to duplicate elsewhere. It sometimes seems as if we're still the lost teenagers we were twenty-five years ago—ducklings imprinted on one another in the absence of an attentive mother. To all appearances, we're mature, successful adults, but inside—the interior that Gina and I had never let anyone but one another see—we're still those terrified teenagers, loving one another out of loyalty rather than zeal.

I should be angry about the affair, but as time goes on, what I feel is a curious sort of encouragement. One of us should experience the real thing, and it seems to me that Gina is the more likely candidate. Aloneness is something I've learned to manage. Despite appearances, I believe that Gina is the more fragile of the two of us, surely the more needy.

My thoughts switch to Jack, whom I imagine to be sprawled across his futon in the ell downstairs. I can tell he misses Gina, too. His mood has darkened; he has even less to say than usual. He's made three trips into the city since she left, and I suspect he sees her then.

Jack continues to work in exchange for his room, which he has re-wired and painted and set up like a studio, with a Persian rug he found at a thrift shop and a club chair from who knows where. I went in there, once, while he was in Manhattan. Books were lined up on a desk rigged of pine planks laid across sawhorses. A goosenecked lamp, a washed-out tin can full of pencils. I opened a notebook that contained random thoughts and what looked like scenes from a play, all in his swift angular hand, then closed it quickly and set it back on the smooth old boards.

The interloper. I admit there was something thrilling about being there in Jack's room, among his things—the silence, the manly heft of his spare furnishings, the scent of his books and the wood he'd used to transform the room. That room, it seemed, was Jack—simple, sturdy, tidy. Standing there by his desk, running my fingers over his notebooks and papers, I envied him his apparently uncomplicated life, while suspecting there was more to it than I'd been allowed to see.

Over the weeks since Gina left, Jack and I have adjusted our routine to accommodate her absence. He works on various projects during the week, while I see patients at my office in Manhattan. When I return to Connecticut on Thursday, he has dinner ready, and we eat in the crackling glow of the fire. He tells me what he's accomplished around the place—as proud as I am of all the changes—and I tell him about an article I'm working on or a meeting I've had with a colleague in one of the professional organizations I belong to. It strikes me that this is the life I had wanted with Gina, discussing our independent pursuits, but without the feeling of separateness.

Then one night, unable to sleep, I roll onto my back. A pale angle of light from a sliver of October moon stretches across the plank floor and up onto the sheets. Slowly, I make out the shape of a man standing by the bed looking down at me.

"Jack?" I say, propping myself on my elbows, feeling my pulse quicken.

"Sorry. I didn't mean to scare you."

"What's wrong?"

"Wrong?" Jack's wearing only boxer shorts. His hands hang at his sides, like a boy's.

"What do you want?"

"To sleep with you," he says, plain, straight-forward.

Jack is tall and broad-shouldered, like the only man I ever had sex with, my music teacher back in seventh grade. In fact, Mr. Dean's face and his long, angular body flash across my awareness right then, sending a painful shock into my chest.

"Why?" is all I can think to say. I pull myself all the way up and lean against the headboard, hearing how ridiculous that question sounds.

"Because I like you."

Jack has a way of making complex things simple, which has served us well with the renovation. My penchant, on the other hand, has always been for convolution. While a surge of adrenalin thrusts most people into action, I seem to be paralyzed by it. How long had Jack been standing there, watching me toss and turn? Hadn't we had a conversation a few weeks ago about being friends? Did he mean "sleep" or sleep?

"Jesus, Jack," I say, turning to the window where a maple branch grates against the glass. "I thought you said no surprises."

"I guess that means no."

Deep down, no doubt, some part of me longs for Jack to crawl in beside me. But that truth, like so many of my impulses, is buried under heaps of shadowy debris. He stands a while longer, as if I might change my mind, or at least say something more. Then he turns and walks out of my room and I hear his bare feet skimming the stairs.

I don't sleep at all after that, getting up and staring out the window, sitting in the chair by the dresser, wishing the sun would hurry and end this night. For years I've done whatever I could to put sex, or even love, out of my mind, to make it unimportant. What do I really feel for Jack? I imagine him climbing back onto his futon, and then, like me, unable to sleep. The idea of going down there, even just to talk, fills me with dread.

The next morning, while I make our usual fruit shake of bananas, apples and orange juice, Jack stumbles into the kitchen, boots in one hand, gray cotton socks in the other. He ducks as his rumpled hair dusts the fresh-stripped wood of the doorjamb and sits at the table to pull on his socks and boots. It's still dark. An autumn chill sweeps under the door. I pour the shake into glasses and hand him one. There's a piece of lint caught in the stubble of his chin. I resist the urge to lift it away, suspecting it isn't my need for tidiness that compels me to touch him.

"About last night," I say. I want to apologize for being so abrupt, make everything as smooth as it's been since he arrived here four months ago.

He stands and steps to the coat rack. "Let's forget it, okay? I'll start bringing up those two-by-sixes." I've noticed, recently, that Jack's chin quivers slightly, as it does now, when he's upset. I can see he feels embarrassed, or maybe ashamed. I want to tell him there's no need.

He jams his fists into the sleeves of his jacket. The blinds bang the window as he closes the door behind him.

I watch him make his way down the walk as the sun clears the trees along the road and blasts orange off the barn windows, as if the whole leaning mass were on fire.

Jack told me once that he'd grown up on a farm in Nebraska. I imagine him heading down to his own family's barn as a teenager, as he does to mine now, a wake of misty breath trailing behind him in the cool, morning haze. I wonder what Jack was like at thirteen or fourteen—tall for his age, strong from farm work, awkward and shy as the farm boys I knew in high school in western Massachusetts. Absurdly, I think we would have been friends, had we grown up in the same small town. We'd have broken through one another's reticence and spent all of our time together, as boys sometimes do, immersed in intense emotional crushes that are just on the cusp of being replaced, magically, by a less mysterious attraction to girls.

But, of course, that switch in attraction hadn't intervened for Jack, and somehow he got himself to New York, where he could have the sort of life he wanted. I envy him the way I have always envied Gina— people who know exactly what they want and don't let a density of complications get in their way.

Jack carries the two-by-sixes up to the house and starts building a storage area in the cellar. I work at my desk most of the day, distracted by his sawing and hammering and his occasional trips to the kitchen, the sound of the refrigerator door opening and closing, the faucet turning on and off. I have always liked Jack's busy presence in this house, and I worry now that things might change.

At the end of the day, we take turns cleaning up in the bathroom, with its 1950s flesh-colored fixtures. Jack's razor sits next to mine on the sink. Two toothbrushes stand in the glass, where five weeks ago there had been three. I miss the scent of Gina's bath oils, though the musky man-smell that has taken over the bathroom has its appeal, too.

I work on dinner while Jack sits at the kitchen table, thumbing through a restoration catalogue. Occasionally he reads a description out loud of some gadget or tool that might come in handy for one of our projects. Then he mentions the steps he wants to build at the front door, our quiet chatter reassuringly easy again. He draws a plan on the back of the envelope the catalogue arrived in, showing the steps in perspective, as elegant as any architectural rendering. I study it and nod. "That looks perfect," I tell him.

He smiles and turns back to the catalogue. I sit down across from him at the table. "Can we talk about last night?" I ask.

"What's to talk about? I was out of line. I'm sorry." His eyes continue to scan the pages.

"It's a lot more complicated than that."

He sets the catalogue aside, rests his elbows on the table and looks to me to go on.

"I don't know what I want, exactly," I say. "I like you a lot. I don't know what's happening with Gina. Sometimes I think . . ."

"You don't have to explain anything, Corey. I had no business...." He gets up, goes to the stove and stirs the stew. "Other things are a lot more important. We're friends. Gina and I are friends. That's the main thing."

"Have you seen her?"

"Yes."

"And?"

"We talk about work. She doesn't mention Jim, and neither do I."

"Do you know this guy?"

"I've met him. That's all. It's awkward now, being with Gina, neither of us talking about the elephant in the room."

I think about those wonderful June weekends when Jack first came to this house, when he spent hours working with me and an equal amount of time talking to Gina.

I pick up a pencil and start shading Jack's drawing of the steps. But my crude strokes only detract from the pristine elegance of his rendering. I have always been drawn to talented people—Gina, Jack—perhaps because I'd been a promising piano student as a kid, something I'd abandoned, abruptly, when I was sixteen. I used to believe that career was the most important thing in life. Now I'm not so sure. Lately, I feel as if I missed out on a whole lot.

Jack pulls the baguette out of the oven, slices it, and drops the pieces into a basket. "I was thinking of going into the city tomorrow," he says.

Jack and I usually spend Saturdays working, but I don't say anything.

He ladles the stew into bowls and sets out spoons and knives, the bread and butter. "I'm going to meet up with a friend. We'll have dinner, maybe go to a bar after."

We eat in silence. I have to admit I'm jealous.

"You got a letter today," I say, after a while. Jack doesn't get much mail here, but this is the second letter postmarked Chadron, Nebraska, with no return address.

His eyes flash up at me.

"I just want to make sure you saw it."

"I saw it."

I get up and set my half-empty bowl in the sink. Sitting back at the table, I pick up a pear, slice it and give Jack half.

"The letter is from the friend I mentioned," Jack says. "He's going to be in New York this weekend." He takes a bite of the pear, wipes the juice from his chin. "He was my lover, when I was nineteen. A professor at Chadron State, where I went to school, in Nebraska."

I look down at my hands, picturing Jack walking a tree-lined campus, lanky and boyish, awed by the attention of some distinguished professor. "And you've stayed in touch?"

"On and off." Jack turns to the window, as if he can see the professor out there rather than his own reflection in the black glass. It strikes me just how important he has become to me. "It was a long time ago," he says, turning back to the table, stretching his legs out in front of him.

Jack's legs are as lean and tight as a runner's. I've always observed how men—straight men—pretend they don't notice one another's bodies. But it's clear that they do. Maybe it's a competitive thing, or maybe it's sexual. Or maybe competition is part of sexual attraction between men. I don't know. It all feels so muddled.

Jack changes the subject back to the new steps for out front, saying he would pick up the two-by-eights the next morning, before he leaves for the city.

When we stop talking, it's late. The dishes are dried and put away. I wonder if Jack is going to the city because of what happened last night, though he doesn't seem that upset about it now. Still, on our way to bed, we are like a couple of wary dogs, easing our way to opposite ends of the kitchen. He waves and ducks into the ell as I turn up the stairs. I think about how few words there are to describe the fullness I feel for Jack. Affection isn't strong enough, and love makes me feel like I'm running along the edge of a cliff. I close my bedroom door behind me, comforted by the soft click of the latch falling into place.

The bedroom is large, the same size as the dining room directly underneath it, with the same arrangement of small-paned windows and a tiny fireplace sharing the chimney with the big one downstairs. It's a peaceful place to escape to during the day or collapse in at night. But as I undress, it seems cold and empty. If I feel this close to Jack, shouldn't I go downstairs and be with him?

Gina and I and our straight friends in the Hamptons were always so accepting of gay people. We all agreed that love between two men or two women was as worthy as the love of a man and a woman. And, of course, we had gay friends. But it seems to me now, that that acceptance had been a little smug, easy from the secure distance of our presumed heterosexuality. Even the term acceptance, as I think of it now, seems arrogant. What is there to accept if homosexuality is neither inferior nor wrong?

Such questions plague me as I lie in bed, my relentless uncertainties as thick and suffocating as the Kudzu vine that creeps into the field from the gully along the road out front.

Beyond the windows, low clouds lurch along the horizon that glows faintly from the distant city lights of Danbury, sixteen miles south. I picture Jack stretched long atop his futon downstairs, his arms flung out like a diver's. It occurs to me that what I really want is to be Jack, to possess his intensity, his resolve, his integrity. But then, I get up and stare out the window at the silhouette of the hulking barn, wondering how often I've told myself one thing while the truth lay somewhere else.

A week later, Jack and I are working on the front steps. He miters the breadboard ends, a refinement I would not have considered, setting the steps off like a frame does a picture. He never said anything about his night in New York with his ex-lover. And I haven't asked.

About four in the afternoon, unannounced, Gina's Volvo slows on the road and pulls into the driveway, sending up a wake of dust and fallen leaves. My stomach tightens. Jack squints into the sun, looks over at me and then back down to the miter joint. I can't tell whether he's pleased or not to see Gina. I don't know myself.

She bounds up the walkway, looking glamorous in a long black cardigan. I can see she's nervous. She hugs me, then Jack. We're all eerily silent—Jack glancing down at the step, Gina watching me and me trying to read Jack.

"Welcome back," I say, stiff and unconvincing. Already, I can imagine myself being drawn to her like a drifter to the town he grew up in, though everything has changed.

She takes my hand and leads me through the front door and up the narrow stairway to our room, my room now. She sits in the rocker by the dresser. I lean against the window frame, feeling like I'd lost my place in a book and can't find it again. Out the window, I see Jack head down to the barn. He's removed his carpenter's apron.

Gina is saying how she's missed me. "I've been thinking about trying again," she says, getting up and coming to me. "What do you think?"

Gina is always way out ahead, switching gears as adeptly as a race car driver. I've hardly adjusted to her arrival, and she's proposing we go on as if nothing had happened.

I wonder when things soured with the director. The anger I felt resurfaces and then blurs. It's becoming clear to me now that the pride I've taken in being faithful to Gina has been a function of a good deal of denial and fear of my own impulses. She kisses me. Reaching for her, I hear the pickup's engine turn over. Jack is leaving. Gina's waist is small, feminine. She tugs the flaps of my shirt out of my jeans. The truck idles as Jack eases it past the Volvo at the front door and then revs at the end of the driveway.

We kiss more deeply and move to the bed. I try not to think about Jack killing time at Kmart or Agway so that Gina and I can have this time alone. Under the blanket, I push inside her, wanting the coherence, the certainty of her grip on me.

And no doubt, Gina wants that, too. I know she felt rescued by me when we were kids—from her aloneness, her general alienation, her disastrous relationships with the older boys she dated in ninth grade. And I suspect she felt rescued a second time, when we married three years ago—from the tenuous life of a struggling actor, and from the unsuitable men Gina still found so electrifying, one who'd thrown her down the stairs, another who had simply disappeared after three months of marriage. Ironic as it seems now, I was the picture of stability to her, as grounded as a pyramid, the "right" sort of guy that she has never found exciting.

Lying next to her afterward, I tell myself that nothing in life is perfect, that the trick is to grab what happiness you can. But is happiness lying here next to me right now or is it out there wandering the local back roads in the pickup? Of course, I know it isn't here or there, it has to be in me somewhere, hiding where I'm afraid to find it.

The tension has faded from Gina's face. I wonder where it has gone, when it will be back. I want to go finish the steps so Jack can admire them when he gets back. Instead, I rise and go down to the kitchen, where I make sandwiches and bring them back to the bedroom. I hear Jack come in around nine and go to his room in the ell.

At five the next morning, I'm in my bathrobe, sitting alone at the kitchen table. The robe is a gray tartan, with red and green—I don't know its name—given to me by my parents when I was sixteen. I never used it then, never felt chilled as a teenager, at least not physically.

I watch the light go from purple to dawn red, setting the oaks around the barn aglow. Their leaves rain down in a gentle breeze.

A week has passed since Jack came to my room. Now, he's asleep in the ell just beyond the kitchen wall. Morning brings the promise of work to eat up my bemused thoughts, with some sort of solace in the new light itself. I stand and look out the window. The yard is black beneath swells of mist. The field, the driveway, the barn roof, the shed, even my pickup are all covered with blackbirds, their cries so loud I can't believe I haven't heard them before now. The whole landscape is darkened with their feathers, a blackness stippled with iridescent purple and green, a fluttering quarrelsome blanket. I turn and pass through the doorway to the ell.

Jack is boyish in sleep, his mouth slack, his hair spread across the pillow. A pulse throbs in his neck and I feel frightened, as I imagine a new mother must, observing the precarious miracle of her infant's life.

Slowly, I creep to the window. The birds still cover the ground. I watch them a while longer. When I turn back to Jack, my dim shadow falls across his legs, bent under the rumpled sheet. I step slightly to one side, edging my shadow up to Jack's hips, his stomach, his outstretched arm with its delta of blond hair just below his wrist. I reach out and lay the shadow of my hand gently across his face, as the scent of dry leaves drifts through the window screen.

I love Jack, a truth presenting itself—finally, awesome, simple.

He stirs and looks up at me. I picture Gina asleep upstairs, Jack walking around Times Square with his ex last weekend, the front steps with their elegant mitered joints. "Look outside," I say.

Jack stretches, pulls back the covers and gets up. At the window, we stand stock still—Jack in his boxers, me in my robe—as if any movement might startle the birds away. I sense the warmth of his bare shoulder, smell the dry odor of sleep on his breath. "Amazing," he says.

The birds are my cloak of fear, I'm thinking, a quivering black mantle of worries. I view Jack and me from above, surrounded by them, part of their darkness, yet together in the emerging light. I consider reaching my arm around him, but he turns and I watch his reflection in the window as he ducks under the door to the bathroom.

As if the sound of water splashing in the sink disturbs the birds, they rise from the yard, the fields and the barn in one huge rustling flap of a magician's cape, and Jack and Gina and I are left down here with one another, and our expanding predicament.

Chapter Four
1985

The blackbirds rise in a swirling exuberance that darkens the sky. I watch them regroup into a startled trapezoid and disappear over the hills to the south. For the first time in weeks, I feel clear. I love Jack. I love our life here, rescuing this house from oblivion. The anxiety of a week ago, when he appeared by my bed, vanishes with the birds, and I decide, finally, to trust what seems an outlandish impulse—though, of course, it's far more than impulse. I'm trusting feelings I had twenty-five years ago, with Bill Dean, feelings that had ended in disaster.

There's another problem—Gina, my wife and Jack's best friend, asleep upstairs.

I hear Jack brushing his teeth at the sink now, can almost smell the minty toothpaste I have detected on his breath so often. I step into the bathroom just as he steps out of his shorts and into the shower. He pulls the curtain behind him and ducks under the spray. I savor that glimpse into what I am already envisioning as our life together—bathing, carrying in groceries, doing laundry, things we've done all fall that will feel new and different now. I want to lean against the sink and watch Jack bathe, make him laugh, tell him everything I know about myself, make him love me. I settle for tossing two cupped palms of cold water over the curtain.

"Ah! You bastard." He jumps back, nearly falling out of the flaked tub.

"Just making sure you're awake."

"I owe you."

Drying my hands on my robe, I catch my reflection in the mirror over the sink, surprised that my face looks the same as it does every morning—a day of stubble, a timid look of anticipation. "I have to go upstairs. Gina and I may take a drive. Not sure." My wife, who has driven up from the city to tell me she wants to put our marriage back together. I cringe. Caution, my nemesis, is putting up a fight.

"I'm going to finish up the steps out front," Jack says over the curtain. "If we're back in time, I'll help."

I often picture myself at some point in the future, not five or ten years, but an hour from now, or even four hours. The potential for radical change is a function of moments, not years. Standing there, watching Jack tip his head under the spray, the frothy soap descending to his shoulders, I suspect that when I return from talking to Gina, my life will be altered considerably.

"There's not a whole lot more to do," Jack says, his voice muffled by the water.

"I'll see you later, then," I say, forcing myself to leave, thrilled by the anticipation of loving Jack.

Crossing the dining room to the stairs, I decide to suggest to Gina that we drive to Kent and park along the Housatonic River north of town, walk its shoreline and talk the way we did when we were kids, perched on her parents' front porch in Williston. She'll be surprised—maybe shocked—to hear about Jack and me, but I dare to hope that we can sort all that out together. Gina can be reasonable or outlandish, there's no telling. This time, I hope she'll at least listen. I even imagine us coming back to the house in the afternoon, Gina fixing dinner while Jack and I finish up the steps out front.

Being in love can taint your judgment.

Upstairs, Gina lies awake in our bed, her arms folded behind her head. She doesn't turn to me when I come in and close the door behind me. She is often thoughtful in the morning, uncharacteristically quiet until she's had her coffee, her mood difficult to read. You can almost see her energy grow throughout the day. Gina is a night person. I, of course, am a morning, waking at six at a fever pitch.

I have no idea what time it is, only that I left the room at first light, and now the sun glints off the barn roof with the steady glow of a welder's torch. I take off my robe and slide into bed beside her.

"Where have you been?"

"Downstairs," I say, trying to sound nonchalant. "I couldn't sleep."

"Me neither. Maybe I shouldn't have come."

"Why did you?"

"Something told me I should."

"That's pretty vague. Are things over with what's his name?"

"Jim is not the issue." Gina pulls herself up in the bed and leans against the headboard.

If Jim isn't the issue, then Jack isn't, I tell myself, taking heart. In fact, I've been so involved in sorting out my feelings for Jack these last weeks, I haven't exactly been consumed with jealousy about the director. "What is the issue, then?" I ask her, truly interested in how she sees things.

"Us. We started slipping away from each other when we bought this place."

"Really? I thought we were slipping closer together."

"You've been different."

"Excited, you mean? Happy?"

"This house is your thing. It was never mine. It's come between us."

"And this Jim? He hasn't come between us?"

"It happened, Corey."

"Come on, things don't just happen." Don't they? Haven't I fallen in love with Jack without intending to? I can feel Gina stiffen beside me. She's always hated having to account for herself.

"We can talk about Jim, or we can talk about us," she says, fidgeting with the frayed edge of the spread. "I think it might be more productive to talk about us."

"Of course you do. Then I can be wrong again, and you don't have to deal with the fact that you left me six weeks ago for someone else." I pull myself up in the bed to be at the same height as Gina. "Besides, I'm not sure they're so separate, your affair and us. People don't take up with someone else unless they're unhappy, right?" Clearly, I'm speaking about myself.

Gina pushes back the covers and starts to get up.

"Wait," I say, taking her arm. "Don't go."

She sits back. Unlike me, Gina has never been afraid to be selfish. She's done pretty much exactly what she wanted—moving to New York, acting, road shows all over the country. And for the last three years, I've been along for the ride, often literally, her own little cheering section in this theater or that. Wasn't that what she had wanted? But I've said all these things before, and I don't want to distract us now from what we really need to talk about.

"What about my affair?" I blurt out.

She turns to face me. Gina, the actress, can feign astonishment or tranquility, either one seamlessly. She chooses the latter. "You're having an affair?" she says, as calm as if I'd told her I'd bought a new suit.

"Kind of."

"It's like being pregnant, Corey. You either are or you're not."

Gina prides herself on how well she knows me. She often tells people that we met when we were only thirteen years old. That's true, of course. But this has always seemed to me a source of undue satisfaction for Gina, or perhaps reassurance. My announcement doesn't fit with the Corey she knows.

I have always believed that Gina's devotion to me, if you can call it that, has to do with the idea that I am the only man who really knows everything about her—her history, her fears, her dreams. It isn't true, of course. There are huge gaps in my understanding of my wife, things she deliberately keeps from me—this director, Jim, is a good example. Gina is an enigma, and like most enigmatic people, she needs to believe that there is someone out there who knows her whole story. No one knows anyone's whole story, of course, but I suppose I'm the person who comes closest for Gina.

I can see that her interest is piqued. Has it never occurred to Gina that there might be a little verve lurking in me somewhere? It hits me that, in hiding my will or spirit or whatever it is, I've been as selfish as Gina. And far more cowardly.

She rearranges her legs under the sheet. "When do you have time for an affair?" she asks me. "You're either working until nine in the city, or you're working until nine on this place. Where would you find the energy?"

My hands lie at my sides, pulling the sheet taut over my hips, revealing the head and shaft of my long-neglected dick. Of course, it isn't my dick I've neglected all these years, but the complex of emotions that ends up there, so to speak. "Gina, my worldly one, having an affair isn't about time or energy. It's about joy, right? Isn't that why it's such a big deal? And it's about risk, restlessness, excitement. But, of course, you know all that."

She gets up, her body still lithe yet more solid than when we were adolescents. She pulls on the robe I shed and turns to the window. If she'd been in a 1940s film, she'd have lit a cigarette. I feel a rush of affection for her, one of the few times Gina has ever appeared vulnerable.

She told me once, after a somewhat uninspired session of love-making, that she'd been born to love me. Those had been her exact words— "I was born to love you," muttered half under her breath. What exactly had she meant? That some cosmic predestination had linked us forever? That she felt bound by guilt because of what had happened when we were sixteen? We both knew that more worthy pursuits occupied her, so I hadn't quite bought the whole notion. Yet, the idea that Gina loved me out of a sense of obligation had depressed me.

"What are you thinking?" I ask her now, knowing she has always hated that question.

She continues to stare out the window. "I was thinking about ninth grade. We were such good friends then. I was thinking how innocent we were."

Gina is rarely frightened, something she reveals with a mere quiver of her elegant left temple. It pains me to see her upset, somehow especially because she can't or won't show it. Yet I don't want to comfort her now. I get up and step into yesterday's jeans, left in a heap by the chair. The floor boards are cold under my feet. My chest flutters. "I think I've fallen in love," I say, buttoning my jeans.

Tears brim in her eyes. She walks to the mirror over the dresser, where she fingers her hair into place. She's pulling herself together. I can see it. She's regrouping.

"I didn't plan it. It was just there all of a sudden, this amazing, incredibly intense feeling."

She looks at my reflection behind hers in the mirror, still forcing nonchalance. "So who's the lucky gal?"

This conversation is not going the way I had hoped. I can see that we are not going to work things out in some amicable way, at least not for a while. And we probably aren't going to go on living in this house, the three of us. The urge to turn back grips me. I could say I imagined the whole thing, some fictitious, local single mom, made it all up out of jealousy. We could go downstairs and have breakfast, the three of us, together. Suddenly, I'm terrified of losing Gina.

Then I'm equally terrified of not allowing myself to love Jack, that I might never allow myself to really love anyone.

"It's not a woman," I say.

Gina looks at me as if she doesn't understand what I'm saying, as if she doesn't have a more complete context for my revelation than anyone I know. As teenagers, we had inhabited our own willful self-confinement, a little world-for-two of aloofness. She knew about Mr. Dean. No one knows me better, even now, than Gina. Feigning confusion only convinces me that she knows exactly what I'm saying, and that she understands it only too well.

"Jack," she says.

"Yes, Jack."

Stung, she turns back to the mirror, trying to maintain her composure. "You've got to be fucking kidding me," she says, eying my reflection behind hers.

With my thumb and forefinger, I count the change in the left pocket of my jeans—three quarters, four dimes, two nickels, seven pennies—eighty-two cents in all.

"What's happened to us?" Gina says, turning to me. "What have we done to our lives?"

Still, I resist going to her. "I don't know," I say. "We're just living them, I guess. It's always felt kind of random to me, life, ours anyway. Maybe this is just more of the same, you know?" I'm backpedaling, trying to downplay the magnitude of what's happening here.

"I had a feeling," she says, turning back to the mirror and fiddling again with her hair. Gina hates surprises. When they occur, she denies them. "I always knew you might be gay."

The smell of coffee wafts up the stairs into the bedroom. Jack is making breakfast. "Jesus, Gina. If you thought I was gay, why did you marry me?"

"Why did *you* marry *me*?" She's streaking on lipstick now, two heavy swaths across her mouth, Baby Jane-ghoulish.

"Because I loved you? Because I've loved you since we were thirteen?"

She presses her lips together. "You should have told me you were attracted to men." She turns to me, toughened by the redness of her mouth and the pinched pain around her eyes.

"I probably would have," I say, "if I'd known."

"Oh, fuck you and your innocence. How could you not know?"

"I haven't even had sex with Jack."

She smiles, derisively. "Then, what the hell is this affair?"

"I love him, Gina."

"Love is a silly fucking fantasy, like thinking you're never going to die." She slips the lipstick back into its case and drops it on top of the dresser. "And does he? Love you?"

"I think he might."

"That fucking Brutus."

A gust of wind blasts against the window. I pick up my sweatshirt off the floor and pull it on.

"You're making a fool of yourself," she says. "Imagine what our friends will think."

"I don't much care what they think. Do you?"

"I'm always embarrassed for people who fuck up their lives in the name of love. Like it's the most important thing. What if it's just some silly, narcissistic fantasy? What if it just brings out the worst in people— their lust and envy, their spite?"

"Probably for some people, it does."

"You know as well as I do, the only relationships that last are the ones you work at. And that's what we've got, a working relationship."

"One in which you're free to indulge and I'm not."

"We're getting older, Corey. Before you know it, your muscles are sagging, your arches are falling, your skin's dotted with spots. We share a past, a history, and a present worth holding onto."

"I've always believed that, but it never seemed that you did. Now, I feel as if I want some passion in my life, you know? Before my arches fall."

"Good luck."

"Maybe you're right—about everything. You usually are. But how am I going to feel if I never try?"

Gina turns back to the mirror, opens her lipstick and takes another swipe at her mouth.

"I know the whole thing sounds ridiculous. Yes, I've felt drawn to men at times, but it never felt like this."

"Talk about control. You never let yourself feel sexual, when obviously, you felt sexual."

"I don't know," I say, picking up my socks. "Are you attracted if you don't feel it?"

"You always make everything so fucking complicated. Does a goddamned tree falling in the woods make a sound? Of course it does, if you have the fucking sense to pay attention." She recaps the lipstick, drops it and pulls an eye pencil out of her purse. Looking into the mirror again, she lowers one eyelid and draws a solid black line above the lash. "You mean you never wanted to fuck a man until now?" she says.

I notice the window is open a crack, and wonder if Jack has started working on the steps just below and can hear every word. "No, I don't mean that."

"Then what the hell are you saying?" Having lined only one eye, Gina looks like some Estée Lauder advertisement for witches.

"Maybe I felt attracted to guys sometimes, but it also horrified me—the idea that I might . . . do that. Again."

"Christ! You've been attracted to men all along!"

"And I was attracted to you. But you left."

"Fuck you, Corey!"

I stuff my hands back into my pockets. "You never gave a shit what I thought. You just left, Gina, and you never came back."

She gives me that questioning look again, as if she doesn't remember how abruptly she left Williston, and why. She sits down heavily in the chair by the window.

I sit on the edge of the bed and count the number of floor boards between my bare feet and the wall. I am as much to blame for the bizarre twists in our relationship as Gina is. Yes, she left me, ending our adolescent romance. And I have never forgiven her. But she's right, I should have known a whole lot more about my own sexuality than I ever have.

Suddenly, she's on her feet. "I should go," she says.

"Please don't leave, Gina, not now. We're finally talking."

"Talking? Christ! My husband's gay and he's having an affair with my best friend who just happens to be living downstairs in our house. Doesn't that sound like an exit situation to you?"

She sloughs off my robe and pulls on the jeans and tee shirt she was wearing when she arrived yesterday. With one violent swipe of her arm, she whisks her wallet and lipstick, the eye liner and her keys off the top of the dresser into her bag.

"Gina, please don't go."

She stands in front of me, frantically pulling on her boots. "We were sixteen, for Christ's sake. And you know exactly why I had to leave." A tiny fleck of her spittle lands on my cheek. I brush it away. She picks up her cardigan and tosses it over her shoulders. "We're a fucking joke, Corey."

She looks around the room for anything she doesn't want to leave behind, or maybe to survey it for the last time. She opens the door and starts down the stairs, slips, grabs the railing and steadies herself. She turns back to me, as if she's thought of something more cutting to say, but then changes her mind.

"Gina!" I yell as she disappears at the foot of the stairs.

I start after her—barefoot—taking the stairs two at a time, turning into the hallway just as Gina flings open the screen door and sprints past Jack who is just setting his tools down on the front step. Jack, our best friend, standing, appropriately, right there in the way.

"Fuck you," she says as she pushes past him.

I take in Jack's look of bewilderment as I clear the front steps. I hop across the stony driveway and catch Gina just as she slams the Volvo door and locks it. "Gina, don't leave," I yell through the glass. "Please. Don't leave."

She jams her keys into the ignition and starts the engine. I cling to the door handle.

"Gina," I yell again.

She shifts the car into reverse and hits the accelerator. I run alongside. She stops, shifts into gear and hurls us ahead, past the front door and down the driveway. I hold on in a barrage of dust and gravel, unable to let go of Gina and our grueling, lifelong link. And she drags me along with her, as she so often did, not even looking back.

I hear something tear, and I'm wrenched to the ground as the car's rear tire spins past my face. The roar of the exhaust recedes as I roll into the dead grass at the side of the driveway. Spitting dirt, I come to rest on my back, squinting up at the dazzling morning sky, taking in the dry, earthy fragrance of dead leaves.

Jack's startled face appears above me. Bloated clouds drift in the distance behind him. He kneels down next to me. "Are you all right?" he asks.

My cheek stings as he brushes sand from around my eye. I blink at the blood on his fingers. "I'm not sure," I say.

"Can you stand?" He takes my hand and pulls me to my feet. My knee burns where my pant leg is torn, but nothing seems to be broken. Blood drips from a cut over my left eye. He leans down and pulls my tattered pants away from my leg. "I heard this tear all the way from the steps," he says, looking underneath. "Lucky it was just the pants. Do you want to go to the emergency room? There's a lot of dirt in these cuts."

"No. Just help me up to the house."

We make our way to the back door. Jack helps me inside and lowers me onto a chair by the kitchen table. At the sink, he fills a pot with soapy water, takes a fresh towel and soaks it. He leans over my chair. "This is going to sting," he says, dabbing at my forehead and cheek. I wince. "Are you all right?" He keeps dabbing. "I would suggest you avoid a mirror for a couple of days," he says, grinning.

I can smell his mint breath and the straw-like scent of his hair as he leans closer to dislodge some stubborn grains of sand from my chin. I've never been this close to him, never noticed the fine spiky lines between his eyebrows, the tanned, naked space between his sideburn and his ear.

Watching him wring out the towel in the pan, I think how grateful I am to have him here. We're both loners, sharing the qualities of the loner—the competence, the self-sufficiency, the hiding. And yet, the truth is I have never done so well on my own. I had to turn too far inward, ignore too much. I don't want to be alone anymore.

Tears well up in me at the sheer joy of Jack's presence. Suddenly, it seems no accident that we met, or that we were so drawn to each other.

I feel as if I have met my twin, only he seems stronger, more mysterious, maybe even more hidden than me, if that's possible.

He dumps the bloody water into the sink and refills the pot. He pulls a second towel from the drawer, dips it in the warm water and kneels next to my chair. He parts the torn leg of my jeans and dabs at the bloody abrasion. "Why don't you slip these off," he says. I start to get up, but then remember that I'm not wearing any underwear.

"I can't," I say.

He continues dabbing at the scrape, which I can see now extends from my calf to my thigh. It's a mess, just as he said. He rinses the towel several times and goes back to his gentle daubing. He's so handsome, it almost seems worth getting bloodied, just to have him crouch here at my feet. Soon, he'll go back to working on the steps. I'll help. Together we'll countersink the nails, sand the edges and apply a coat of sealer. We'll have dinner. Time will pass. I will love him.

"You need to take these off," Jack says, "so I can finish my nursing duties."

He undoes my belt and unbuttons my jeans. I lift my hips and he slips the jeans from under me, eases them by my erection and the abrasions on my leg. He smiles, then bends and touches his lips to my thigh, just above the nasty scrape. A spasm of pleasure ripples up my spine.

I long to return his touch, but my hand, my whole body, feels leaden. I don't know what will please him. Even what I want is vague and cloaked in dread. Jack's touch is specific, skilled, knowing. Mine, I fear, would be awkward. He knows the subtle, calibrated pressures, the profound tactile conveyances of life. I know nothing.

Minutes pass and it feels as if the whole of Jack's being is concentrated in the delicate pressure he applies to my thigh. I feel a sudden terror like the percussive blast of an explosion. But then, just as quickly, it's gone, leaving a silence in its wake as peaceful as the light gracing the kitchen this Sunday morning. Not that my past with Mr. Dean doesn't still threaten to pin me, but the curtain I had long ago draped over that entire episode lifts enough for me to see how different Jack's touch is from Bill Dean's.

I lean down to him and let my cheek rest in the manly fresh scent of his hair. I lift my hands to his shoulders and let them slide down his back, taking in the firm knolls and valleys beneath his shirt. I have the dizzying sense of flight, up and away from the life of thrilling wonder I had begun as an adolescent, and then so abruptly ended.

Jack's lips are soft and dry. I run my fingers into his hair as he moves gradually up the inside of my leg, the stubble of his beard a pleasant tingling sensation against my skin.

Chapter Five
1962

Williston was a quiet, picture-postcard town, nestled into the drowsy Berkshire Hills of western Massachusetts. The white spire of the Congregational Church poked up amid the naked branches of elms and maples and oaks that winter of 1962, its simple gold cross gleaming in the dazzling, morning sun. The white clapboard houses lining Main Street, their cedar roofs drifted with snow, dated from the early 1800s, when the library was built and the general store, which eventually became the home of the local Historical Society. It appeared that the early nineteenth century was the last time that anything noteworthy had happened in that town. But don't be fooled—people prided themselves on the secrets they knew about one another, meting them out in whispers behind fingertips.

Like that frigid Sunday morning in February, when my mother learned that our church organist had left town with Mr. Beatty, the owner of the hardware store who had a daughter in my class. And, of course, a wife at home. People disappeared. Like the orthopedist who hadn't shown up at the hospital one day, and then was spotted a year later in San Francisco. I imagined Mr. Beatty, slipping out his back door in the icy pre-dawn, the only sound the click of the door latch and the guilty crunch of snow underfoot. Did he turn and look back, or half-run to his pickup, head down, eager? And Mrs. Beatty, when she rolled over and found the bed empty. Did she run to the window? It was scary, at twelve, to think that your whole life could change as easily as dropping a new slide into a projector. Scary, but exciting too—the organist waiting at the end of the street, clear-eyed, clutching her bag, a freezing gust flinging her neat, page-boy haircut.

We winced in our pews that Sunday as Father Ryan, the tone-deaf pastor of Saint Francis Church, wailed through chants and blessings without the support of the organ. A week later, desperate, the priest came to our house for dinner, and to propose that I take over in the choir loft until a permanent replacement could be found.

Setting down my knife and fork, I began to explain to him that the organ was a very different instrument from the piano. "The touch is lighter," I told him, "and the volume range is huge. And there are the pedals to think about."

Actually, I was flattered to be asked, but I was concerned about how faggy I might look, perched at those four set-back keyboards, high above a congregation that included many of my school friends and their parents. For the past year, I had begun assessing any new activity for its potential to earn me the dreaded "fairy" epithet at school, particularly in light of my obvious favor with Mr. Dean, my central position in the school's orchestra, and my conspicuous absence from its athletic fields. Not that Mr. Dean was faggy, not at all. Just that any sort of prominence, other than athletic, invited scorn at Williston Junior High, and "fag" was the most damning epithet you could suffer.

"How different can it be?" my mother interrupted, pointing to her empty wine glass. My father stood, walked to her end of the table and poured. "Of course. Corey would be glad to help out," she assured our priest.

I should have known my mother would make a civic duty out of my filling in on the organ.

"You have no idea what a relief this is," Father Ryan said, puffing out his pasty cheeks and expelling a sigh. "The church is very grateful to you, Corey. And to you, Joy." He sipped his water and sat back in his chair. "Now, about compensation. Your predecessor received a modest salary. I thought that, given your age and the opportunity this experience affords, the church might provide organ lessons in lieu of financial compensation. What do you think, Corey?"

Actually, I was thinking that five bucks a shot would allow me to buy a couple of new shirts and some new records each month, maybe a present for Mr. Dean. "Who would be teaching me?" I asked him.

"I've approached the organist at Saint Joseph's in Pittsfield, and he was open to the idea."

"What about Mr. Dean?"

"Who?" said Father Ryan, raising his bushy salt-and-pepper eyebrows.

"The new music teacher at school," my mother put in. "He's doing a great job with the kids. He's getting a chorus going, now that the orchestra is up and running."

"You've probably seen him at church, Father," my dad said. "Tall guy. Actually, he's joining us for cocktails next Saturday. You'll meet him."

"A Catholic, then," Father Ryan replied. "Oh yes, I think I have seen him. But is he an organist?"

"He plays everything," I said.

Father Ryan seemed amenable to just about anything, as long as his music crisis was resolved. "I'll approach Mr. Dean," he said.

My mother raised her glass to Father Ryan. I could tell she was pleased at the reflected attention she might expect from her son, the new church organist. That was fine with me. I would get more of what I yearned for that winter—time with Mr. Dean.

Why would I want more time with Mr. Dean, after what happened in the storage closet? What was my problem? I couldn't explain it. I just longed to be with him, no matter what. He was the most exciting person I'd ever known, he liked music, he liked me. And anyway, a day or two after a trip to the storage closet, the memory grew as dim as the closet itself, all that went on in there padlocked inside.

I smiled at my mother and raised my water glass to Father Ryan.

The following Saturday afternoon at four-thirty, I had my first lesson on the organ. The intense quiet, the lingering smell of incense and polished oak, the giant pipes soaring straight above us into the open space, all added to the thrill of being alone with Mr. Dean there in the choir loft. We spoke in low, confidential whispers, intimidated by the solemn atmosphere and the presence of God, Himself, who supposedly resided on the altar below. His saints peered out at us from their perches around the apse and in the bright greens, reds and blues of the clerestory windows, while the Blessed Virgin, to the right of the altar, smiled down at the infant Jesus, protected in her adoring embrace.

This atmosphere posed a serious conflict, since, at nearly thirteen, my penis had acquired a stubborn mind of its own. Stiff and soaring as one of those organ pipes, it stood adamant and self-satisfied against my stomach much of the time, particularly around Mr. Dean. Bewildered, I carried books or a music score or my jacket in front of me wherever we went, hiding my body as I had already learned to hide my thoughts. But in the presence of God, my pathetic state felt particularly outrageous.

Mr. Dean sat close, his arm occasionally resting on the choir rail behind me. His leg brushed mine as he pumped the pedals of the lower register that I would have to master as soon as I could reach them. Chills darted down my legs with that touch, leaving goose bumps in their path. The second hand on his watch ticked away our precious time together.

"Try starting the run with two, then three, and thumb under on the G. Then you'll have one, three and five there for the arpeggio."

I did as he said, the notes reverberating around the huge empty space, the power of the final chord sending a heavy vibration through the bench beneath us.

"No, like this," he said, arching his hand over mine to demonstrate the passage. The heat of his hand, the throbbing bench, the quivering pipes, whatever it was, I came right there in my pants—startled, bewildered, bent with the force of my first ejaculation. Pulsating contractions in my throat matched those in my groin, as a warm wetness spread to my thigh. I turned away from Mr. Dean.

"Are you okay, Corey? What's wrong?"

"I'm fine," I managed.

"Try it once more," he said, taking his hand away.

Always good in a crisis, I played it correctly this time.

"There, you've got it now."

I dropped my hand to the spot, sick with self-reproach. In a church? Without even touching? What kind of disgusting pervert must I be?

"Maybe that's enough for today," Mr. Dean said. He reached and shut down the organ, the hum of the giant pipes slowing and coming to rest with a thin click, like a TV screen going blank. "You played really well. You're going to be good, Corey." He put his hand on my shoulder. I grabbed the music score and closed it in my lap. As Mr. Dean stood and lowered the lid of the organ, I slipped off the bench and turned my back to him. I lifted my parka from the pew where I'd left it. A package tumbled out onto the floor—the present my mother and I had bought for Mr. Dean that week, in Pittsfield.

Mr. Dean looked over at me. "What's that?" he asked.

I dropped the music score and pulled my parka in front of me, feeling my shrunken penis in its damp little nest. "What?" I said, too loud.

"That box on the floor."

"Oh, that. It's for you." I bent down. "Here," I said. "For teaching me organ."

I could see he was surprised as he eased the box out of my hand, probably thinking my sudden awkwardness was about the present. As he tore off the paper, I put on my parka, which luckily covered me in front.

Mr. Dean opened the box and pulled out the white, extendable conductor's baton. "This is so beautiful, Corey," he said, pulling out the extension and raising the baton toward the empty nave, where he conducted an invisible orchestra. "It's a perfect weight. I love it. Thank you." He looked as if he was about to hug me, or kiss me, but then, thank God and his angels hovering over the choir loft, he reconsidered.

For some reason, I pictured Mr. Beatty right then, hunched behind the wheel of his pickup, rolling it silently down the driveway, jump-starting it as he hit the street. Nervous, crazed, yet excited, about to enter a whole new world. Like him, I felt unprepared for my own expedition into the unknown, yet somehow undeterred. Leaving the church, I walked behind Mr. Dean, admiring his athletic walk, wondering if one day I would be like him. It was nearly five-thirty, and he was coming to our house for the cocktail party my father had mentioned to Father Ryan. I wanted nothing more than to get to my room and change my pants.

We drove in the new Impala past the brick school building, rosy in the fading sun. Drifts of old snow littered the playing fields out back. As he always did, Mr. Dean took a roundabout route to my parents' house.

"Who's going to be at this party?" he asked me.

"The usual, I guess." My parents entertained a lot—people who bought Fords from my father; my mother's women friends from

Pittsfield and their husbands; Mr. Daley, my father's business partner and Gina's father; and Mrs. Daley, whom my mother tended to ignore. "You're probably the only teacher. I guess they like you."

"That's good," Mr. Dean said, smiling across the seat. "I like them, too." He drove with one hand on the wheel, half facing me, as he always did. "Are you happy, Corey?"

That was not a question people asked then. At least not anyone I knew. In fact, I wasn't sure exactly what he meant. "I guess," I said.

"That doesn't sound very enthusiastic."

"Sure, I'm happy," I said, brighter this time.

"I'm real happy," Mr. Dean said, staring at the road ahead, as if he saw a whole lot more out there than the dull smooth blacktop surrounded by gray fields of dirty snow, the occasional white house and red barn. "My father wasn't a very nice guy, you know? He was drunk all the time, and he hurt my mom a lot, me and my sister too. It wasn't like your family. I always dreamed about leaving there, about teaching in a town just like this, with friends like you and your parents." He looked over at me, and then he reached out and took my hand and held it there on the seat, a touch that felt completely different from the one half an hour before. My palm sweated into his as we drove over Prescott Hill, past the Prescott's dairy farm, into the fading light.

"You're my best friend," he said, as we approached the turn onto my road.

"I wish we didn't have to go home yet."

"What would we do?"

"Drive somewhere."

"We'd miss the party."

I shrugged. "We could just keep driving, past Pittsfield, maybe all the way to New York City. Think of the concerts they have there. We could go to Carnegie Hall. I'd give anything."

"Someday," he said, taking his hand away. He pulled his convertible up in front of our house where a dozen other cars were parked along the driveway. "Maybe someday we'll go to New York," he said, turning off the car's engine. "Just you and me."

Mr. Dean seemed to stiffen all of a sudden, to grow up maybe, when he stepped through our front door and said hello to my mom. "How are you, Mrs. Moore?" he said, extending his hand.

My mother kissed the air by his cheek. "Oh please, Bill, call me Joy. Mrs. Moore sounds so old."

"I saw you and Mr. Moore in mixed doubles with the Cushmans down at the indoor courts this morning," Mr. Dean said, "and I have to say, you and Betsy made the men look a little slow."

I could see he was warming up, catching on already to how people talked in my parents' circle.

My mother laid her hand on his arm. "Well, I could say the same about you, running the socks off Daryl Brown, that adorable shop teacher. Oh, to be in my twenties again."

"I didn't know you were out of them."

Score one for Mr. Dean, I thought. He changed so quickly, you never knew quite what to expect. He had already shed that weird initial formality as easily as his topcoat. With me, he could go from gentle and supportive to rough and scary, all in the space of a few minutes.

"Oh, Bill," my mother said, pushing her newly streaked hair back behind her ear.

She led him into the living room, making the most of having a handsome man on her arm. From where I stood in the hallway, they both seemed to be exactly where they had always wanted to be in their lives, doing just what made them happy. How had they managed that? I wondered. Would I ever feel that way?

Then I realized I was still wearing my parka. I dropped my book bag by the stairs and glanced down at my pants. The telltale spot had dried. I stuffed my parka into the bottom of the coat closet, got myself a soda in the kitchen and wandered back into the living room where I grabbed a handful of peanuts from a silver bowl. My mother handed Mr. Dean a drink and led him over to the Cushmans and their week- end guests, a couple from New York City. I followed them, unnoticed.

"They're not married," I heard my mother whisper to Mr. Dean as they crossed the room. "Living together." She smiled up at him. "Things are so different nowadays. I missed all the fun."

Right! No one had more fun than my mother.

"I doubt that, Joy," Mr. Dean said, winking at her. She sure brought out the best in him.

When she introduced him to the Cushmans and their friends, the woman from New York said, "Bill Dean? Oh my God, *the* Bill Dean? From BC?"

They all turned to Mr. Dean, who blushed the color of a winter sunset. "Yes, I went to Boston College," he said.

"Class of '59, right? Claire Ferguson was one of my best friends senior year." The woman's voice was loud, as if she'd already had too much to drink.

Mr. Dean took a tiny step backward. My mother looked from the woman to Mr. Dean, and then back to the woman.

"She never stopped talking about you. I feel like I know you."

"Tell us," my mother said. "We're all ears."

The woman was suddenly silent, her eyes cast down to her shoes.

"That good, is it?" my mother said. "We'll have to talk later." She whisked Mr. Dean away, not so much rescuing him, I didn't think, as keeping him to herself. Mr. Dean looked befuddled now, and grateful to be in the safe keeping of my mother. "I bet you broke poor Claire Ferguson's heart, didn't you?" I heard her say, as I turned away and made for the stairs to my room.

In the mirror above my dresser, I stared at my reflection—my eyes set deep under my new bushy brows, my long chin, my floppy hair, all like hers. Mr. Dean sure seemed to like my mother. Was it because she always had something clever to say? Maybe I was too quiet. I needed to think of how to make Mr. Dean laugh the way she did.

I lay on my bed and thumbed through a book of organ music that I'd brought home from my lesson. The chatter of voices downstairs built into a steady crescendo, as new people arrived. I pictured Mr. Dean talking and laughing, my mother taking him by the arm and introducing him to everybody, never returning to the woman from Boston College.

An hour or so later, I heard footsteps outside my door, probably my dad, coming to check on me as he sometimes did. But it was Mr. Dean who peaked around the door of my room and stepped inside.

"How come you're not downstairs?" I asked him, sitting up.

"Got a little boring," he said, pushing the door not quite closed behind him.

"How did you know which room was mine?"

"Just a guess." He was unsteady, his eyes narrow as if he were squinting to see.

"Where's my mom?" I asked him.

"Downstairs. They're all down there. I snuck off, just to say hi."

He seemed especially tall, looming above my bed. I set the music score down next to me and leaned back against the headboard.

"Do you mind?" he said.

Did I? I had thought of showing him my room some day, but now it felt strange. He smelled like liquor.

"What are you reading?" he asked, leaning over to the organ book.

"The stuff we were working on today."

Mr. Dean swayed as he thumbed some pages. The glass in his other hand tilted until an ice cube tumbled out and hit the floor. "Oops," he said. He bent further to retrieve it, and for a minute, I thought he might fall onto the bed. He swayed as he stood up and dropped the cube back into his glass. He looked down at me. "Guess I'm a little drunk."

"It's okay," I said.

He reached out and ran his fingers through my hair. My mother had probably missed him by now. She might even come up here looking for him. Still, I wanted to take his hand and hold it the way he had held mine in the car. I wanted him to tell me more about when he was a boy, growing up with a mean father. But not here, and not when he was drunk.

His fingers moved to my shoulder. I could feel my heart pounding. "We should probably go downstairs," I said, moving to get up. He pushed my shoulder back against the headboard.

"You know how much I like you, don't you, Corey?"

Looking up at him, not knowing what to say, I thought I heard someone on the stairs.

"I think you're great," he said. "I really do." He ran his hand from my shoulder down across my stomach to the belt of my jeans.

"Mr. Dean. . . ."

"It's okay, don't worry." He slipped his fingers down inside my underwear.

"Don't, please."

He leaned over as if he was about to kiss me. I pushed him away and jumped up, just as my father stepped into the room.

"Bill!" my father said, tilting his head, surprised. He glanced around the room, as if he expected someone else might be there, maybe my mother.

"I came up to say goodbye to Corey," Mr. Dean said, stepping back, knocking into my bedside table. He reached out to steady the lamp.

"I came to check on him, myself," my dad said.

We all stood around my bed, awkward and self-conscious. My father turned to me. "Are you okay, son?"

What had he seen? Was I okay? How was I to know? "Sure," I said.

"Do you want to come down and get something to eat?"

"That's okay. I'm kind of tired."

"Why don't I leave you two," Mr. Dean said. "It's time for me to be going, anyway."

"Wait," my dad said. "Joy's been monopolizing you all evening. By the way, singles tournament at the indoor next weekend. Think about it." He poked Mr. Dean in the arm, then turned to me. "Goodnight, son."

Stay, I thought. Sit here with me a while. Tell me something about people. Anything. But my father took Mr. Dean's shoulder and guided him out of my room. I listened to their heavy steps on the stairs, imagining my dad arriving a little earlier than he had. A shiver rippled down my back.

Soon I heard Mr. Dean at the foot of the stairs. "Wonderful evening, Joy, really." I pictured him embracing my mother and shaking my dad's hand. Did he even know how reckless he was? To me, he was like some crazy, out-of-control kid, himself. Probably people didn't know what to make of him. Probably they were too polite, or naïve, to even wonder.

I heard the door close downstairs and ran to the window, where I watched Mr. Dean walk to his car, open the door and angle his long body behind the steering wheel. He looked up to where I stood and flashed his most beautiful, conspiratorial grin. Then he started the Impala and turned it around, leaving a trail of blue exhaust as the car crept slowly to the end of our driveway.

Chapter Six
1988

Three years have passed since Gina left this house for good and Jack moved upstairs to my room. For months, her absence pained us both. I sometimes wondered if my relationship with Jack, born of hurt, was destined to drown in the wake of its own offense; that it was only a matter of time. Though Gina had been the one to sever all connection with us, guilt and regret interlaced our first months together.

Still, things moved along with a speed and vigor that outdid my imagination. The wildflowers Jack and I planted emerged that first June with a flourish that surpassed our most romantic expectations—daisies and black-eyed Susan, bachelor buttons and Queen Anne's lace, Indian paint brush and thistle. As he had predicted, their blossoms were reflected in the placid surface of the pond each evening, as the sun descended in a throbbing, red glare to the horizon. It also seemed to me that our interaction was reflected in those vibrant blooms—the sweet optimism of the daisies, the delicacy of the Queen Ann's lace, the sharp thorniness of the thistle.

We returned to that first summer's habit of dining on the grass by the shoreline, the ground still warm from the day and smelling of wild mint and chive, tree frogs and crickets breaking into song as a lambent darkness made us feel small. My spirits soared in an unprecedented and frenzied rapture until some incidental spark ignited a conflict and our wills collided. Silence engulfed us then and I retreated, frightened and doubting the whole enterprise. But, with a conciliatory smile or fingers slipped under my thigh in the middle of the night, a bunch of those wildflowers set in a glass by the sink, I rebounded with the force of an inflated raft held under water. The strain of our emotional connection seems directly proportional to its intensity.

Some people think friendship ruins the possibility of romance, all those hours of chaste conversation, habits and schedules that have nothing to do with the reckless ecstasy of sex. But Jack and I made love in the barn, in the fields, in the pickup at the end of a long-closed dirt lane. We washed each other in the cramped shower downstairs, dried one another with towels warmed on the radiator, made spent spoons of our bodies under flannel sheets. We accumulated private jokes, developed our own language of affection and dismay, cherished the most mundane activities of shopping and shoveling snow because we did them together. We became a couple, by some miraculous process neither of us understood or could ever have anticipated.

We're best friends, lovers, antagonists. Holding hands, secretly, in the pickup still sends a shiver of excitement through me, as if two men having such a connection were unprecedented, a brand new concept, unique to us. I want to lean out the window and proclaim, "I love him, and he loves me. Isn't that amazing?"

Other times, I wonder if this feeling of newness that still pervades the relationship means that I haven't really gotten to know Jack. He reveals so little. The occasional story about his past bursts from him as if it had escaped, and he rushes to close the gate behind it. The few times I asked about the lover he had in college, he bristled. Covering up seems like it's just Jack's way. I wish he would trust me, be as vulnerable as I sometimes feel around him.

On this particular Saturday, a stubborn storm front threatens the sunny, high-pressure system of our interaction, frustrating us both. We're painting a mural on the dining room wall. Actually, Jack is painting. I mostly move the ladder and clean up, lean heavily against the butternut-paneled fireplace that dominates the room, or would if Jack weren't here. I'm the gofer, my least favorite role, the one I played when I was married to Gina. I look around the dining room in an attempt to distract myself. The Quakers, who initially inhabited this house, would have cooked and eaten in this room, lingered before the fire on an October Sunday like this one. I imagine myself present at one of those dinners—a chicken slaughtered that morning, produce from the garden, sparse conversation. And loving Jack at the far end of the table, which curtails the fantasy—a scowling congregation, disdaining the feelings I have for this man.

The dining room is the soul of the house, with tall twelve-over-twelve windows letting in plenty of light, and four doors leading to the hallway, the kitchen, the cellar, and to the ell attached in the nineteenth century—Jack's room before he moved upstairs. The ceilings are over eight feet, high for an early house and allowing plenty of wall space for the mural.

This morning, Jack and I emptied the room of all but the plank table, which we covered with newspaper, brushes and tubes of acrylic paint. I watch now as Jack, his tongue pressed into his cheek, draws his brush down the wall, the heavy, dark line as straight and steady as a tree trunk, which I can see now, is exactly what he intends it to be. And which, in fact, is how I see him—sturdy, solid, rough on the outside, vulnerable within. He dabs his brush in brown and then yellow and runs a line out from the trunk. A branch, foreshortened, appears to jut into the room. Jack, so serious, so utterly involved, so irritated by any distraction.

"I wish you were as comfortable with a conversation as you are with a paintbrush," I mutter.

He doesn't respond. Did he hear?

Sometime during the past year, he stopped taking my complaints about his aloofness to heart, which, ironically, has freed me to complain more. Not that I'm a model of openness, myself. I'm beginning to see how all the words I spew don't reveal that much about me. Words can obscure as readily as silence. Actually, I'm glad Jack doesn't use phrases like "emotionally available" or "getting in touch with your feelings." I hear plenty of that in my practice in the city.

He rinses his brush now and dabs at the black, then the yellow again. He runs a line from the branch across the trunk of the tree to the ground, and a shadow appears, almost as if some errant rays of sun had materialized from the hallway. I contemplate a chair turned upside down on the table, which I would set on the floor and sit in a while, if it didn't feel so much like resignation. All day, I've wanted a little more creative input, but haven't been able to squeeze it in around Jack.

"Grab the ladder, will you?" he says, paint dripping off his brush onto the damp rag in his other hand. His strong jaw warps into a boyish petulance when he's concentrating, a look I find amusing, for a while.

I remove a cup of water from the top rung and slide the ladder over next to the fireplace, a few feet beyond where I know he needs it to be. I set the water on the window sill. A breeze, smelling of dry leaves and sun, drifts through the open window. Isn't this exactly the sort of moment I had imagined, living with a man?

I decide, after all, to turn the chair over, and sit at the far side of the room. Jack jiggles his brush in the glass. Swirls of gold and russet cloud the water. He kicks the ladder, screeching across the wood floor.

I love this man, I tell myself. And it's true, a love that whirls like a beacon in the shroud of heavy weather that sometimes envelopes us, an intensity that flashes brilliant and then vanishes in a feverish, yet predictable pattern. Not that I feel particularly appreciated, or even understood. I feel desired in a way I never experienced before, and stunned by the still-exhilarating unreality of being with a man.

At breakfast this morning, while chasing a few lingering raisins around the speckled bottom of my cereal bowl, I brought up the idea of painting the dining room. Jack was noncommittal. "Actually, I was thinking about a mural," I persevered.

Jack's eyes, a dazzling cerulean blue that still causes my heart to flinch, darted to the bare walls, then back to his coffee. Did he know the effect of those eyes? That they were enough, almost?

"Like you see in old taverns or those restored manor houses in Virginia. You know, a painting of the house, the barn, fencing, maybe some animals. An Edward Hicks knock-off."

Jack continued to stare at the wall. I suspected, from his relentless heel tapping, that his lack of enthusiasm masked a deeper worry. He had started his own small contracting business after that first summer here, and he was probably fretting about a recent job he'd taken, shoring up a barn in Kent. There'd been unforeseen problems—a dry-rotted ridge line, cracked sills under two windows—and Jack was afraid he was going to lose money.

Giving up, I'd been about to pick up the empty cereal bowls and take them into the kitchen, when Jack said, "Murals are so formal. Might look pretentious in here."

"We could keep it simple."

Jack got up and walked to the wall next to the fireplace, taking his coffee with him. He ran his free hand along the old plaster, assessing it. I read somewhere how the senses compensate for one another—if a man loses his sight, his sense of smell becomes more acute. In that case, Jack was like a blind, deaf person with a serious cold. He always explored through touch, running his hands over a breached beam or a jammed window sash, diagnosing the problem tactilely. A talent I appreciate a whole lot in bed.

"What about a Noah's Ark?" he said.

I picked up our bowls, then stood, contemplating the bare wall. I was pretty stuck on the idea of a rendering of the house, but I was willing to compromise if it meant that Jack would take an interest. "What if the ark were a huge hull with this house set on top of it?" I asked.

Jack brightened. "Yes! But with a twist. A gay Noah's Ark. Male and female pairs of animals filing all around the room, led by two men—you and me, holding hands."

Excited, I set the bowls back down. "Followed by two lesbians in flannel shirts and jeans, with bad haircuts."

"Then two stallions, two hens."

"Two bulls, two ewes."

I took Jack's arm and pulled him on a march around the room, as Jack put the list to a tune—Three Blind Mice. "Two red cardinals, two sleepy lionesses, two Tom turkeys, two horny rams."

"The genders need to be subtle, but clear."

"The point is, God will save his gay creatures."

"Because they have better taste," Jack cried, turning me in a do-si-do.

"Because they won't destroy the planet with their cute little procreations."

"The point is, the world won't survive with these couples."

"The point is, who cares?"

"The point is we're all dying, anyway."

We collapsed back into our chairs, knocking my cup and spilling coffee onto the table. We both had friends in New York who had died of AIDS. That last mural joke was bitter-sweet.

"Sounds like a plan," I said.

Jack jumped up. "Let's get going."

"Now?"

"Why not?"

No one was more eager and yet more methodical than Jack. In restoring the house, he had always wanted to determine exactly how things had been done initially—why two beams had been joined in a particular fashion or whether a remnant of trim had once extended all the way around a window frame or just across the top. And then he would try to remedy the deterioration using the early logic he'd found so appealing in its simplicity, or sometimes in its complexity and attention to detail.

Savoring the pleasure of being in sync with Jack, I cleared away the breakfast dishes while he made a list of the things we needed—sponges, water colors, brushes.

"We should probably sand the plaster first," he said, poking along the wall gently with his fist, testing its solidity.

He steps back now, after completing a pair of great blue heron. The damp plaster emits a faint odor of the sea. It's late in the afternoon, we're tired, and it's obvious from the tension in Jack's jaw that he's not happy. "It looks like a fucking kindergarten in here," he says, surveying his work.

It's true, the room has taken on a whimsical but amateurish look—two plump elephants, two bug-eyed frogs—not at all the effect we were after. I chuckle.

"Let's erase them," Jack says, dropping his brush on the newspapers.

I am reminded how devastated Jack gets when things don't work out as he envisions. Only recently did I realize how depressed he was about having quit acting. How could I have missed that? Does Jack's reticence have to do, at least in part, with my insensitivity?

"Don't give up so soon," I say. "They're not that bad."

"Easy for you to say."

"What's that supposed to mean?"

"Everything you touch turns to gold—your practice, this place." He tosses the paint water into a mound of ashes in the fireplace, sending up a cloud of dust.

"And you're creating a contracting business."

Jack grimaces and sets the empty water glass on the table. He thrusts his hands deep into his pockets, surveying the room. "These paintings still look like shit."

"What if we found some drawings of animals in one of my folk art books? We could copy them, trace them even."

"They would still need more definition, more depth. I'm no good at that."

"I think you're deep and well-defined," I say, grinning.

A smile flickers across Jack's lips. "Maybe we should go back to the original idea, the hills and the pond and the woods."

I take the sponge from the bucket, wring it out and begin wiping away the pairs of animals. Sadly, I watch them begin to disappear.

"Wait," Jack says. "They look good like that. The elephants can go, but keep the herons."

I step back and consider the half-erased depiction of the long-necked, graceful birds that sometimes stalk the pond beyond the barn. They're impressionistic now, as if they'd been worn away by time. "You're right," I say, wiping my hands on my jeans. "They look like they've been there forever."

Jack picks up his brush and, despite the hour, begins painting around the herons, a scene of birds and trees and ferns native to Connecticut. I watch as a red-tailed hawk, head bowed, wings arched, seems to soar out of the plaster near the ceiling. I set to wiping away the vibrancy of the colors.

Apparently we're abandoning the ark idea. I picture two gay rats, their suitcases packed, diving astern of the great sinking ship. I try not to read too much into this painting-erasing process. I'm always telling myself I want Jack to let go more, yet here I am, helping to diminish his vivid images. With the sponging, his quirky trees seem to emerge out of the two-hundred year old plaster like the epic pre-Renaissance paintings on the intonaco walls of a duomo. We're a good team, I want to believe, watching him put the finishing touches on a roosting goose.

"Why not put some more background around the goose," I say, "maybe the pond, some cattails?"

But Jack has lost interest, as he sometimes does, crashing with the same imposing force that sparks him initially. He heads to the kitchen to wash out his brushes. It's evening and the last of the light drains from the dining room, taking with it the golden ruddiness of the mural's first successful panel. I think maybe I'll try my own hand when Jack is back in Kent tomorrow, working on the barn. The mural needs some people, a couple of guys, Jack and me.

I follow Jack into the kitchen and stand next to him at the sink, where russet-yellow blotches drip from the brushes onto the old porcelain and flow in golden rivulets to the drain. I turn and pick my jacket off the back of a chair. "I'm going to go for a walk, okay?" I say, waiting to see if Jack might want to come along, but he only sets one brush in the dish drainer and picks up another.

Outside, it's dark and the sharp air, smelling of dead grass and vaguely of sleep, stings my eyes. It's good to be by myself. A ring of keys clinks in my pocket, and I abandon the walk-in-the-dark idea and head to the pickup. The old truck turns over with the dependable, mineral odor of gasoline. I flick on the lights and head down the driveway, tires hurling gravel as I pull out onto the highway.

Twenty minutes later, I pull into a rest area and kill the pickup's engine. The headlights' afterglow throbs behind my eyes. I churn inside. Jack admires independence. I want most of all to bond. So where's the connection? At times like this, I can't help but imagine life on my own again, selling the house and moving back to the city, throwing myself back into career, research, publishing papers. But then, dread overtakes me, a hollowness in my stomach. There are times when being with Jack fills me with a vibrancy I never knew, something so important I can't, or shouldn't, think of letting it go, something worth working for, worth cherishing, even when the effort seems overwhelming.

A truck pulls into view down the highway, its giant cab outlined in tiny orange lights. I imagine the driver, high on his plush seat, a tape playing his favorite songs, his only concern a safe arrival in some distant city. The truck's headlights swirl through the pickup like a search beacon as the giant rig slows and turns into the rest area. The pickup seems to shudder as the rig pulls past and slows to a stop, its brakes exhaling a piercing hiss.

The urge to have sex stuns me like an electric shock. I've been faithful to Jack, as I was to Gina. But it's as if being with Jack these last three years has awakened some sleeping sexual monster—starving from its years of dormancy. I cruise men sometimes in New York, though I never let anything come of it. Something drives me, something murky and unsettling. A fuzziness obscures the fantasies. I can hardly make them out, only the crushing drive. I don't know how to explain these longings to Jack without him thinking I'm dissatisfied with us sexually, which I'm not.

I watch the driver as he opens his cab door, pauses, looks back toward me and swings down to the pavement. In the orange overhead lights of the cab, I can see that he's a large man, forty-something, wearing jeans, boots, open shirt. He drops a cigarette on the blacktop and stomps it out. He hitches up his pants and heads around the truck into the woods that line the far side of the rest area.

My heart races. It doesn't take a genius to figure out that the eroticism of this situation has to do with the sex I had with my teacher twenty-five years ago, sex that linked arousal with danger and illicitness. And I know that I am more vulnerable to sexual impulses after a day of tension, like today. But knowing all that doesn't seem to detract from the desperation I feel now. I'm not even attracted to this truck driver. I want to be monogamous with Jack, the man I really do care about. And yet, I can't start the truck and get out of here.

The driver reappears at the edge of the wooded area. He zips up his fly, which, obviously, he might have done before now. He stands there, not moving toward his truck. My mouth dries to chalk. I reach for the key, but continue to watch the driver. Neither of us moves. It's obvious he's waiting for me to approach him. I let my hand fall away from the ignition.

I roll down my window and rest my arm there. The driver pulls a cigarette from the breast pocket of his shirt, lights it and exhales a thin, blue haze into the night air. I imagine the smell of the smoke. My heart races with excitement and dread, a mix so familiar, so irresistible it almost makes me wince.

He looks both ways, up and down the rest area, which is deserted except for us. He drops his cigarette and soon he is at my open window. "How you doin'?" he asks me, his breath stale with smoke and coffee.

I can't speak. I don't even look at him, just stare ahead.

"Quiet type, huh?"

Still, I don't say anything.

"That's okay. I just wondered what you're up to, that's all. Just sittin' here like this, not doin' anything."

My neck aches. I look at my watch—eight-ten. I've been away from the house over an hour. I reach for the ignition key again.

"No reason to be rude," the guy says.

"I have to go," I say, turning the key.

The truck doesn't turn over. It has a loose battery connection I've been meaning to replace.

"Problem?" the guy asks.

"Just my battery cable," I say, releasing the door handle. The guy doesn't move out of the way.

"Excuse me," I say.

He steps back. I slip out of the pickup, walk around to the front and raise the hood.

He follows me, leans in over the engine, squinting in the weak light from his truck, parked nearby. "Nice truck," he says. "They don't make 'em like this anymore."

I reach in and tighten the positive lead cable.

The driver reaches in too, lets his hand fall on top of mine. "Watch out," he says. "Don't want to shock yourself, do you?" He laughs, spraying spittle onto the engine.

I pull my hand away. A bead of sweat glides down my sideburn. We stand there, looking at each other. His eyes drop to my crotch. As he reaches for me, I turn away and walk around to the driver's door. I pull myself up onto the seat and turn the key. The engine starts.

The driver pushes my door closed behind me. "You take care now," he says. "Maybe you'd be better off stayin' home with the wife and kiddies, you think?" He laughs again.

I shift into gear. The pickup rumbles reassuringly as I pull out onto the highway toward home.

Whatever this urge is, it has to stop, I think, as the pickup rounds curves, its headlights flashing ghostlike into the woods along Route 7. I gain speed, vowing never to let anything like this happen again. I take an indirect route home, waiting for that vow to calm me, which eventually, it does.

Lights blaze in the kitchen and dining room, as I pull into the driveway and park next to the barn. Opening the back door, I smell chicken cooking. The newspapers and paints have been cleared off the dining room table and plates and wine glasses set out. On the wall, Jack has painted the house into the mural—its classic lines, solid brick chimney, even the small-paned windows. A man stands with his hands on his hips at the front door, another pushes a wheelbarrow alongside. No doubt, I'm the one with the proprietary stance and Jack's the worker. Still, tears sting my eyes. I'm so happy he's entered us there among the birds and trees, so happy to be home. I want only Jack, only us.

In the kitchen, I open the oven door and stare inside. The chicken appears to be drying out, as are the mashed potatoes on top of the stove. I turn off the oven, take off my jacket and drop it on the chair. I set plates on the counter and serve up the food, find a candle stub in a drawer, press it into a candlestick and place it on the table.

Jack doesn't join me, though he has to know I'm back. A narrow boundary of light spills from under the doorway to the ell. I walk past the empty bathroom with its fresh smell of soap wafting into the hallway. I knock on the door to Jack's old room and push it open.

The room is long and narrow, with a large window on its outside wall. I adopted it as my study, after Jack moved upstairs. My desk occupies the wall nearest the kitchen so the afternoon sun warms my shoulder when I work there. Jack's old futon extends from the opposite wall, covered with an Indian fabric and half a dozen mismatched pillows, an ideal spot for a nap. More than any other, this room seems to belong to us both. Jack's worn kilim covers the floor, extending under a cracked leather club chair by the window where he sits now, reading.

I want to go to him and kneel next to his chair. I want to bury my face in his chest, take in his lush scent, tell him we can never leave one another. But instead, I say, "Do you want to eat something?"

He looks up from his book, eyes steady. He shrugs. "I guess." He gets up and follows me into the dining room. "How was your ride?"

I set plates on the table. Jack lights the candle. The newly completed portion of the mural takes on a glow that inspires hope. "I really like what you did," I say, pointing to his addition to the mural. "It looks great."

"I like it too," he says, smiling a little.

As we eat the tepid chicken, I picture the truck driver, smell his foul breath, hear his derisive laugh. "It looks as if the house is in flames," I say.

"Feels like it sometimes, too." Jack cuts a pat of butter. The stick is hard and his knife clangs against the dish. He drops the butter onto his tepid mashed potatoes, where it sits, not melting.

"We should talk more." I say, knowing there's an explosion lurking beneath the placid surface of our relationship that we're both afraid to ignite. Jack told me once, early on, that he didn't believe in psychotherapy. Most of his New York friends had seen shrinks, he maintained, with no noticeable results. His statement had felt like a slap, since therapy, in addition to being my profession, had gotten me through a pretty desperate stretch of time during college and graduate school. I knew that Jack's attitude protected him from looking too deeply into a painful past of his own, but I should probably have thought more about what his comment had meant about our future. Our rapport has always been physical—replacing beams, clearing brush, and that amazing, wordless, sexual connection. But now I have this need for more.

Jack tries another bite of chicken. His shirtsleeves are rolled, his muscular forearms tanned from working outside. I often desire Jack in the midst of these tensions, some strange synaptical misfiring, no doubt. But tonight, that desire is even more marked. I am desperate to be consumed by Jack.

The candle flickers between us. I sprinkle salt over my chicken in a hopeless attempt to enhance its appeal.

"What should we talk about?" Jack asks.

"I don't know. Ourselves?" I consider asking him what he and Gina had been talking about that day, three years ago, when I overheard them in the kitchen. The fact that it comes to mind tells me it still bothers me. Or maybe, now, I can say more about what happened with my teacher back in junior high. Maybe that would put us on a new path. In fact, I did mention it to Jack once, though I'd been cryptic about the details of what had actually happened. I'd never told anyone, other than my shrink, about my teacher. And frankly, I still wasn't sure how that whole experience had affected me, so I hadn't known exactly what to say to Jack. Had I been gay since childhood, and Mr. Dean had simply picked up on that? Or had my teacher awakened the homosexual potential present in any adolescent? Had the experience been so upsetting that I'd hidden my sexual feelings for twenty-odd years, even from myself?

Jack hadn't asked for details, which had been both a relief and a disappointment. No doubt, he'd been sensitive to my need for privacy, yet I had wanted him to show more interest or concern, maybe even to help me understand the effects of what had happened, like the truck driver, which seems to me such an obvious repeat of that early experience with Bill Dean. And yet, I fear that if I were to tell Jack about it, he'd never trust me again. Can a relationship unravel that easily? Is our hold on one another that tenuous?

"Remember when I told you about being molested, in seventh grade?" I ask him now.

"Your teacher?"

"You never asked me what happened."

Jack sticks his fork into his mashed potatoes where it stands erect, a monument, to what? Our general impasse? "You told me about him two years ago," he says. "Why are you bringing it up now?"

"Because it was such a big thing for me. I guess I had wanted you to ask more about it." I hated the petulant tone of my voice. And I was being unfair, putting the responsibility all on him.

"I told you I thought the guy was off base."

"It's more complicated than that, Jack."

"How so?"

"First of all, I liked the guy. He was the only person who really took an interest in me."

"Don't all abused kids think it's some sort of love they're getting?"

"I knew so much more than I should have, so much more than other kids. Or at least I thought I did."

"What do you mean?"

"How adults worked, how they behaved. In a weird way, I felt like an adult, myself, around that guy. Now, when I see a kid that age, I'm amazed. They're such boys!"

"The guy was out of line."

Anger ripples across my chest and then subsides. Maybe Jack is right to see things so simply. Maybe complication is a means of holding onto unhappiness, making it all easier in a way because there's nothing definitive you can say or do. Complicated is easy, simple is hard. I reach for Jack's hand. "I love you, you know."

Jack allows his hand to be held.

"How's the barn going, in Kent?" I ask him.

"Okay, I guess. I'll probably break even. Guess I need to be a little more careful when I take on a project, particularly an old place."

"Like this one," I say, grinning. "Do you think we got in over our heads here?"

"Are you speaking metaphorically?" he asks.

We both chuckle. Jack turns to the mural. "I like it," he says, "the house, you and me."

"We've been together over three years."

"From when?"

"From when Gina left, I guess. That's when I think of things really starting between us."

"You mean that day I cleaned up your cuts?"

I grin. "You could have gotten at those scrapes without taking off my jeans, right?"

"Probably."

We chuckle again. Jack retrieves his hand and gets up. "Had enough?" he asks, reaching for my plate.

Never, I think. Never will I have had enough of you. "You go back to your book," I say. "I'll clean up."

At the sink, I chip the burnt chicken juices off the pan, then decide to run water into it and leave it until morning. As I reach for the light switch in the dining room, I pause once more to examine the addition Jack made to the mural. I run my fingers over the two men, obscuring one and then the other. With the loss of each, the mural seems incomplete. We need each other.

Dwelling on the mural in the stillness of the house, imagining Jack slipping into sleep upstairs, I hope that things will be okay with us. We'll work things out, I tell myself. I vow never to let anything like that truck driver happen again. And I vow to tell Jack more about the time with Bill Dean. How can he understand, if I don't tell him the whole story?

I pull newspaper from the bin by the fireplace and spread it across the table. I set out paints and brushes and a cup of water. In the woods behind the house, I paint a boy, not as accomplished as Jack's figures, yet credible. The boy sits at a grand piano, his hands perched above the keys.

Chapter Seven
1988

On a March day that smells hopefully of spring, Jack enters the kitchen. Smelling of turpentine and new wood, he pulls off his jacket. He's been refinishing a chest of drawers he picked up at the flea market in New Milford. "Somebody bought the Thomas place," he says, reversing his New York Yankees cap and stepping to the sink. "At least they're in contract."

The Thomases had lived in the next house on our road for over sixty years. They'd been our closest neighbors when Gina and I arrived in 1985, though you can barely see their place, and only in winter when the leaves are down. Mr. Thomas used to stop by that first year to check our progress with the restoration. He loved telling stories about the previous owners' skating parties on the pond and their vegetable garden that had produced seven varieties of tomatoes. Mrs. Thomas sent over a rhubarb pie that first July, before Alzheimer's sapped her ability to cook or to remember who Gina and I were. She moved into a nursing home about the same time that Gina left, and she died not long afterward. Jack and I looked after Mr. Thomas for a year, running errands and shoveling his walk, until he died, too. During that year, Mr. Thomas never inquired about my change of partners. Freedom of choice is a conservative, Yankee value, and Mr. Thomas was both, in spades. He would have said it was none of his business, and I suppose he'd have been right.

For two years after he died, the place stood empty, the two Thomas sons apparently reluctant to part with the memories of growing up there.

"It's only been on the market a couple of weeks, hasn't it?" I say.
"Three."

Jack pushes up his shirt-sleeves and begins washing his hands. I take in his worn jeans, the sound of water splashing in the sink, the hum of the old refrigerator, and I feel as if I have stepped into a lambent stillness, a narrow ray of golden-flaked sun. I blink, then move behind Jack and slip my arms around his waist. I kiss the back of his neck, under the hat-peak. The fresh scent of hand soap mixes with the smell of Jack's saw-dusted neck. He turns, his hands dripping, and I step back, feeling the stirrings of an erection pressing against my jeans.

We've both been trying to talk more, since that tense day painting the first mural panel. And I can sense a difference.

"The new owners were walking around the place when I got back from New Milford," Jack says. "I stopped and welcomed them to the neighborhood."

I'm impressed. Jack is not usually that friendly to strangers. "You should have invited them over," I say, immeditiately regretting the implication that he'd done something wrong.

He clasps his wet hands to my cheeks. "Ah!" I shout, jumping back. "That's cold."

He lifts the dish towel off the rack and dries my face. "They're gay," he says.

"The new neighbors?"

"Two guys, obviously a couple."

I take the towel from Jack and finish drying my face. "That is so cool!"

"One's older, Wall Street type—mergers and . . . whatever."

"Acquisitions."

"He told me before I had a chance to ask. The other one's probably my age—thirty-five, tops. Not sure what he does. He said, but I didn't follow it. That one is not hard to look at. You'd probably like him."

"You mean he's hot, like you?" I say, slapping Jack's butt with the damp towel. I turn to the stove and lower the heat under a saucepan, where a cylinder of frozen lentil soup stands like one of those giant rolled hay bales that dot the fields around here in summer. "I can't believe two guys are moving in next door," I say, pushing the soup around the dented pan with a knife. "That is so great!"

"They want to do some work on the place—new bathrooms, an addition. The house needs a roof. I gave them my card."

I sense tempered excitement in Jack's tone, something I haven't heard in a while. "Jesus, Jack. Gay neighbors and maybe your first big job. When are they closing?"

"Let's not get carried away."

"Why not?"

"Maybe they were just talking. You know how people can be." Jack moves to the window and looks in the direction of the Thomas place. "Maybe they're assholes. Who knows?"

"But Jack, I want to get carried away. Why go through life expecting disappointment?"

"Don't play shrink, okay?"

"But it's true. We've always felt kind of isolated here. This is a real opportunity to make some new friends—gay friends."

"Maybe." Jack moves from the window and peers over my shoulder at the soup. "I should shower before dinner."

I watch him cross the kitchen. He's put on a few pounds in the three years we've been together. Extra weight or no, he still does it for me. "Want some company?" I say.

He turns and smiles. "Sure. Why not?"

I switch off the soup and follow Jack into the ell. Pulling off my shirt in the bathroom, I glance out the window toward the Thomas place, wondering what the buff new neighbor really looks like.

George and David hire Jack to take charge of renovating their place. In turn, Jack hires an array of subcontractors—plumbers, carpenters and painters, all of whom he supervises in the biggest job he's ever taken on. In three months, there's a new roof on the house, a new kitchen and screened porch, remodeled bathrooms, everything freshly painted in colors chosen by a New York decorator. And a pool is installed in the back, complete with outdoor shower and Jacuzzi. As I watch the place being transformed from a simple nineteenth-century Cape to an up-scale weekend retreat, I sometimes wish Jack and I had that kind of money to throw at our house. But actually, when I really think about it, I prefer the slower pace we've taken, restoring more than renovating, and doing the bulk of the work ourselves. I want to feel personally attached to my home, to know how the heat and plumbing work, to look at the foundation and recall when Jack and I rented a hydraulic lift to replace the sill under the kitchen.

Jack was both right and wrong about the new owners. On the one hand, they did sometimes promise more than they delivered. The pool house got nixed, for example—too expensive. But with George, the older one with the money, you always know where you stand. Whatever comes into his head comes out of his mouth. David, the cute one who is sometimes up from the city without George, is harder to read. During the renovation, he sometimes invited Jack to stay for a drink after the workmen finished for the day. Weekends, I joined them, but on their own during the week, David and Jack occasionally had dinner. I try not to feel jealous of what appears to be David's ongoing flirtation with Jack.

On a Saturday evening in July, we are invited to dinner, along with two other couples who are George and David's guests for the weekend. The steaks are thick and rare, and the wine goblets are huge. The conversation centers on money, its acquisition and management—its care and feeding is how I think of it. My eyes travel from one successful, forty-something year old gay man to the next. Money and houses are the children of gay men, their financial offspring, an ongoing source of pride or disappointment. David drops a lot of names—who was seen doing what with whom in the Hamptons. Jack is oblivious. He is happy to receive their compliments about his transformation of the house, but their social concerns carry no weight with him. Ironically, the other men seem to find this aloofness alluring.

Jack's lack of pretension, his basic honesty, pleases me.

Late in the evening, after a long cocktail hour and an even longer dinner, I find myself alone with George. Their guests from Manhattan have gone to bed. Jack has disappeared to the bathroom, and David was last seen crouching in the garden, examining the new lilies. I have long since lost track of the amount of wine I've consumed. You can't set your glass down in this house without George refilling it. I sit on a wicker sofa on the new screened porch, admiring Jack's work. Maybe this will launch his career as a builder, I'm thinking, though I don't know if that's what Jack wants. He's never said, but I suspect he harbors the fantasy of returning to acting one day. We're talking more, but Jack's career is a sensitive subject.

The underwater lights from the pool, which sits on a raised bluff just out of sight of the house, cast a tall, undulating light show onto the mature trees brought in to shield the property from the road. George returns from the kitchen, his glass in one hand, an open bottle of an excellent Pinot Noir in the other. "What are you smiling about?" he asks me.

"How great this house came out. And what a fine evening this was."

"Can I freshen you?" George says.

"No thanks." I cover my glass with my hand. "I've had enough."

George pours for himself and sets the bottle on the coffee table. He sits in the wicker chair adjacent to the sofa. George is probably in his mid-fifties, his plain looks enhanced by a relentlessly upbeat manner. In no time, he's on his feet again, and I wonder if all financially successful people are restless by nature. He shuts off the overhead lights, and the screened porch falls into a pleasant semi-darkness which highlights the play of light in the trees. I lean my head back against the plush cushion, thinking that Jack and I need to invest in some pillows and a couple of upholstered chairs. But then, like George, we so rarely sit.

I close my eyes and take in the distant lapping sound and the occasional splash in the pool. "What's it all about?" I hear George ask.

When I open my eyes, he is standing behind the sofa, directly over me. "What's what all about?" I say, raising my head off the cushion.

"This!" He gestures with his glass to the garden, the pool, the place in general. "All this." The glass overflows and a splash of red wine spreads across the pale upholstery like a gash. I slide out of the way.

"Shit," he says, reaching to brush it off. "Sorry."

"Shall I get a sponge?"

"Leave it." He sips his wine. "We like you guys. You seem different—not so caught up in the scene."

The scene, I think. There is no scene around here to get caught up in. Why did George and David choose Connecticut rather than Long Island, where their friends spend weekends? "We like to be alone," I say. "But sometimes it feels a little isolated. We were really glad when you guys bought this place."

George's fingers slip into my hair, and I notice the spicy smell of cologne on his hands. Relax, I tell myself. The guy is just being friendly. He's had too much to drink. I hear him set his wine down on a table behind me, and then there are two hands massaging my scalp, then my neck and shoulders. Despite myself, I tense.

"I'm not going to hurt you," George whispers.

George's touch is skilled, as if he'd taken massage lessons at some point. His comment, intended to help me relax, has the opposite effect. Mr. Dean used to say something similar, when we first met. He must have known, even so early on, that he was, in fact, going to hurt me. Why make such a statement, unless you've considered the possibility of hurt?

Yet, despite myself, I do begin to relax. George kneads my shoulders and back more deeply. I can feel the stirrings of an erection, which I hope George doesn't notice. It's the wine, I tell myself, the setting, the long evening.

"What are you thinking?" George asks me.

That you're coming on to me, that it feels good, that I should probably stand up and go find Jack. "How comfortable this couch is," I say. "How tired I am."

I lean forward, out of George's reach. "It's late," I say. "We should probably get going."

George moves around the sofa with the deliberate gait of the intoxicated and drops onto the cushion next to me. I imagine the wine stain seeping into his linen trousers and wonder what it might cost to replace the cushion, and now the pants, and whether I could ever be so nonchalant.

He rests his hand on my thigh. "You and Jack are very attractive guys," he says.

I take George's hand off me and hold it, feeling awkward, yet still trying to appear friendly. I feel at once irritated and vaguely aroused.

"David and I do it with other couples, sometimes," he says in a tone that is probably not intended to be sad. "Some company kind of helps us keep going with each other, you know?"

Where the hell is Jack? I'm wondering as I sit there, feeling ridiculous, holding hands with my neighbor.

"What about you guys?"

"No. Actually, we don't."

"There's always the first time," George says.

"We're looking forward to being friends with you and David," I say.

"Isn't sex a friendly thing?"

A yelp comes from the direction of the pool, then a violent splash. Of course, that's where Jack went! He's in the pool. With David. I jump up. "Is Jack. . . ."

"Who did you think was riling the water out there, a couple of deer?"

I walk to the screen door, feeling suddenly dizzy. Jack and David. I open the door and step outside. The flashing light on the trees slows as I make my way past a teak table and chairs and through the terraced flower beds. The night air feels cooler than it had under the protection of the porch. I can smell the chlorination of the water as I clear the hill to the pool.

"Corey?" George calls after me.

I stop. Why am I feeling so desperate? Haven't I been tempted by guys far less attractive than David and George? Being faithful to Jack has always taken precedence, though I know very well how few couples are monogamous, gay or straight. Am I trying to control Jack, or just myself? "Let them be," George says, catching up with me. "They're having fun."

Fun is one thing; having sex with our neighbor, something else. I arrive at the pool, where Jack and David float straight up in the deep end, their arms outstretched toward one another on its glowing surface, their fingers not quite touching. Their naked torsos are refracted by the water so that they appear as short and broad as sumo wrestlers. Jack's chin and nose are highlighted by the light, his mouth and eyes black holes. He ducks under, then comes up laughing, a splashing exuberant guffaw.

George, standing beside me now, drops his wineglass on the grass and kicks off his Ferragamos. He pulls off his stained trousers and paisley boxers in an awkward, one-legged bounce, losing his balance and winding up on his back on the grass, his testicles exposed in a clump of graying hair. There's something endearing about his clumsiness, like an adolescent who's trying too hard. He stands, naked and hirsute, and regains his balance before walking gingerly down the pool steps.

In the distance, I can make out the roof of our barn, and I remember how Jack and Gina and I swam naked in the pond that first summer, a nakedness that felt natural in a way that this does not. I recall the day Gina left for good.

Jack leaves David and swims over to the side of the pool. "Come on in," he says to me.

He has not had sex with David. Not yet, anyway. It would show in his eyes, which gaze up at me now—boyish, guiltless. I want to leave before anything does happen. More than that, I wish Jack wanted to leave, though it's clear he's enjoying himself. Would I want to have sex with David and George? Why are my sexual impulses always so shrouded in layers of turmoil? I undo the buttons of my shirt.

Jack smiles. David ducks under the water and comes up by George in the shallow end. I pull off my jeans and stand naked at the side of the pool. Suddenly I don't feel shy anymore. I feel sexy. I dive in.

"Thanks," Jack says, when I surface next to him. Then he plunges under and comes up halfway across the pool. I dive after him, and we cavort like dolphin back and forth across the pool until, exhausted, we pull ourselves into the hot-tub at the side, wincing at the scalding temperature. I notice George off in a flower bed, vomiting. David stands next to him, his hand on his back, an oddly tender scene.

Under the swirling water, Jack takes my hand. Steam roils around our faces. "You thought David and I were having sex, didn't you?"

I duck under the hot churning water.

"Didn't you?" Jack says, poking me when I come up.

"Yes," I admit. "I don't think I could handle that."

In the distance, David turns from his sick partner to look in our direction. I wave. Jack and I settle back against the thrusts of the underwater jets. Trust Jack, I tell myself. Soon we will pull on our clothes, damp with dew, and head home to our bed where, still smelling of chlorine, we'll make love and then snuggle under the sheet until we fall asleep.

Three months pass in this up-and-down pattern Jack and I have fallen into. For days at a time, we both try to talk more and that seems to work—we feel closer and sex is less perfunctory. Then, a minor resentment, an argument, or sometimes nothing I can pinpoint, sets us into a stony distance that can last for days or even weeks. During those times, I wonder if we did the right thing—Jack staying on in this house when we hardly knew one another. But the thought of him moving out is enough to goad me into trying harder, and eventually that works.

One Sunday morning in October, I awaken before Jack. It's after ten when we get around to breakfast and the New York Times I picked up earlier, in town. I try not to make too much of the fact that I have enjoyed the three hours on my own before Jack came downstairs. I glance at the mural, which neither of us has touched since summer—the two men outside the house and the boy at the piano in the woods. I look across the table at Jack, his nose buried in the Arts and Leisure section, and I recall an old friend of my mother telling me once how she and her husband used to renew their commitment to one another every year, on their anniversary. They both believed that it didn't make sense to pledge more than one year at a time. People changed too much, circumstances, needs. There were days, the woman had said, when she didn't know whether or not she would "re-up," as she put it. Jack and I have been together for over three years now. Would I commit to another year?

The phone rings. Jack looks up at me. I don't move. On the fourth ring, I say, "You get it and I'll do the dishes."

"Deal," he says, getting up and going to the phone in the kitchen. I half listen to his monosyllabic responses—yeah . . . okay . . . right—as I turn to the Week In Review.

Jack hangs up and returns to the dining room. "My mother died," he says, standing in front of the ash-strewn fireplace, his hands at his sides like a boy making his first communion.

"What?" I say.

Jack shows no discernable emotion. As far as I know, he hasn't spoken to his mother or to his brothers—I think there are two—since I've known him. Far younger than his siblings, Jack has referred to himself at times as an afterthought, or worse, a mistake. "When? What happened?"

"This morning. She died in her sleep, I guess. My brother went out to her place when she didn't answer the phone and found her on the kitchen floor."

I don't ask him how his mother ended up on the kitchen floor if she died in her sleep. Clearly, Jack is distraught.

"How did he find you? Here I mean?"

"I guess he looked in her address book."

I stifle the impulse to stand and hug Jack, thinking he might not want that right now. "Was she sick?" I ask him.

"I don't know. She had a heart condition. She was old."

Jack looks like the twelve-year-old boy I sometimes feel that he is. I don't mean this disparagingly. I feel like a lost child, myself, at times. It's something I think we have in common. "Are you okay?" I ask, and I do stand now and hug him. "I love you," I say into his ear. When I pull back, his expression is the same—blank, bewildered. "I'm sorry," I say, "about your mom."

He seems to take in my words, and for a moment it looks as if he might cry. But, instead, he says, "I should go pack."

"Why don't you sit a minute?"

Dutifully, he sits back at the table.

I am struck by this void of emotion in Jack, and feel vindicated, in a way that lacks gratification. It's not my fault that our connection hobbles along as it does. Jack doesn't even respond to his mother's death. Is it simply a lack of emotion that makes him seem so straightforward? "What else did your brother say?" I ask him. "What's his name, anyway."

"Jeb."

"Did he say she'd been sick?"

"I told you, he just went out there and found her."

I try to think of how to engage Jack without upsetting him. "When was the last time you saw your mother?"

He glances at me, then turns to the fireplace. "She never even knew me," he says.

I wait, hoping he'll go on.

Jack stares blankly into the cold ashes. "She only saw me on the stage once, other than high school stuff. She came up to Chadron State for a play. She seemed so vulnerable, so out of place there. I remember being distracted by her silhouette in one of the side rows—motionless, concentrating, or maybe just lost, I don't know. Jeb brought her. The whole visit felt awkward. I was pleased, you know, that she came, but nervous and ready for her to leave when it was over. We had so little to say to each other."

"But she must have wanted to see you, in the play, I mean."

Jack turns to me, then picks up his fork and stabs a piece of cold bacon which he pushes around the perimeter of his plate, leaving a greasy wake. "The weird thing was, she really hit it off with the professor, my ex. That was the last thing I would have expected. We all went out to this hamburger place after the performance, and the two of them talked and carried on. I'd never seen my mother like that. It was getting late, and she and my brother had to drive four hours home. It was so odd to me—that someone I liked, liked her. I'd written her off, you know? Suddenly I had to question what was me and what was her. The professor came to her house with me a couple of times after that. I wondered what she thought about my relationship with him. If she even thought about it at all."

"It's nice when people you care about like each other," I said, sounding feeble. I know so little about either of these people, and I fear that if I say the wrong thing, Jack will clam up. "So, what did they talk about?"

Jack parks the bacon next to his abandoned toast and puts his fork back down on the table. He picks up his napkin and twirls it into a bandanna. "Are you jealous, Corey?" he asks, glancing at me.

I'm jolted by this question. "You mean that the professor got to know your mother and I didn't?"

"Maybe."

"Are you saying you trusted the professor more than you do me?" This whole turn of the conversation seems odd, but I excuse it. Jack is probably in some sort of shock. I just want to give him whatever he needs right now, and not worry about anything else. "I think I'm more curious than jealous," I say. "I just want to know what goes on inside that handsome head of yours."

"All you have to do is ask."

"But I don't know what to ask about." I get up and walk to the fireplace mantle, turn and lean against it, trying not to assume the officious stance of the man in the mural.

Jack only smiles, as if that were sufficient response. Perhaps it is.

"Will you see the professor when you're out there?" A surprise jab of anxiety crosses my chest. I guess I am jealous, just as I was when Jack went to New York to meet up with the guy three years ago. How strange that this man who Jack never talks about remains a haunting presence in our life. I wish I knew more about him.

"I'm sure he'll want to come down to the funeral, though he hasn't seen my mother in years."

"Or you, except that one time." I immediately regret this remark. It's obvious I'm seeking reassurance, or at least information, at a time when Jack is off guard. I have the fleeting fantasy that the professor has visited Jack here when I was working in New York. Three years together, and what I know about Jack is mostly limited to what I observe. Of course, I don't talk much about Gina or my family, either. It's as if neither of us has a past, only this marooned present.

"Or me," Jack says in a tone I can't decipher.

"Should I be jealous, Jack? Do you want me to be?"

"No, and no."

I can hear the wind hissing through the new spruces we planted along the driveway last month. "How old is the professor?" I ask.

Jack grins. "Friends of mine always used to ask that. Everybody thinks age is so important." He reaches for his glass and downs the last of his orange juice.

"I'm sorry," I say. "Now's not the time for us to be talking about him. I would like to hear more, though, someday."

"You know that I loved him once." Jack's hair has dried from his morning shower, though his shirt collar is still circled with a damp ring. He looks distraught. This conversation is all wrong. We should be talking about his mother, though he doesn't seem to want any more of that.

"Let's see," Jack says. "He was forty-one when I met him. I was nineteen. So he's twenty-two years older than me. That makes him—what?—fifty-six now, fifty-seven, maybe? He never looked his age. Or acted it, for that matter."

I had always pictured the professor with white hair and a trimmed beard, a ratty tweed jacket, the stereotypical aging academic. Men in their fifties can be sexy. I don't want to compare myself to the man, but how can I not? "What does he look like?" I ask.

Jack grins again. "He's tall. Average looking, I guess."

"What's his name, anyway?"

The phone rings again. Jack goes to the kitchen and picks up. I can tell from his laconic responses that it's Jeb, again. I stack the plates and take them to the kitchen.

"That was my brother," Jack says, hanging up the phone. "He says he'll pick me up in Omaha, if I let him know when."

"Shall I call the airline?" I say. "Do you want to fly out this afternoon?"

"That would be good." Jack gets up and heads toward the stairs.

Should I have offered to go to Nebraska with him? I would like to meet Jeb, and be with Jack at a time like this. I stare at the half-finished mural, thinking I should paint a child-Jack, standing by himself in the very depths of the woods in the far corner, where sunlight rarely reaches. Not so different from the kid at the piano at the other end of the room, I suppose.

I pull the telephone directory from the closet shelf and turn to the Yellow Pages. The airline keeps me on hold longer than I can tolerate. I'll try again, later, I think, hanging up and taking the stairs two at a time to our bedroom.

Jack sets two shirts on top of a pair of gray flannel trousers he's folded into his duffle bag. "Can I borrow a tie?" he asks me.

"Of course."

He stares at my tie rack in the closet, seemingly unable to choose.

"How about this one?" I say, pulling a tie Gina had given me—subdued, expensive, one I know Jack likes.

He takes it and folds it on top of the shirts. Perhaps I should have held back and let him choose. Jack's pace is slower. When am I going to learn that? I feel as if I'm walking on eggshells.

"Do you want me to come with you?" I ask.

It's obvious from his expression that my going to Nebraska is a new thought, and so I have my answer. But I don't give up. "I don't know your family, so that might make it awkward. But sometimes partners can sort of run interference, you know? I don't want to make things harder for you. It's up to you. I mean, whatever works." I rein in my nervous jabbering, finally, and stop.

"Yeah," Jack says.

"Yeah?"

"Maybe it's better if I go this one alone."

I resist the impulse to retrieve my tie from Jack's bag. Go it all alone, then. "I'll go try the airline again," I say.

Downstairs, while dialing, I imagine Jack with the professor in Nebraska—all the reminiscing, and of course, the support of someone who knew and liked his mother. A tightness grips my chest.

While on hold for the airline, I wonder if I will paint the professor into the mural one day, or if Jack will.

Chapter Eight
1963

I got friendly with Gina Daley the year she got breasts. Ninth grade, our freshman year at Williston High School, the year I turned thirteen, an official teenager. The Beatles were big, even in our quiet little corner of Massachusetts. The A-list kids—the jocks and cheerleaders—wore wrap-around sunglasses and madras Bermuda shorts, a curious mix of Hollywood glitz and New England prep. They smiled, knowingly, never letting on that they were probably as scared as any of us of not fitting in. Like most shy kids, I hadn't yet figured out that the way not to be noticed was to join in. You didn't have to say much, just grin and nod agreement once in a while. If I had at least jettisoned a few bad habits, like looking away when someone made eye contact, biting my fingernails, mumbling to myself, adolescent life would have been a whole lot easier.

Gina wasn't a joiner, either. Not that she was afraid, or had monumental acne or answered every question posed in class, though she probably could have. Her problem was that she didn't appear to want anything. She raised indignation by not noticing which clique had shunned her. Decidedly plain in grade school, with a space between her teeth she hid by not smiling, Gina had kept her eyes on the floor over an armful of books, navigating the school hallways with some foolproof radar that kept her out of direct contact with anyone.

Until that September of ninth grade, when she walked into home room taller and slimmer, yet filled out. Her yellow hair was somehow richer and thicker and pulled back in a bouncy ponytail. Pubescent boys followed her with their eyes as she made her way between the neat rows of desks to the back and took the empty seat next to mine. You could see she hated this new ogling that pursued her like a noxious scent. Perhaps because our fathers were in business together, or perhaps because she saw nothing in me that posed a threat, Gina sought refuge with me. We were both loners, suffering that dreaded adolescent condition of being outsiders for reasons we could do nothing about.

She dragged me to Mass mornings before school, where she pleaded with Jesus to take back her breasts. Kneeling, hands clasped, hoping she hadn't offended Him already by bringing up the subject, she appeared tiny and lost in the immense empty space of Saint Francis Church. She draped a black mantilla over her head as we entered so as not to insult the Holy Ghost who was to put in a good word for her with God. "But he *is* God," I protested. "It's a trinity—Father, Son and Holy Ghost, so how can He intervene for you when He's all three?" But she only put a finger to the determined straight line of her lips.

Her mother had given her the mantilla, believing that a young woman's head and shoulders should always be hidden from God, another thing that didn't make any sense since He supposedly could see everything, including that Gina had suddenly become the sexiest girl at Williston High. The black lace made her look grown up, her blue eyes round and pale as robins' eggs.

Gina believed that her breasts were a spiritual test, like Abraham who'd been willing to kill his son, Isaac, just because God told him to. Personally, I found this disturbing. The Bible was full of such hair-raising tales. So we're supposed to take a lesson from a guy who's willing to cut off his own son's head because somebody suggested it? What sort of God would even ask a thing like that? But then, God had let Abraham off the hook. Gina was hoping for some similar sort of dispensation regarding her breasts. She was willing to cut a deal. She would take them, but in a year or two. She just wasn't ready yet. In return, she promised to stop baiting her mother. I offered to pray for her too, strength in numbers, but Gina believed she had to face everything, even a confrontation with the Holy Spirit, on her own.

The Daleys lived in a Victorian house with aggressive trim just beyond the church and directly across the street from school. That fall, Gina and I took to sitting on her front porch with our feet pressed against the railing, turning the spindles with our sneakers until the smooth raw wood showed through the paint. A couple of fat black flies swarmed lazily around our empty Coke bottles, lined up like bowling pins along the porch. Wadded Baby Ruth wrappers were balls heading for a strike.

We snickered at classmates on the playground across the street, who no doubt saw us as an unlikely pair now that Gina had experienced this caterpillar-to-butterfly transformation and I was still showing less than substantial definition of any kind. But our duo made perfect sense to us. We were both terrified of sex. I had long ago filed Mr. Dean's furtive gropings away in some locked compartment of my meager consciousness, a place, strangely enough, that didn't have to do with sex. Rather, I saw it as some unanticipated and yet thrilling aspect of the adulthood I was so impatient to inhabit. Our secret bore no resemblance to the moonstruck ninth graders who made out under the stairways at school. I had no idea how to take the lead with a girl, what to put where, what to say. Similarly, Gina dreaded having to go along with a guy for fear of hurting his feelings, when nothing she could imagine of a sexual nature was anything less than repelling.

With Gina, my loneliness was suddenly dispelled. I began to fill the bewildering cavern of my detached life with all the space she took up. Reflected in her, I glimpsed an acceptable self, an inkling of hope. Four months into ninth grade, I discovered that I had developed a crush on my new friend. I was inextricably involved with the two most fascinating people in school—Gina Daley and Mr. Dean—and they seemed, miraculously, to want me.

Gina had recently begun saying whatever was on her mind. Unlike me. It was as if all those years she'd been quiet, she had simply refused to say what people wanted to hear. Now, all of sudden, she wouldn't shut up, whether it was about the tight corset of control her mother had wrapped her in, the pair of pink Capezios she'd seen in a thrift shop in Pittsfield, or a play she'd read in some Tennessee Williams anthology. Then, for no apparent reason, she could lapse into a period of brooding restlessness, and we would just sit, rocking side by side on her porch, staring across the street to the manicured athletic fields stretched behind school like the wake of some great ship.

One day, she broke the silence with an appalling announcement. "Kevin exposed himself to me yesterday," she said, gesturing to the house next door, where Kevin Tatro lived with his stepmother, who was also his aunt. His real mother had dropped him off ten years before and hadn't been heard from since. Kevin was seventeen now, with muscles and enough growth to shave every other day.

Gina took the sting out of the most shocking things by making them sound run-of-the-mill. "What do you mean?" I said, aghast, my voice making its embarrassing octave leap.

"Kevin. Remember him?" She pointed again to the house next door.

"Of course I know Kevin. Jesus, Gina. What happened?"

"Don't swear. It's a sin." She crossed herself. "My mother sent me over to borrow their Electrolux, but Kevin's mom is nowhere around, so I head up the stairs to the linen closet. I grab the vacuum, turn, and there's Kevin, blocking the hallway with his you-know-what in his hand."

"You're kidding me! What did you do?"

"I just stood there looking ridiculous with the vacuum hose around my neck. What was I supposed to do?"

I shrugged, picturing Kevin standing with his dick sticking up out of his pants like a surface-to-air missile. "Did he have a stiffy?" I asked her.

"What?"

"Was it hard?"

"I didn't exactly stare at it. What a stupid question!"

"Did he touch you?"

"Of course not." Gina gaped at me in disbelief. "What is wrong with you, anyway? I would have slammed him with the upholstery attachment."

"Well, what happened, then?"

"It's too embarrassing."

"Come on, you told me this much. I won't tell anybody."

"Cross your heart?"

I crossed it and raised my right hand.

"He, sort of, came."

"What?"

"Ejaculation. Into an ashtray on the hallway table, right in front of the window. It was totally gross." Gina grimaced and reached for her Coke, which was empty. "Then he laughed. It was unbelievably disgusting."

"What did you say?"

"Nothing. Wish I had, though. Where'd you get the mouse? or Need a light? Would have shown him I wasn't scared. All he wants is to scare you."

Gina was a master of rationalization. Reason took the fear out of peril, the insult out of rejection. I envied the way she saw through people like Kevin, the snotty, insecure cheerleaders at school, the gawky boys who plagued her in the hallways. Not that she forgave them. Gina forgot nothing. "While he was busy spurting into the ashtray, I just eased around him and left," she said.

I pictured Kevin standing there, coming, and a barrage of confusion descended on me like a squall. Gina was so clear about everything, while the most obvious responses eluded me.

"Did you tell your mother?" I asked her.

Gina's mother was a heavyset woman who seemed to resent everything—her lowly status as the wife of a car salesman, her daughter's fierce independence, that people tended to ignore her. When she wasn't praying, she was complaining or criticizing, and Gina took the brunt.

"Right! Can you see her? First, she wouldn't believe me, and then she'd probably think it was my fault."

"What about your father?"

"He hates me. Ever since this happened." She gestured toward her breasts. "He's always looking at me and asking if I've been to confession, like I've done something wrong."

"Parents are weird."

"Anyway, Kevin's okay. You just have to stay out of his way, that's all."

Just then, Mr. Dean emerged from the back door of our school building, across the street. Gina and I watched in silence as he walked to his car in the parking lot, opened the door and sat behind the wheel. The engine roared into life, then idled. I imagined him adjusting, as he always did, the stack of orchestra scores he kept on the seat next to him. He backed the car out of its space and drove to the exit, where he paused before turning onto South Street. He didn't see Gina and me.

For two years, Mr. Dean had been my teacher and my friend, words that failed to describe the force of our peculiar connection, which was in fact not primarily educational—except in the broadest sense—nor, in retrospect, particularly friendly. Blindly, I was feeling my way through some uncharted space between childhood and adulthood, between pleasure and fear, with Mr. Dean as my unlikely guide. I took my lessons from him on the organ, and attended weekly orchestra rehearsals. We talked about college and a potential career for me in keyboard. Our trips to the storage closet were sporadic. It might happen for several weeks in a row—after rehearsal, when everyone else was gone—and then not for a month or two. Ironically, it was during those interim weeks that I was most uneasy, wondering if Mr. Dean had lost interest in me, or if there might be another boy in school he preferred. When we finally did go to the storage closet, I felt reassured, but also worried and somehow resentful. Everything was under Mr. Dean's control.

Gina picked at a thread in her baggy jumper. She'd drawn that familiar, invisible barrier around herself that I no longer tried to penetrate. What happened with Kevin had probably upset her more than she let on.

It occurred to me to tell her about Mr. Dean, maybe as a way to console her. Gina was my best friend. Yet I felt competitive with her. The idea of seeing Kevin Tatro's dick, had I been honest with myself, intrigued me. I was probably envious of Gina, the same way I'd envied a kid from school who'd escaped his burning house that winter by leaping down a flaming staircase. I wanted to experience an escape from peril; I longed for a chance to prove myself.

Gina had taken one more step up in my estimation. She hadn't been frightened by sexy Kevin Tatro, or worse, excited. She hadn't let herself be taken over, the way I always seemed to. In a casual trip to the Tatros' to borrow a vacuum cleaner, she had demonstrated her essential coolness, her imperviousness to danger, her shocking lack of intimidation.

She slumped in her rocker, fingering its frayed wicker arms, and stared, unblinking, into the empty street. Maybe I thought that by telling her about Mr. Dean, I could join her on that elevated ground I had just allotted her.

But what would I say?

"Do you want another one?" Gina asked me, leaning over to pick up her Coke bottle.

"No, thanks."

My mind sprinted through a variety of possible disclosures. Mr. Dean and I loved each other and some day we were going to live together in New York City. Even I could hear how far-fetched that sounded. And I could imagine Gina's derisive guffaw. She'd think I had really lost it.

I could tell her that Mr. Dean had exposed himself to me just as Kevin had to her, and I had responded in a similarly nonplussed fashion. Just thinking that made me realize how far it was from the truth, how far I had strayed into the pathetic and depraved territory Gina considered the domain of Kevin Tatro and his ilk. I had returned, willingly, to the storage closet with Mr. Dean so many times by then, I had lost count. Where else was I supposed to go with my secret, but back to him? Gina would be horrified that I was actually pleased to be the one he had chosen, and that I still liked him. And she'd figure right away that I must be a homo. She'd tell Father Ryan, just to save my soul, and he'd make a beeline to my parents' house with the news that their son was a fairy. There'd be some giant explosion and when the smoke cleared, I'd be standing alone in the rubble with every kid in Williston pointing at me and laughing.

Still, I pressed on. "You know Mr. Dean?" I asked her.

Gina tipped her empty Coke bottle to her lips, turned it upside down and licked the meager drop it produced. "Of course I know Dean," she said. "What about him?"

"My dad says he's a real good tennis player."

Gina knew that I spent a lot of time alone with Mr. Dean after school—practicing piano, setting out music for rehearsals. She even knew about the Pittsfield concerts and shopping expeditions to find old music scores. Maybe she suspected something. Mentioning him, I was testing her, wondering if she would say it instead of me. As ashamed as I was about what happened in the storage closet, I was also proud of my friendship with Mr. Dean, who in two years had become one of the most popular teachers in Williston.

"Everybody likes Dean," she said. "He's not your standard nerd-ball music teacher. And he's cute."

"He's really nice, too."

"Personally, I don't trust the guy."

"What do you mean?"

"I mean I know you're best buddies and all that. It just seems—I don't know—like he's trying too hard to be cool or something. He's just a little too perfect."

"I don't think so."

"Fine. Just watch out. He's hiding something."

I both admired and resented Gina then. She was right, of course. Mr. Dean and I were both hiding something so big and amazing it defied description. And Gina knew it, though I doubt she could have said what it was, exactly. She had picked up on something, though, something about Mr. Dean that everybody else seemed to miss. I wondered if she saw things in me, too, things she didn't let on.

It was beginning to get dark. Gina's mother would be home soon from her weekly trip to the hairdresser. Suddenly, I couldn't remember why I had wanted to tell Gina about Mr. Dean. What a stupid idea! He was my special secret—a glowing, fretful, hot feeling in my chest that nobody else would ever understand. Mine, though, all mine. "I think he's cool," I said.

"I know you do."

We stared across South Street at the wall of our school building, as if something of the mystery of life might be revealed in that wide blank expanse of brick and glass. Just thinking about telling Gina had made me nervous and the weirdness of my secret more real. I couldn't believe I had considered breaching the solid wall of secrecy I had constructed around Mr. Dean and me.

"I should confess this," Gina said.

"Confess what?"

"The thing with Kevin, of course. My soul is in danger of spending eternity in Hell." She stood and began pacing the porch. Her abandoned rocker groaned back and forth, back and forth. "No wait," she said, stopping, raising her finger to the space between her teeth. "Not if I didn't enjoy it, not if I didn't want it to happen."

The hold Gina and I had on one another seemed to be slipping. Was I going to perish in Hell? Did I want Mr. Dean's body rubbing against mine in the storage closet? Was I that sick?

Gina stared at me, biting her lower lip in concentration. Then she sat back against the porch rail. "I could offer it up," she said.

"Offer what up?"

"The misery of the experience. Father Ryan says that any suffering can be offered up to Christ. It's like penance, in advance. You can use it for the forgiveness of future sins."

"You mean like a savings account?"

"God knows I've run up a positive balance, just living with my mother."

I pictured myself standing in the storage closet of the music room with my eyes skyward, my hands clasped around my gleaming celestial savings book, my pants down around my knees. I could never tell Gina or anyone that I liked Mr. Dean, despite everything, and that he liked me, and that I felt as if I had just betrayed him by even thinking of telling her. I couldn't say that I'd never known anyone who took an interest in me the way he did. I couldn't say that sometimes I dreamed about driving across the country with him to somewhere no one had ever heard of. All I said was, "Jesus, Gina."

"Will you please stop saying that? I keep telling you, it's a sin." She grabbed our empty Coke bottles and walked across the porch. As she pulled open the screen door, she turned back to me. "It's all so dirty, you know?"

She crossed herself one more time as the door slammed shut behind her.

Chapter Nine
1988

It's Wednesday, and I make notes in patient charts at my office in the city. I haven't heard from Jack since he flew to Nebraska on Sunday. I wish he wanted consoling from me, but I give him the benefit of the doubt. He's busy making arrangements for his mother's funeral and visiting with his brother. He's got plenty on his mind.

I file the charts, return phone calls and check for a message at the house. Nothing.

This morning, I phoned Gina and arranged to have dinner with her. The last time we met for dinner was four months ago, back in June. A good looking guy—significantly younger than Gina, in black spandex running shorts—had dropped her off in front of the restaurant. His hand had fallen to her rear end as she reached up to kiss him, and I'd felt my jaw stiffen—more sad than jealous, a sense of something age-less and profound having been lost. Love? Union? Devotion? I'd known all those things with Gina, once. Or twice.

Of course, she's not lost to me. We talk in spurts lasting a couple of weeks until one of us, usually Gina, doesn't call back and we're out of touch for a while. Ironically, I feel closer to her now than I did when we lived together.

Robert, the gay friend Gina used to say I had a crush on, keeps me informed about her. For a while, he had worried about her drinking, though he said she seemed to have gotten that under control. He has known her to disappear for two or three weeks at a time, between act-ing gigs. Robert suspects she holes up somewhere with a bottle or a man or both. Eventually, she reappears, thinner and drawn-looking, as though she'd been battling some secret, powerful demon that had knocked her around and left her sapped.

Robert has never understood why Gina continues to see me, after what happened. He underestimates her determination. She has never, as far as I know, let feelings get in her way. Gina holds onto me, which may seem strange given that she walked away without so much as a goodbye when we were fifteen. Or maybe her persistence now is a reaction to that decision back then.

Not that seeing one another wasn't difficult after she left. Our first meetings were brief, cordial, superficial, and always initiated by me. We never spoke of Jack. Never anything of a personal nature, for that matter. And then, gradually, Gina seemed to move beyond her sense of betrayal to a sincere, if guarded, interest, without ever approaching the intimacy we'd shared as kids.

When I arrive, she is already at Shumai, her favorite Japanese restaurant on Lafayette Street near New York University. It's always crowded there, and the tables are small, but the sushi is fresh and delicious. I should have suggested a place that offered more privacy, I'm thinking, as I squeeze by an attractive, hip crowd waiting for tables. But, after all these years, I'm still reluctant to be at odds with Gina, even over something as trivial as choosing a restaurant.

She's wearing a black turtleneck, black jeans and black boots, her signature outfit. Her hair is drawn back and fixed with a tortoise-shell clip. As she studies the menu, she fingers a jade pendant that accentuates the green tint of her eyes. Gina is the sort of woman I would seek out at a cocktail party if I didn't know her, a sure bet for animated, intelligent conversation. My love for her feels dependable, with a genuine respect and fondness taking up the space once occupied by a barrage of less reliable feelings, from exhilaration to resentment. It's as if I'd been able to remove some troublesome ingredients from a favorite dish and found it more appealing than ever. Because our encounters are infrequent now, I always recall our adolescence when I see her—our reliable, almost sacramental loyalty, our unqualified belief in one another, our categorical commitment. And then I remember how all that had changed so abruptly, how Gina had disappeared from my life for nearly twenty years. That thought still causes a painful ache in my chest, and so I dismiss it and smile across the room.

Gina, looking up from her menu, smiles back. When I reach the table, I kiss her and slide into the chair opposite. "Am I late?"

"No. I was early. Thought I'd grab us a table."

Very Gina—always out ahead. I can feel her eyes assessing me. Each time I see her, I feel as if I'm attending some sort of audition. I usually believe that I get the part, whatever it is, knowing that Gina probably still loves me in our familial way. The saki she's ordered arrives. The waitress, a butterfly tattoo on her neck belying her angelic heart-shaped face, pours the warm wine into tiny green cups. We order, amid chatter about the new play Gina is directing at the Public, a real break for her career.

"So, what's up with Jack?" she asks, removing her chopsticks from their paper wrap. In the last year, since talk of Jack has become fair territory, this has been Gina's first question. I attribute this to the remnants of pain that still dwell in the emotional space she reserves for her ex-husband and her ex-best friend. By asking, she takes control of the subject.

"What do you mean?"

She splits the chopsticks, rubs them together and drops them onto the table. "I could hear it in your voice when you called this morning. It's not that difficult. I usually hear from you when something's bothering you."

She's right, of course, yet I feel put in my place. Gina is so direct. Let the chopsticks fall where they may. I want to say that maybe I could be helpful to her in the same way, if she trusted me more. But I don't go there. "Jack's mother died last week," I tell her.

"Oh, I'm sorry."

"Me too. He's out in Nebraska. I haven't heard a word in three days."

"He hasn't called?"

"And he didn't leave a number." I don't say that I suspect Jack is staying with his former lover, a professor at Chadron State College whose name I don't even know. I don't want to appear petty.

"He's an enigma," Gina says. "Always was."

Like you, I'm tempted to say.

She sips her wine, resting the warm cup against her lower lip, a gesture I find sensuous. No doubt Gina is still sexy to a lot of men.

I decide to risk sounding foolish. "Did he ever talk to you about a professor he was involved with at Chadron State?"

Gina puts down her saki and rearranges her napkin in her lap. "I think I do remember hearing about someone in Nebraska and thinking he was the only guy Jack seemed to have bonded with. At least the only one he ever mentioned."

I notice two men in their late twenties sitting at the sushi bar, obviously a couple. They're laughing. I have the painful sense of time wasted. My whole twenties and well into my thirties, I'd been alone, focusing only on my career, afraid of anything else. How do you make up for so much time lost?

"He's so damned attractive," Gina is saying. "It's not as if there weren't guys hitting on him. Women too, for that matter. But he never gave anyone the time of day. I think the older guy came to New York a couple of times. I remember thinking he wasn't a good match for Jack, even though I never met him. Maybe just because Jack kept him so hidden."

"A good match for Jack," I say. "What's that?"

Gina smiles. "A little older, attractive, professional."

I grin, assuming she means me, and I have a moment of believing Gina has forgiven us. "Seriously. I wonder what Jack wants sometimes, if anything."

Gina pours more saki. "Jack needs a lot of affirmation," she says. "He doesn't know how special he is."

Again, I think the same is true of her.

"He used to get a lot of praise, when he was acting," she goes on. "From other actors, mostly, and teachers. Now he doesn't even have that satisfaction. And you're so successful. It must be hard for him."

This is the first time in three years that I have heard Gina be sympathetic to Jack, who tried for a long time to mend things with her. I wonder if her sense of betrayal is more anguished with Jack because she was closer to him than she was to me. Or is it just our long history that accounts for Gina forgiving me? Whatever the reason, I still hope that one day we can all be friends again.

The waitress sets our sushi in front of us. I think I remember Jack telling me, before he left for New York to meet the professor that first summer, that he hadn't seen him since he'd left college. If Gina is right about the New York visits, Jack was lying.

"You two had the work on the house to keep you busy. Now that the restoration is complete, you need to find some other connection."

"Golf?" I say. "Skiing?"

"I'm serious. Love isn't always enough." Gina holds my eyes a few seconds longer than she ordinarily might.

I pick up a bit of wasabi and set it in the tiny saucer next to my plate, pour soy sauce over it and dab the mixture with my chopsticks. "He came out to New York, the professor?"

"I'm pretty sure. It's so long ago." She lifts a piece of salmon sushi, dips it in soy and deftly bites off half. "Are you jealous or something?"

"Curious. Do you remember his name, the professor?"

"Why all the questions? Is Jack seeing him out there?"

"They stayed in touch, and Jack's mysterious about him."

"Jack's mysterious about everything."

I lean into the hard back of my chair. "Things aren't so good between us."

"Now we're getting somewhere."

I smile. "Can't get anything by you, can I?" With my chopsticks, I flatten the mound of wasabi drying at my place. "I just don't know how to reach him."

"No one reaches Jack. It's part of his charm. The real story, whatever's going on underneath that lovely exterior, if you could even get to it, would probably be a lot less appealing than what shows. I think Jack knows that."

"The real story is always more interesting than the cover."

"You have to believe that, you're a shrink. But I'm not so sure. There's something to be said for self-invention, being the person you want to be versus the one your parents gave you."

"And you? Are you who you want to be?"

Gina picks up a piece of California roll. "I love my work. I'm good at it. I've had some relationships that worked and others that didn't. I no longer blame myself every time something goes wrong. It's a life. And not a bad one." A familiar naughty-girl expression commandeers her face, then she slides the piece of roll between her teeth.

"Are you seeing anyone?" I ask her.

"Me?" She scoffs at the question. "Most of the men I meet are gay, and the rest are married for the umteenth time. Sure, there's this one or that one, but none of it amounts to a whole lot in the end." She drops her chopsticks onto the straw mat at her place, as if the sushi, like men, couldn't hold her interest for long.

"I still wonder, after all this time, what makes you tick," I say.

Gina smiles and points to her heart. "You know what makes me tick," she says.

I would have pointed to her head, Gina's ever-curious and agile mind. But then, perhaps heads and hearts aren't that easily separated. "Actually, I'm not sure I do."

"I'm working on compromise," she says, "the idea that I can't have everything, as I always believed I could. Resignation is like death. It scares the shit out of me."

The waitress sets down two cups of green tea.

"I put my whole life into one thing. I'm so afraid of going back to my apartment some day after some awards dinner and spilling bourbon all over my pretty little statuette."

"Even your dreads are dramatic!" I take a sip of my tea.

"You have Jack. It's different, having someone like that in your life."

It strikes me, once again, what a terrible loss Jack was for Gina. And I recall the time I overheard bits of their conversation and suspected they were hiding something from me. I decide to risk asking Gina about it, at long last.

"One time, when Jack first came to Connecticut, I overheard the two of you talking in the kitchen. I was in the cellar, getting some wine."

Gina smiles again.

"You remember that day?"

"I knew you'd heard us. I could tell. Your whole mood had changed when you came up the stairs. How much did you hear?"

"Very little, actually. But enough to get the sense that you and Jack were hiding something."

"We were supposed to tell you everything we talked about?"

"No, of course not, but this felt deliberate, like you had a secret or something. Did you?"

"And you want to know? Now?"

I feel suddenly uneasy. Maybe I don't want to know.

"Jack and I slept together a couple of times—maybe three, I don't remember. It was before you came back into my life, the previous Christmas, I think. We were both lonely. It just happened."

I picture Jack and Gina in bed together. It doesn't seem that odd to me, this physical manifestation of their intimacy. "Why keep it a secret?" I ask her.

"I don't know. I guess we thought it would be better that way."

"You thought, or Jack?"

"I guess both."

"It was the sense of being left out that hurt. I hate secrets."

"And now you're worried that Jack has a secret with this professor in Nebraska."

"I guess."

"I think people need secrets. They give us a much needed sense of power. We can't know everything about each other. Like I said before, being enigmatic is part of Jack's charm."

The waitress takes away our empty wooden trays and sets the check on the table. "This one's on me," I say, reaching for my wallet.

"I'll do next time," Gina says.

My smile feels a little forced, and wistful. Strangely, knowing that Jack and Gina had been sexual only adds to the sorrow I feel that we're not all still friends. How bizarre life is sometimes. I leave a generous tip.

"What are you doing for the weekend?" Gina asks, when we're outside.

Surely Jack would be back by Friday, I think, startled at the idea that he might not be. "I don't know," I say, taking in the cheerless neighborhood along Lafayette Street, the drab university housing across the street. An ache of missing him rises in my chest.

"Some friends are coming to see the show Saturday," Gina says. "Join us, if you want."

I kiss her. "Thanks," I say. "You take care, okay?"

The narrow tree-lined streets of the West Village feel less claustrophobic now that the leaves have mostly fallen and the October air has freshened. Walking west to my studio on Perry Street, I recall making my way there from NYU as a graduate student, fifteen years ago. The few friends I had then, fellow doctoral students, I no longer see. Again, I picture Jack having sex with Gina, and now I'm titillated. If they'd told me back then, might something have developed among the three of us? We'd have ended up where we are now, anyway, I decide.

I let myself into the lobby of my building. I had sublet this apartment when Gina and I moved in together six years ago, and then returned to it after we were divorced, my crashpad in the city now, little more than a hotel room to return to after a long day at the office. The elevator grinds to the sixth floor with the heaviness I feel all over my body now, being away from Jack. Inside, a sense of failure permeates the tidy, familiar layout, my lifelong failure with Gina, and potentially now with Jack. Still, I love them both, and I vow to try harder to trust Jack more and maybe to bring Gina back to us in some way.

I should get a different place, I think, as I look around the small apartment. No, Gina's lingering, practical presence shouts over my shoulder—the rent is cheap, it's only three nights a week and it's steps from your office. And besides, she adds, wherever you go, you take yourself with you.

I check the machine for messages—none from Jack—then stand at the window with its sliver view of the Hudson River, reduced to a narrow, black cavity since the construction of several new high-rises further west. Fifteen hundred miles or so beyond the river, Jack visits with his brothers, or walks the Chadron State campus with his old friend, or maybe sits alone in his mother's empty house. How can you love someone, miss him, desire him, and still feel like you hardly know him?

Chapter Ten
1964

By tenth grade, Gina had no more time for Mass. The baggy jumpers she'd once hidden herself in were abandoned in favor of tight sweaters that accentuated her amazing breasts. She'd lost her bargain with God, and she was paying Him back in spades. She straightened her hair and let it fall around her face like a blond Cher. Her whole mission was to break the Catholic strangle hold her mother had on her, and boys were her surest tack.

First, there was Rick Ferraro, the mechanic at the Esso station who had sold Mr. Dean his Impala convertible two years before. Rick was twenty and had dropped out of high school to work on cars, the only thing he cared about other than Gina, whom he'd been flirting with since she was eleven. Everything about Rick was slight, except for his hands which were broad and solid, their roadmap creases permanently stained with black grease. He sported confrontational, dagger-like side-burns, and affected a bemused broodiness that obscured a complete lack of inspiration. The breast pocket of his shiny red Esso shirt was permanently squared by a bulging pack of Winstons. Low-slung jeans hung perilously from his narrow hips and dwindled into clunky black boots that served to anchor him to the ground.

Rick and Gina cruised Main Street in his Dodge pickup with the crudely-patched rocker panels and flame-painted hood. She sat almost in his lap and lit his Winstons when she wasn't searching the radio dial for the latest from the Beatles and the Rolling Stones. It was obvious that Rick hoped to convince Gina, one day, to settle with him in his shabby little bungalow behind the Esso. He had no idea just how much "settling" that would have required of Gina. Everyone but Rick knew that he had more to do with her war against her mother than any future she might possibly have as a housewife. Second only to quitting Mass, Rick was her prime weapon, and it was open combat now. You could hear her mother across South Street and out onto the ball fields behind school, calling Gina an offense to God and threatening her with eternal damnation.

But then, to Gina's dismay, her mother grew to like Rick Ferraro that winter of tenth grade. While Gina struggled with algebraic functions in class across the street, Rick sat with Mrs. Daley mid-mornings, drinking pale coffee and listening intently to her stories about sightings of the Blessed Virgin. Rick was sharper than anyone had realized. His strategy: divide and conquer, get to the mother first. They even devised a plan to take Mrs. Daley's diabetic father to Lourdes for a divine intervention, until they learned that the famous site of healing wasn't wheelchair accessible. He worked on her Mercury and replaced the window in the breezeway, shattered that previous Halloween when Gina slammed the storm door, wearing full woman-of-the-night costume—spike heels, mesh stockings, a shiny black jersey that provided a second skin for her breasts.

Soon it was evident that if she was going to fuel this battle with her mother, she was going to need more potent firepower than Rick Ferraro. She found it in Harry-John Lane, a senior on the football team. Harry-John was one of the few black kids in Williston then, perfect for the role she'd cast him in opposite her mother. This was a new manipulative and intimidating Gina. Curiously, she made me wonder about myself. Was I using Mr. Dean in some twisted way to get back at my parents? For what? Sure, they were pretty distracted, but they weren't bad parents. Nowhere near as annoying as Mrs. Daley.

The stickler was that Gina kind of fell for Harry-John. I could see it, huddled into our down parkas one February day on her front porch, a tentative glimmer of tenderness when she talked about him, a softening of edges. Of course, her feelings for Harry-John, or Rick Ferraro, or any boy for that matter, were beside the point. Her problem was her mother, not boys, freedom, not sex, leaving Williston, not staying.

She handed me half a bologna sandwich. "My father got in a fight with Harry-John last night," she said, a tinge of anxiety creeping into her voice. I looked at her, not entirely surprised by this news. It seemed to me that something like this had been waiting to happen all winter.

Gina's father was a good enough guy. He was big and gruff, had driven a delivery truck before buying the Ford dealership with my dad. Everybody in that town liked Mike Daley. He always had a good word, and he always said he loved Gina more than life. What does that mean, exactly? Wasn't Gina a sterling part of that very life? It was like the Holy Trinity. How do you break it down? His fervor was a burden for Gina. Unlike my parents, who had had me within a year of getting married, the Daleys had about given up on having a family when Gina finally appeared. They believed she was sent straight from the Holy Spirit to South Street, by way of Saint Francis Church up the block, where Mrs. Daley had spent every afternoon of her then eight-year marriage praying for just such a miracle.

"We were parked right there, in Harry-John's Firebird," Gina was saying, pointing to the curb in front of her house. "I was looking for that good rock-and-roll station out of Albany. Before we knew what was up, my dad pulls open Harry-John's door, grabs his neck and yanks him out."

"What did you do?"

"Harry-John's on his butt in the middle of South Street, and I'm hanging half out of the car with the cigarette lighter glowing red in my fingers. My dad's yelling something about him never coming around his daughter again. Harry-John gets up. He's strong enough to flatten my dad, but he just stands there, doesn't do anything, doesn't say anything. A gentleman, not something you see very often around here. They stare at each other, their fists clenched, while I wish one of them would back off. I mean, this was serious."

"Jesus!" I say around a mouthful of bologna and white bread.

"I know. I'm about to throw myself between them when Harry John turns and gets back into the Firebird and burns rubber halfway down the street. Look, you can still see the tire marks."

I glanced to the curb, but pictured Mr. Dean, standing in front of me in the storage closet earlier that afternoon. He'd been about to touch me, and I'd wanted him to, sort of. It'd been weeks since we'd been back there, and the idea that he might not want me anymore had been plaguing me for most of that time. What would I do without Mr. Dean? So I had teased him some during our practice session this afternoon, making the lingering eye contact I had learned from watching my mother, the same silly jokes. Finally, under the pretense that we needed to set up some instruments and music stands for orchestra rehearsal the next afternoon, Mr. Dean unlocked the storage closet door and dropped the padlock into his pocket, as he always did, with his keys still stuck in the lock. Their muffled jangle set my heart racing. I wondered what he was thinking, or more precisely, what he thought of me. Did he like me, really? Did he think I was talented? We sorted through some music stands in the dim light, then pulled the xylophone out from behind a stack of risers. He stopped me then and turned me toward him. "You're beautiful," he said. "You know that?" He leaned over and sniffed my hair. "And you smell like apples."

And so I got to see his excitement, to sense the hold I had on him, to feel less alone than I usually did. As we left the storage closet, we both knew there had been nothing in there we needed, except each other.

"I hate myself," Gina said.

"Me, too."

"You?"

"It's not your fault," I told her, wanting to believe that Gina and I weren't just bad kids.

"Whose fault is it then?"

"I don't know. Things happen, that's all."

"No!" She banged her fist on the arm of her rocker. "I'm not going to hurt people any more than I already have—Rick, Harry-John, my dad. No more. I'm turning over a new leaf."

I had never felt so wide awake as I did right then, watching Gina hunker down into her parka, shivering with icy conviction. I felt as if I had blinked head-on into our whole happy future together, unfolding before my eyes like some golden scroll. I put my hand on top of hers. Slowly, she turned her hand over and gripped mine, and we sat, not talking, as the sun's fiery red remnant traveled up the side of our school building across the street, smoldered temporarily in the parchment shades of the music room on the top floor, and disappeared.

I was in love with Gina Daley.

But, curiously, our vigils on her front porch fell silent after that day. We sat, holding hands, but for the first time, I felt inhibited around Gina, self-conscious and gawky, feelings I thought I'd left behind in ninth grade. Love changed things, it seemed, and not always for the better. Who knew what Gina's silence contained that spring? She seemed frustrated, her fiery rebellion thwarted by guilt. I always feared she was planning her exit from Williston, a last step in her restless quest for freedom. When she did talk, it was about plays she'd read, drama schools she'd heard of, the cost of an apartment in New York City. I felt powerless to bring our conversations around to us, though the thought of her leaving filled me with dread. I would be left with Mr. Dean, the only other person in the world I believed I could rely on. Even then, I could see the irony in trusting that man. But, unlike Gina, he wasn't going anywhere. I was his favorite student. He would see that I got into the right college in two years. My father had my mother and my mother had her list of causes. Gina would have her acting career. I had Mr. Dean.

"I'll bet you've never even had sex, have you Corey?" Gina said one windy April afternoon, her hand resting, warm and delicate, in mine.

I knew she meant the girl kind, the right kind. "Of course I have," I lied.

A pang of anxiety surfaced painfully in my chest. Not that many fifteen-teen-year-old boys were sexually experienced then, despite what they claimed in the locker room after gym class. Hadn't Gina and I avoided that whole issue for good reason? Hadn't sex been nothing but trouble for each of us, since day one? I'd always considered our relationship unique, in part because it was chaste. Why would we sully it, now? Every day, I did what I could not to think about sex, plagued though I was by hourly erections and a teacher with great oral technique.

I never told Gina about my secret life with Mr. Dean—though she probably suspected. She knew as well as anyone that I was a virgin when it came to the weaker sex, a misnomer if ever there was one. She was the only girl I hung out with, after all.

"Yeah, right," she said. "Who with?"

"Which time?"

"Mr. Don Juan. Hah! You crack me up."

"Why is virginity so fucking honorable in a girl, and such a disgrace in a guy? I mean, there have to be an equal number of guys and girls doing it, right?"

"Actually, no."

"Maybe I'm saving myself."

"For who?"

For her, of course. Didn't she know that?

Two seniors from school, baseball players leaving pre-season practice, sauntered up the sidewalk. They waved to Gina. She waved back. "I'm just thinking about your future," she said. "A guy should have experience. Otherwise, the girl has to show him around, and that, my friend, would not be sexy."

Gina had long since taken the higher ground with me about pretty much everything. I doubted she'd been all the way with either Rick Ferraro or Harry-John Lane. Still, who knew? She had to be more experienced than I was, which, of course, wasn't saying much. My hand perspired around her fingers. "You're my favorite person in the whole world, you know that?" she said.

I did know that. And I felt the same way about her. But what did that have to do with sex?

"Do you want to sleep with me, Corey?" she asked, holding my eyes with hers.

I turned away, chuckled nervously and played with a tear in the sleeve of my parka. "But we're friends."

"Isn't sex a friendly thing?"

She had a point. Maybe sex wasn't all creepy and nerve-racking, the way I had always thought of it. Still, the most likely scenario was that I would fail miserably with Gina, and we'd both be humiliated. It wasn't worth the risk.

"Come on," she said, jumping up, her empty chair rocking back and forth, inching its way across the porch toward me. She disappeared behind the slam of the storm door.

The whole time I'd known Gina, I could never figure out why she liked me. She was the prettiest and most exciting girl at Williston High, to me anyway, and underneath her bluster, the sweetest. Yet it always seemed that something unseen was careening out of control in our direction, something lethal, looming just out of sight. In her reckless fashion, she had loaded a gun now, cocked it and handed it to me.

I rose and stepped gingerly into the hallway, holding the door to stop it from slamming. I even looked into the kitchen, though I knew for sure Mrs. Daley was in Pittsfield at her hairdresser. At the foot of the stairs, I cleared my throat. "Gina?"

"I'm up here."

A hundred guys would give their left nut for a chance like this, I told myself, starting up the stairs. I stopped on the landing and stared out the window, where a budded dogwood bent in the wind. Didn't Gina just say that there was nothing more boring than an inexperienced guy? You had to direct things, get a hard-on, get it inside, decipher the whole damned convoluted riddle right there on the spot, as if it were second nature, as if you were completely cool about it. As much as I loved Gina, or maybe because I did, I couldn't handle the idea of her secretly thinking less of me.

The oak stairs creaked and strained in a way you'd only notice at a time like this. I could see into the Daley's bedroom at the top of the stairs. There was a nightgown hanging off an unmade bed, underwear on a chair. Mrs. Daley must have left in a hurry. I had the urge to go in and straighten things up, make the bed, but I could hear Gina down the hall, calling me. "Corey, come on." I exhaled into my palm to check my breath.

She stood at the end of her frilly pink bed, her jeans and sweater already in a pile on the floor. She was reaching behind her back to unfasten her bra. I looked away. "It's cool," she said. "You can see." Her breasts erupted out of their restraints like a pair of unleashed Great Danes, assertive and secure, nipples golden and erect. She kept her panties on, thank God. "Come here," she said.

We were exactly the same height. We blinked into each other's faces. I bit my lower lip as I felt a tear brim and dribble down my cheek.

"What's the matter?" Gina asked me.

"I love you," I said.

She took my hands and placed them on her naked breasts. They were warm, firm and incredibly smooth. Her hard nipples tickled my palms. I leaned in to kiss her, but Gina turned just then and dived onto the bed, her wonderful breasts jiggling like vanilla pudding. She pulled the covers up to her smooth white shoulders. "Come on," she said, a hint of impatience invading her voice.

I sat on the edge of the narrow bed, frowning at a stubborn knot in one of my sneakers. "I don't know, this is weird," I said.

"What is?" She turned onto her side.

"We're supposed to be studying for the algebra test tomorrow, remember?"

"Corey, you're the nicest guy I know. If we met ten years from now, well, who knows? So, the timing was a little off. Why should we let that stop us?"

I couldn't quite follow her logic about timing. I guess she was saying she hadn't fallen in love with me, as I had with her. Gina had always made it absolutely clear that nothing would get in the way of her acting career in New York. Yet somehow, I had always assumed that I was as important to her as she was to me, that everything was even between us. Suddenly, I felt as if I had walked out onto some rickety ledge and had only just noticed there wasn't a whole lot underneath but air.

I unbuttoned my shirt, snuck a whiff of my armpit and slipped off my khakis without standing up. I had a raging hard-on under my shorts. At fifteen, that's possible—a simultaneous hard-on and dive-bombing anxiety. I took the erection as a positive sign, and chose to focus on the task at hand, so to speak. I slid under the slippery pink cover.

Gina leaned her head on my shoulder; her warm, firm breast pressed against my side. "Everything's going to be cool," she said. "Just relax. This is supposed to be fun, you know?"

I have never found being told to relax very relaxing. Gina ran her chilly fingers up and down my stomach. I hoped we might forget the whole thing, snag two more Cokes from the fridge and open our math books to Chapter 7. But then she lifted my t-shirt and ran her hand along my chest, stopping to circle my nipples. This felt sensational. Still, I shied away.

"Easy," she whispered. "Just relax."

The tension in my legs, as if I had been considering a leap from the bed, began to ease a little. She fingered the waistband of my shorts, probably some signal that I should slip them off. Then she reached inside. "Whoa, Corey Moore, you are definitely not hurting in this department." "I'm not?" Compared to who? I wondered. Kevin, next door? Harry-John? She maneuvered my swollen dick out of my shorts. "Trust me," she said.

Each gentle stroke felt reassuring, but then, abruptly, she rolled on top, straddling me. What was her hurry? A spotty blush had risen from her resplendent breasts up into her neck. "Touch me," she whispered. A sigh surfaced from somewhere deep within her as I reached up and licked her nipple. She pulled the crotch of her panties aside and slipped my hard-on inside her, just like that. It felt so warm and wet, I thought I might blow everything right there. "Don't," she said, as if she could tell what I was thinking. "Don't you dare come."

"Right," I said, holding on, silently reciting the Gettysburg Address I'd memorized for extra history credit back in seventh grade, anything for a little distraction. She moved slowly up and down on me. 'A new nation, conceived in liberty,' I thought, heaving up and down with her. Her eyes were closed, her breathing loud and fast. 'And dedicated to the proposition. . . .' The room had filled with the faint, damp fragrance of a forest floor. Squashed beads of sweat linked her thighs with my hips. 'That all men are created equal, endowed by their creator with certain inalienable rights, and among these are. . . .' I was fucking!

Then, out of nowhere, Bill Dean's face appeared, that mischievous grin of his, widening across his mouth. I tried to blink it away, but it wouldn't leave. I turned to the window, to the fading blue sky and the budding maples lining South Street. Gina opened her eyes and looked down at me. "What happened?" she asked. "What's the matter?"

"Nothing."

She pulled herself off me and looked down at my shriveling dick. "Christ, you didn't come did you?"

I shook my head.

"Are you sure?"

"Of course I'm sure."

"What's the matter, then?"

"I just don't feel so great."

She slid off and lay down next to me. "Don't worry," she said, resting her arm across my chest. "It's fine. Really. It is."

When someone says things are fine, I wouldn't exactly go out and celebrate. Yet, we kept at it, coming to life like the whole greening new world around us that spring. Gina hadn't exactly been as experienced as she'd led me to believe. But each time, things got a little better. I worried less, and Mr. Dean's appearances on the ceiling became sporadic. Gina flattered and sustained us, and I learned some ways to make her happy. We went for long walks as the fields and trees around Williston turned luminous. I felt normal. I was in love. And I believed that Gina loved me, whether she knew it or not.

I look back at that time as the most idyllic and optimistic and blissful of my life. Gina and I were together most afternoons, and on Saturday nights we held hands at the movies or danced with each other at the gym. I continued to see Mr. Dean at rehearsals and private practice sessions. We still bought records and took long rides in his convertible, talking about my future career in music. Our trips to the storage closet assured me that he loved me, not the way Gina did, but in some way I had given up trying to explain to myself. I simply believed it. And I assumed he would always be around when I needed him, which, despite our new togetherness, was not something I could say with any real conviction about Gina. I had a girlfriend and a mentor who were also my best friends. Sure, it was complicated, but like the lilacs and daffodils blooming along South Street that May, I felt surrounded by an enveloping and obscuring mist, and undaunted by the blistering heat that, if I had thought about it, I'd have known was on its way.

Chapter Eleven
1965

On one of those freaky June afternoons when ninety-degree heat taxes tender new blossoms, my mother and I toured one of the better neighborhoods of Pittsfield, Massachusetts. We were playing an old favorite game. "Houses," we called it, an uninspired title, like the game, itself. There were no rules. You just had to find the most spectacular house for sale in whatever neighborhood we had driven to that day. We had categories—prettiest, best yard (grounds in the case of the really grand finds), best design for entertaining (as determined from the street), best location, greatest curb appeal, etc. My mother's whole life had been about helping people she thought had gotten a raw deal, usually poor women, but also blacks, the unemployed, immigrants. She was never one to care what people thought of her nontraditional New England values, and she was not at all ambitious when it came to domestics. Probably the real purpose of these excursions was to spend time with her increasingly laconic son. We made notes, took down addresses, devised a star rating system from one to four, like the Michelin guide. We both knew my father was never going to buy one of those houses. That wasn't the point. These were bonding sojourns, during which she took the opportunity to quiz me on how I was doing in school, how things were going with Gina, what Mr. Dean thought of my progress on the piano.

"I got one," she screamed as we rounded a corner and pulled onto a deserted street of wide lawns and manicured hedges. She braked next to a For Sale sign tacked to an ornate white fence. "Oh, nice," she said, admiring the ornamented stone façade, the fluted columns, the widow's walk along the roof.

"Mom, they can see."

"They want people to look, don't they?"

"By Appointment Only. The sign?"

"You and I agreed on Tuesday to come here today. That's an appointment, isn't it?"

"It's too fancy, anyway."

"I don't know. I kind of like the pilasters. They could use a coat of paint, though."

My mother and I were exactly the same height that spring, five feet eight inches. We looked straight across the front seat of the Galaxy at each other. I longed for the day, not far off, when I would pass her by, in height anyway.

She looked haggard that day. My mother was constantly beleaguered by conservative, local politicians who opposed her work for women's reproductive rights or employment opportunities for minorities, and as a result by my father, who feared her activism might reduce sales at Moore-Daley Fords. Their fights had taken on a new urgency, when I listened from my room over the kitchen. I was afraid, on one of these rides, that my mother would tell me that she had never loved my father, which I suspected, that their values conflicted, which I knew, that his solemn, narrow body had never excited her, which I didn't want to hear. I had enough on my mind, already.

"How are things?" she asked me, turning away from the house.

"What things?"

"I don't know, things. You never want to talk any more. You used to tell me everything."

"I used to be naïve."

"What's that supposed to mean?" She looked at me askance, her hands still gripping the top of the steering wheel.

"How many teenagers do you know who stalk stranger's houses while telling their mothers the intimate details of their lives?"

"Good point." She started the engine and pulled her sun-dappled convertible slowly away from the curb. "How about a burger? I'm starving."

"It's almost five. Shouldn't we be thinking about dinner?"

"Shouldn't I be worrying about that instead of you?"

She reached for her Salems and pressed the lighter. "You just don't seem yourself, lately."

"I'm fifteen. Aren't I supposed to be not myself?"

"I've never had to tell you to study before. I've never found you sleeping in the afternoon. You don't eat much, and your hair looks like a rat's nest."

"It looks like Paul McCartney's hair."

She pressed the lighter to the end of her cigarette, inhaled and set the lighter back in its slot. "You don't seem to care about anything anymore. Is something bothering you?"

How could we be seeing things so differently? My life was going great. I had a girlfriend. I had a teacher who was looking out for me.

"You mean besides you right now?"

She made a right turn. My mother had an infallible sense of direction. And in retrospect, I can see she was pretty intuitive about her son, as well. But nothing she could say would have gotten me to talk that day. I glanced at the houses along the side of the road as she drove.

"Houses are just symbols, anyway," I said.

She took the bait. "What do you mean?"

"They're supposed to show how successful you are, that you're important, that you made something of your life."

She drew on her cigarette. "And do you feel successful? Do you feel important, Corey?" Smoke clouded her lips before being whisked away by the wind. She had slipped off the hook.

"Give it a rest, Mom."

"No, really?"

"More than I ever have, probably."

"Well, that's saying something, isn't it?" She turned north onto Route 20, back toward Williston. "You're important to me, you know. Very very important."

Why did any sort of expression of affection make me uneasy? "This time next year, I'll be driving and you'll be sitting over here," I said.

"Do you think we'll still play Houses?"

"If I can drive."

The following Sunday morning, Gina tiptoed up the narrow wooden stairs to the choir loft of Saint Francis Church, where I'd been "filling in" on the organ since I was twelve. Obviously, Father Ryan had given up on finding someone fulltime, if he had ever tried.

I was surprised to see Gina at church, since she used any excuse now not to attend Mass—illness, homework, a lack of conviction. On those occasions when her mother insisted, she would sit by herself in the last pew, picking at a hangnail or reading from a paperback collection of plays stuck inside a missal. She rose to leave at the earliest reasonable moment, which became my signal to prepare for the recessional.

The day before, my mother and I had driven down to New Haven, Connecticut. Over breakfast, I had expressed an interest in attending Yale, and she'd suggested going to have a look at the campus. No time like the present! For the second time that week, she had taken the opportunity to get me alone in her car and quiz me about the general state of my psyche. Clearly, she sensed that something was not right with me. Though she hadn't as yet zeroed in on the true source of the problem, she was probably close to figuring it out. She knew I was in the throws of my first love. Though my choice of Gina had obviously not pleased her, she was nonetheless supportive and encouraging, probably confident the relationship would burn itself out in time. She was wise enough to know that nothing encourages romance like a parent's disapproval. Aside from Gina, though, my mother had grown increasingly certain that I was hiding something, which made her more attentive that spring. Nothing bothered her more than thinking she was being left out of the loop of my life, which she had been, actually, since Mr. Dean, my parents' occasional tennis partner and cocktail party guest, came to town three years before. I both appreciated this new attention and longed for her former state of distraction.

We'd put the top down on the Galaxy, and, in less than three hours, were walking under the ornate arch onto the Yale campus. "You're going to have to keep your grades up if you think you want to spend four years here," she'd said, taking in the giant freshman quadrangle. I didn't tell her that my interest in Yale was in large part due to its location ninety minutes by train from New York City, where Gina was planning to study acting the moment she left Williston High. I dreaded all the cool guys she would meet there. I dreaded to think she might forget about me. It was absurd to be coordinating our future plans so soon, and yet, I couldn't resist. Picturing where we'd be living in a couple of years calmed me the way an obsession, with its repetitive familiarity, its power to distract and to offer a flimsy sense of control, provides a certain relief. I imagined Gina coming to New Haven on weekends, going to the Beinecke Rare Book & Manuscript Library, renting a room in a guest house on Long Island Sound in nearby Guilford.

Gina leaned over the organ bench now to whisper in my ear, her mantilla brushing my shoulder. "I'll meet you up here after Mass," she said. Don't leave." I nodded. Her perfume smelled like a sweet lime drink, and once again, I felt grateful to have such a remarkable girlfriend. Gina had mellowed in the last year. She seemed to have put aside the anger that had plagued her for so long, which I dared to think might be because she was happy being with me. She was quieter and more polite, if distant, with our few friends. She put all her energy into memorizing scenes, while getting straight A's in school. She was like a filly in blinders who'd only just left the starting gate and was already three furlongs out ahead of the field. I prayed that I could keep up.

As I played the recessional, a Bach fugue, I wondered what sort of scheme she might have concocted now. There were always plays in Springfield or Pittsfield that she wanted us to sneak off to, though we had never actually attended one, thanks to her mom's conviction that we shouldn't spend any unchaperoned time alone. Parents were so peculiar. We'd had the run of Mrs. Daley's upstairs every Wednesday afternoon for over a year, but we couldn't take the bus to Pittsfield together.

I shut down the organ and heard Father Ryan close the sacristy door and start down the walk to the rectory. Still no Gina. A tightness rose in my chest at the thought that anything might be wrong. Finally there was the brush of her pumps on the creaking stair.

We always spoke in whispers in the choir loft, not out of respect for the Holy Spirit which we had both long-since dismissed as a highly improbable presence, but because even a normal voice boomed up there and reverberated to the distant shadowy corners of the nave below. Whether you believed in God or not, there was the sense that you were not alone there, that some presence lurked just out of sight and heard everything.

"Where were you?" I whispered, gathering up my music.

"I wanted to be sure we were alone."

I kissed her cheek, inhaling her limey essence. "What's up?"

"I'm pregnant," she said, matter-of-fact, cool, staring out over the choir rail, down into the nave where a statue of Mary held the baby Jesus. She fiddled with a button on her coat, fitting it in and out of its rope loop. "Like the Blessed Virgin, but neither blessed nor virginal, I'm afraid."

I sat, weak-kneed, back onto the organ bench. "Jesus, Gina, are you sure?"

"I'm sure, two months, I think."

Our whispers were hisses in the huge empty space. Gina seemed surprisingly serene, and she looked more beautiful than ever, with no hint of apology or fear in her gleaming green eyes. "What are we going to do?" I asked her, knowing she'd have thought through all the options.

"What can I do? I've got to get out of here."

"What do you mean?"

"I can't. . . ." She turned toward the stairway, as if she needed to leave right then. Her shoulders were so narrow, it was hard to imagine there was room for another life inside her. "Can you see me with a ? . . ."

This had never been one of my fantasy pictures of Gina and me, but yes, given some time to think, I could see us laughing on her front porch, a tow-headed toddler wobbling between us. I could definitely see it. We wouldn't be the first teenaged parents. "It's not just you, Gina."

"In fact, it is. It's me who's pregnant." She tapped her stomach. "Me."

"But. . . ."

"I'm not going to have this. . . ."

Abortion. That's what she was thinking. She just wasn't saying the word. The idea stunned me like a blow. This was what happened to the young women my mother worked with in Pittsfield. Not Gina, not us.

"What choice do I have?"

"I don't know. We have to think."

"I have thought, Corey. We're fifteen!"

"What about your parents?"

Gina turned away. "Right," she said toward the stairs. "My mother would make me have it, and raise it herself, then use it against me for the rest of my life."

"My mother will help us. She deals with this sort of thing all the time. She'll know what to do." This sort of thing. That expression sounded all wrong. This was not just any sort of thing. It was our baby, Gina's and mine.

"I have to leave."

"Where will we go?"

Gina looked back at me and then out over the nave again, as if I were impossibly dense. "We can't both leave. What are we supposed to say—Gee folks, Corey and I thought we'd take a little vacation?"

She'd already left. I could see it in her eyes. The sickening idea of ending her pregnancy was already a fact for her.

I knew Gina trusted me. She'd just never, in her whole life, relied on anyone but herself. She didn't know how. I had to get her to share this with me, to make it our problem, something we could get through together.

"Remember Jane Brenner from seventh grade?" she said. "She lives in White Plains now. She's always invited me to come visit. I'll find something there."

Something. "Look at me, Gina. Please."

She wouldn't.

"Gina, it's our baby you're talking about."

"It's not a baby. Not yet."

Gina had always seemed hours of study, days of contemplation, years of experience ahead of me. And now she was taking that higher ground we'd both always allotted her, and there didn't seem to be any way I could stop her. "You can't go alone, Gina."

"I won't be alone. Jane will be with me."

She knew how much that would hurt me, the idea that anyone other than me would see her through this. Her face had that same icy look she used to get when she defied her mother. But, of course, she was right. She didn't need me.

I leaned forward and took her hand. "What if we got married?"

She looked at me as if I had sprouted blue hair. "We're fifteen!" she yelled, pulling her hand away. Her voice echoed in the cavernous space. "I got myself into this," she whispered, "I'll get myself out."

"Pregnancy is not something you get into yourself. It was us. We got ourselves into this."

I followed her eyes down into the dim, empty nave below, a space my hands could fill with the thundering reverberations of liturgical music. Yet I was powerless to change an almost inaudible conversation now in one small corner of its upper reaches.

"Do you have any cash?" she asked me.

The choir rail caught my shoulder, painfully, as I sat further back on the bench. "I can get some."

"And maybe you would go with me to the bus."

We stared at each other, the immense quiet of the church all around us. "Gina," I said, holding my hand out to her, again.

Her fingers still fidgeted with the button of her coat. "Friday," she said. "After school." She turned toward the stairs.

It was drizzling as I walked her home. A solid gray wall of clouds dragged itself across the low sky. Neither of us spoke. Gina pulled the lid over that private abyss she'd always reserved for herself during the worst of times, and I felt myself veering away from her on that narrow, cracked sidewalk across from our school, the way one retreats from someone he thought he knew, but suddenly sees is a stranger.

At her front walk, my hand shot out to her elbow in one last attempt to stop her. "Gina," I said. "I wish. . . ."

"I know." She forced a smile and then turned and started up the walk. Tiny jeweled droplets of mist glistened on her coat. Her mantilla, damp from the drizzle, had slipped to her shoulders. I watched her climb her front steps and reach for the railing we'd stripped bare with years of our nervous footwork.

The rain stung my eyelids as I started walking home. The Victorian houses along South Street that had always defined our world looked gray and unfamiliar. I hunkered down against the rain, confident that Gina would survive the abortion, but less certain about us.

On Wednesday afternoon, for the final time, Gina and I took our positions on her front porch, our feet up on the railing, our hands wrapped around sweating green bottles of Coca-Cola. Over the year that we had been lovers, we had talked far less than when we were friends. No doubt that had been part of our lovers' pact—no hassles. I had come to believe that Gina had slipped into being with me because it was easy, because I had demanded nothing. Faced with a pregnancy, it was obvious how ill-prepared we were to deal with one another. Gina had made up her own mind, and it didn't matter what I thought. But wasn't there more to talk about than just what action to take? I wanted to tell her how sorry I was, and how frightened I was for her. I wanted Gina to tell me what she really felt about our baby. I wanted to know if she loved me, or if I had just been someone to bide her time with until her real life could begin. I'd been flying, soaring above my own life for over a year, and now I was crash-landing and stunned into immutable silence.

"What happened to your hair?" she asked me.

"I cut it."

"Yourself?"

"Of course not myself."

"You look like a cross between Pat Boone and Ricky Nelson."

"Thanks."

"You just need to decide and go in one direction or the other. Take a stand."

Taking her at her word, I got out of my chair and stood in front of her. "Gina," I said. "We should be talking about. . . . You know."

"I told you. You're meeting me after school the day after tomorrow, and I'm going to take the bus to visit Jane Brenner in White Plains. I'll be back on Monday for the last week of school."

"I know what your plan is."

"Then what do we need to talk about?"

"I feel a little left out, you know?"

"Sorry."

"No, you're not."

"Should I be? My life is the one that would be ruined by having a kid, remember?"

She looked around me, distracted by some movement across the street. I turned to see Mr. Dean, leaving school with his hand on little

Jimmy Harkness's shoulder, a wimpy seventh grader with curly blond hair and an eruption of zits dotting his chin. My keystone, recently dislodged, slipped entirely out of its slot now, and the soaring arch of my life came crashing down around me.

"Hi Jimmy," Gina called, waving around me. "Hi Mr. Dean."

I turned and waved. They waved back. "Jesus Christ, Gina. Could you be less cool?"

"It looks like you've been replaced as teacher's pet," she said.

"What is that supposed to mean?"

"Your problem is you'd rather be riding home with Mr. Dean than sitting here with me."

"That is fucking bull crap, and you know it."

"Bull crap?" she said, yelling in my face. "Bull crap?"

"You know I'd rather be with you than anybody," I said, shrinking from her. Was what she said true? I had loved Gina and Mr. Dean in ways that were so different they had eluded any sort of comparison. Mr. Dean had felt reliable in a way that Gina never had. But obviously, I'd been mistaken. The only certainties right then were that Gina was pregnant with my baby and Mr. Dean had a new best friend, and neither of them gave a shit about me.

"What I know," Gina hissed, "is that I'm pregnant and you're probably a fucking fairy."

She smiled a phony grin and waved again as Mr. Dean drove past with nerdy Jimmy Harkness peering up over the dashboard of the Impala.

I hopped over the railing to the grass below, and started running.

"Where are you going?" she called after me. "Don't forget, Friday."

I ran up South Street to Route 20, and kept running toward home.

Over the next seemingly endless two days, Gina steeled herself for the task ahead, and I steeled myself against her. We didn't speak on the telephone as we had every evening that whole year. At school, it seemed that Gina only walked with me between classes so that things would appear normal between us. On Friday, she met me for lunch in the cafeteria. But she ran to the girl's room after a few minutes, returning with glassy eyes and a face the color of notebook paper. At three, we left school together, as we always did, but turned away from

Gina's house, toward Cole Avenue and the bus depot. I carried her small, striped suitcase with the rolled leather handle. She carried her book bag over one shoulder. She took my hand, for show or real affection I couldn't tell.

We stood for several minutes at the side of the bus station, out of sight, with nothing to say to each other, or so much that neither of us knew where to begin. "Here," I said, handing her a wad of bills, money I'd been saving for a car, college, a ring for Gina, whatever.

She took it and slipped it deep into her coat pocket. "I love you," she said.

"Yeah."

"I mean it. More than anyone."

But it's not enough, is it? I wanted to say. Down the highway, the bus pulled into view. "Here it comes," I said.

I handed her the suitcase, and she gave me her books. "Keep these for me, will you?"

We watched as the bus swung into the parking lot, the long greyhound on its side frozen in stride, always running but never getting anywhere. The brakes gave off a piercing wheeze, and Gina switched the suitcase to her other hand.

The bus door opened and she walked up the steps. "Gina!" I yelled, holding the door from closing. She turned. Don't go, please, I wanted to shout. Instead, I stepped up and put my arms around her, pulled her to me so hard the buttons of her coat pressed into my chest. She felt small, defenseless, or perhaps I just wanted her to be, so I could protect her, keep her with me.

The driver called "All aboard, Miss." Three guys at the rear of the bus clapped and whistled as I stepped to the ground. I watched Gina walk halfway down the aisle and take a seat by herself. The door hissed closed and the bus roared into motion, pulling out onto Cole Avenue, leaving an acrid gray haze along the macadam.

That was the last time I saw Gina. She never returned for the last week of our sophomore year. Somehow, she managed to stay on with the Brenners in White Plains for a while. She called once, but I wasn't home. My mother talked briefly with her, but didn't take a telephone number. The Daleys stopped coming to our house. I went to Yale two years later, and eventually, to graduate school in New

York. I never tried to find Gina, though I thought about it. We were right there in the same city, walking the same pavements, breathing the same polluted air.

But then we ran into one another on that rainy day, on lower Fifth Avenue, just up from the arch at Washington Square, and started all over again.

Chapter Twelve
1965

I walked the two miles home after putting Gina on the bus to White Plains, her book bag heavy on my shoulder, my own books curled under my arm. The new house, under construction at the corner of our road, loomed hulking and vacant behind a row of newly leafed-out maples. It was after five and the workmen had left for the day, though the sun was still high over those exhausted peaks of the Berkshire Hills, rounded by eons of glacial scraping. I stepped behind the trees and circled the house, tripping on the uneven ground, looking up at the unfinished facade. Screw them all, I thought.

It was hard to believe it had been three years since the organist at Saint Francis left town with Mr. Beatty, and I started weekly organ lessons with Mr. Dean. And over a year since Gina and I had sex for the first time, and I came to believe we would always be together. Two weeks ago, playing Houses with my mom in Pittsfield, I had thwarted her attempts to extract information from me. What would I tell her about my life, now? Beware of complacency? Never trust anyone? My concern about getting into Yale in order to be near Gina seemed so naïve now; and the idea that Mr. Dean would always be my best friend, a nasty joke.

I picked up a piece of brick, still warm from the sun. It felt jagged and heavy in my hand. I turned it over and wiped away the mud clinging to its underside, appreciating its coarse, brutal appeal, how out of place it appeared, clenched in my white piano fingers. Those fingers symbolized everything that was wrong with me—too restrained, too weak, too unmanly. Tears stung my eyes. How I hated those fingers!

I tossed the brick. The sliding glass door to what would be the kitchen quivered and exploded inward in a million tiny shards. The brick thundered onto the plywood sub-floor inside, surrounded by splinters of fractured silver light. I stepped to the shattered window and ran my fingers along a single sharp point, applying pressure until it penetrated their smooth spongy pads. I licked the blood and spit it on the other door, then spread the sticky mix in sweeping circles like finger paint, an artist, an angry, abstract expressionist.

I looked around. The ground was littered with fragments of broken bricks. I picked up one, threw it, and another glass door gave way. Then more bricks, more windows, one after another, in great collapsing sheets. I looked toward the road, thinking someone must have heard, but there was no one. I lobbed a piece of cinderblock through the large beveled window above the entrance, and then smaller pieces into the bedrooms upstairs, throwing and throwing, on fire, sweating, licking my fingers and spitting out gritty blood. Finally, I sat heavily on the ground, exhaling in short thin breaths, and stared up at the gaping façade. I laughed. Getting good grades in school, always trying to do the right thing— what did any of that matter? Gina left anyway, to rid us of our unborn child. Mr. Dean had obviously taken up with a new wimp. I'd fooled myself. What a jerk I was! What a pathetic dreamer!

The ground was damp. Dirty blood dripped from my fingers and marred the pristine surface of Gina's book bag. I needed to get out of there before someone came along and noticed me. The road was deserted when I stepped from behind the trees, and I felt a bizarre sort of composure as I made my way home.

My parents were out. At the kitchen sink, I dressed the stinging cuts. I took some left-over chicken to my room, where I changed out of my soiled clothes. My fingers throbbed beneath the bandages. My mother yelled up the stairs around eight o'clock, when she returned from one of her meetings. I yelled back that I had already eaten and was staying in my room. I faked sleep when she stuck her head in the door an hour later.

The next afternoon, on returning from school, the new house at the end of our road was as eerie and forsaken as a tomb. My mother greeted me at our back door. "Your father wants to see you," she said, eying the bandages she'd asked me about that morning. My mother asked a lot of questions, but was often too distracted to focus on the answers. I told her that morning that I'd had an accident, and she'd asked if there had been any calls while she was out the night before.

"What's up?" I asked her now.

"I hope nothing, but I'm worried. He's in his office."

I was worried, too. Did my dad know about the house? Had someone seen and reported me? Had Mr. Daley told him that Gina was missing? I wanted my parents to know everything and to know nothing. I wanted to be left alone and I wanted their help.

The door to his office was closed. I knocked. "Mom said you wanted to see me," I said, stepping inside. My father sat at his desk in the far corner of a room shaded by heavy drapes and smelling of cigar smoke. He looked tired. The weight he'd gained in the last few years made his face puffy. His forehead gleamed in the light from the window.

"It's about this ugly damn business at the new house down the road," he said, turning to me. "What happened to your hand?"

"I cut it."

"How?"

Outside the window beside his desk, the swimming pool glistened in the waning sun. The wind had overturned a wicker chair. I had the urge to go set it right. My father ran his fingers through his thinning hair and exhaled through tense lips, a barely audible sputter. He played with a yellow pencil, running his fingers down the length of it, turning it on its head and repeating the procedure—eraser, point, eraser, point. He glanced up at me. "The contractor says he knows you. Says you've been by there. Is that true?"

"Sometimes, after school."

"Over two thousand dollars worth of damage. A hell of a mess." He dropped the pencil. It rolled and came to a stop where the leather surface ended and the polished wood began. "I asked the man what he was implying. He said he just wondered if you'd seen anything." He paused, glanced down at his fingernails, looked back up at me. "Well, did you? See anything?"

"Yes."

"Really? What?"

"I did it."

"You did what?"

"I broke the windows."

My father's head dipped to one side like the RCA Victor dog. I suppose he was trying to decide whether to believe me, and if he did, what then?

"Corey. . . ." He scratched the back of his head. "He said there was blood all over the place."

I held up my bandaged hand.

He winced. "Jesus Christ. What the hell?"

My father and I had never discussed anything beyond the complexities of edging the lawn or vacuuming the swimming pool. He was not someone I really knew. And he certainly didn't know me. "I'm going to go get your mother," he said, getting up. I followed him with my eyes. He turned at the door, perhaps hoping that he had only imagined the last five minutes. I raised my bandaged hand again, and he left the room.

I waited, wishing things would slow down a little. What did you ever really know for certain about anyone? How did people like my parents, who didn't seem to have much in common, get together in the first place? I loved Gina, but I was beginning to see what an unlikely couple we were, just like them. If I'd been honest with myself, I would have known something would drive Gina and me apart, eventually. Gina was like some kind of bird, a hummingbird, maybe—frenzied, never coming to rest anywhere for more than two seconds. She had one goal only, and if I'd had my eyes open, I would have noticed that it had never included me.

Mr. Dean was harder to figure. We'd talked so much about music, about college, about a trip to Carnegie Hall one day. I had played in the orchestra since he started it, studied the organ with him at Saint Francis. I was more than just his favorite student. He had taught me what it felt like to be loved by somebody, somebody who chose to love me, not just because they had to, like a parent, but because they liked who I was. Being loved that way had been something completely different, something you never expected, something you can't describe. What had happened in the storage closet, among those discarded band instruments and moldering music scores, was just part of Mr. Dean's affection for me, something he couldn't resist, as I think he tried to during those weeks between visits to that room, proof of how important I was to him. I had consigned those illicit and, in truth, sometimes thrilling moments to some sealed-off cellar of my mind, away from the sound and smell and light of the real world. It had been our secret, and it had bound us together, the way secrets do. That's what I had believed. Was none of it true?

My father returned and sat back behind his desk, like some chief inspector in a TV movie. His face had that contorted expression it got when he fought with my mother or when not enough new Fords were moving off the lot. My mother followed him in and took the wingchair next to mine. She lit a Salem and sat back, staring at me. Uncharacteristically, she let my father take the lead.

"Is anything bothering you, son?" he asked me, holding his breath and puffing out his cheeks. Beads of sweat had surfaced on his upper lip. I could see he was trying really hard not to explode.

Only the two most important people in my life, I thought. "Like what?" I said.

"That's what we're asking you," my mother put in, her tone laced with what sounded to me like anger. "Your teachers say you're messing up in class, and now this . . . this . . ." She gestured toward my bandaged hand. "What's going on, Corey? Is there some problem with you and Gina?" Then she softened, as if a velvet approach might be more productive. "We want to help."

My mother took a long drag on her cigarette and exhaled through her nose and mouth. She'd always bailed me out of scrapes. She would have known what to do about the pregnancy, had I been able to tell her. She would have been disappointed in me, but she would have flown into action, dragging Gina and Mrs. Daley along with her. The baby would have been saved, quietly, probably with Gina spending a few months out of town next fall. And Gina wouldn't be in White Plains right now, sneaking into some clinic on some back street.

"What is it, son?" my father persisted. "Is it Gina? Did something happen?"

What shocked me then was the realization that it hadn't even occurred to them that my problem might be with Mr. Dean. Hadn't they noticed that for over three years I'd gone to concerts with my teacher, gone shopping in Pittsfield, been away three hours for a one-hour organ lesson? Wasn't that a little unusual? What was suddenly frightening about my whole time with Mr. Dean was that no one had even noticed.

Sitting there, looking from my mother back to my father, I had no idea what to say to them. How was I ever to explain, even about the house? The bricks were there. The windows were there. The connection, at the time, had seemed obvious. The bandaged fingers I stared at now seemed as if they belonged to someone else. So did my deteriorating grades at school. How was I supposed to sort it all out and make them understand? I had to say something, yet I knew that if I said what was foremost in my mind, it would change things forever.

"I've got a lot going on right now," I said.

"Like what?" my mother asked. "Is it school? Is somebody giving you a hard time? Just tell us."

Dark roots labored under my mother's cropped red hair. Her nostrils spread and then narrowed again, like fish gills. Her lipstick had worn away on her smoking side. I recalled, before I was old enough to go to school, helping her plant flowers in pots and put them at the front door where everyone would see. I remembered her holding me up in the shallow end of the pool, her strong hands pressing against my stomach, encouraging me to kick. I missed her now. I wanted her back. But that woman and that kid didn't exist anymore.

"Mr. Dean," I said. The sound of his name made tears brim in my eyes.

My father switched his gaze from me to my mother, then back to me. "What about Dean?" he said.

When I was four or five years old, I used to look at people I didn't know—couples I saw in the grocery checkout line or walking up the steps to church—and wonder what it would be like if they were my parents. I know, that sounds weird, but already it had seemed to me that so much in life happened by chance. Why not whose kid I was? I used to imagine what it would be like if I'd been born to some lady in a house dress I'd seen shopping at Sears, and her tall skinny husband with no uppers. I'd have looked different, had different friends. I might even have been born in China or Singapore, been awake when everyone I knew now was asleep. It used to scare me, the idea that the world was such a random place, that anything could happen, and did, all the time.

As I wiped my eyes and looked from my father to my mother that afternoon—my busy, well-meaning parents—I felt as if I hardly knew them. They wanted me to say something that would make everything okay, but I couldn't think what that would be. Nothing could make things okay now. But one word, it seemed, one word might stop the dizzying eddy inside my head.

"Sex," I said.

My mother crunched out her cigarette, the smoke trailing pink as it rose into a dying angle of sun from outside. "Jesus Christ," she said.

She stood and walked to the window. Though I couldn't see her face, I sensed her sorting through the years since Mr. Dean arrived in Williston, putting things together, all those late afternoons I'd arrived home in his convertible. Maybe she recalled, feeling foolish, her own flirtations with Mr. Dean. "Are you homosexual?" she asked into the drapes, like whether I wanted strawberry or raspberry jam on my peanut butter sandwich.

My father squirmed. "Of course he's not," he said. "He's fourteen, for Christ's sake. What does he know?"

"Fifteen," I said.

"We're not judging you, Corey," my mother persevered, turning back into the room and sitting back in the wingchair.

Not judging? Hadn't we all *judged* that something was wrong, something terrible, and wouldn't we—or they—soon be *judging* what to do about it?

I could see now that my mother, too, was doing everything she could to maintain her cool. Her voice had the vibrato of a lyric soprano; her fingers dug into the upholstered arm of her chair. "We're just concerned. We want to help." She reached—rigid, cool—to touch my arm. I looked down at her bright red nails and pulled away. What was going on under that phony, placid veneer, all the more scary because it was so rare in her?

"Has that. . . . Has he touched you?" my father asked.

I looked at him, across his desk, then back to her. The mantle clock tallied the last unnerving moments before everything in our lives would change.

"He's touched him, Warren," my mother said. "I think that's obvious."

"Bill Dean?" my father said, incredulous. "A fucking fairy?"

My mother's eyes narrowed and a delicate twitch traveled across her upper lip. She looked at me with what I took to be a mix of embarrassment and revulsion, but with maybe a brief, detached instant of envy, to the extent that I had broken free of the conventions that bound her so awkwardly to my father and to that community she was always trying to change. For a moment, she seemed to glimpse the incredible exhilaration of the runner who emerges from the pack with nothing ahead of him but the delicate, gleaming string of the finish line. But that glimpse froze and shattered in her icy stare. There was no track, no finish line, only a giant wall of dread.

"Maybe Corey should talk to you," she said, getting up.

No, I thought, don't leave. Maybe she was icy, but she was all I had right then.

"Sure," my father said, adopting his authoritarian tone. "Of course."

"Mom?" I murmured, watching her walk away.

She paused, with her hand on the doorknob. Then she pulled open the door and left the room.

My father and I stared at each other. What had we ever said to each other that could possibly prepare us for what we needed to say now? I looked down at my hands again, thinking they were the problem. If it weren't for my thin, white, capable fingers, none of this would have happened—I wouldn't have played the piano for Mr. Dean that first week of seventh grade, I wouldn't have thrown the bricks, I wouldn't be sitting here now, trying to think how to avoid betraying the man who had been my friend for as long as I could remember. Or did I want nothing less than to betray him, since that day, a week ago, when I saw him driving up the street with Jimmie Harkness?

My father stood. "What do you say to a ride?" he asked me.

As if we were heading off on a fishing trip, we piled into his Country Squire and drove south on Route 20 until he pulled off at a rest area, a place I'd been to plenty of times with Mr. Dean. Suddenly alone together in the fading light, without the distraction of driving, our awkwardness returned. He stared straight ahead down the highway and said nothing. I thought about Gina, alone in the guest room in Jane Brenner's house in White Plains. I thought about Mr. Dean, eating a sandwich in his apartment, sorting through tests and grades for the end of the school year. What could I do? My parents were not going to forget about Mr. Dean, the way they did so many problems that had vexed them for a day or two and then evaporated with a little judicious neglect.

"He blew me," I said.

My dad's foot shot to the brake, as if the Ford were careening out of control, not us. "And I sucked him." That word, ice hard and sharp, flew from my tongue, hovered briefly between us and then dove like a dagger for my father's chest.

"Oh, my god," he whispered.

I turned away. I wanted to hurt my father, but I didn't want to watch. And shame rose in me like bile.

When I finally did turn to him, he continued to stare down the highway, gripping the steering wheel, wringing it like a wet towel. "Do you still like Gina?" he asked me.

"I guess so. Sure."

With that, he lunged across the seat and grabbed me in a stiff bear hug, our first. I remember being surprised at how little I felt, how precarious his hold on me really was, how alone we both were. My link to my parents, and to Mr. Dean and to Gina, seemed as flimsy now as frayed thread. I imagined my father fretting about me, as if one of his new Fords had been hijacked and taken for a joy ride, but miraculously returned to him undamaged. I dared to hope that he would breathe a sigh of relief and forget the whole thing.

As I endured his embrace, a truck pulled into the rest area, and I imagined the driver staring into my father's car as the headlights of the huge rig passed over us. I imagined that he thought we were making out, that he might pull my dad out of the car and smack him. I thought to myself, you're a little late, buddy.

We drove home in silence, my father squinting into oncoming headlights. He seemed angry, and maybe disgusted, thinking about me getting sucked by Mr. Dean. Looking back, I wonder if he was sad, too, unable to really talk to me, as his own father had probably been afraid to talk to him, years before, and his father before that, in an endless line of fathers afraid to talk to their sons. Afraid of the closeness that would come of such conversations. Afraid that that closeness, itself, might feel sexual. My father was afraid of exactly what I needed to talk to him about.

I realized then that my parents couldn't fix all that was wrong, as I might have hoped they would, in that naïve way that kids believe their parents can fix anything. I tried to rid myself of the dread that Mr. Dean was in serious jeopardy now. My father was nothing if not a fighter. He would go for Mr. Dean's throat, fixated on revenge. The more I thought about it, the more I realized nothing would be worked out that would spare Mr. Dean. For the first time, it occurred to me that I might never see him again.

That evening, after my father had driven off to meet with a lawyer, I tried to talk to my mother about Gina, and maybe, depending on how that went, about Mr. Dean. She was my hope, the only one who might derail this train that seemed to be hurtling toward destruction. But when I asked her if we could talk, she picked up the telephone to call someone about a meeting. For once, she was letting my father handle things. In the end, she needed him to be strong, to restore the protected little world she'd always seemed so eager to defy.

Chapter Thirteen
1988

At five-fifteen on Saturday morning, I'm wide awake. Jack has been gone nearly a week and I still haven't heard from him. I roll over and stare at a familiar roadmap of ceiling cracks above my head. My feelings rove from understanding into worry and get hung up on angry before I reign them into indulgence. This time is about Jack, I tell myself, not me. Losing a family member you've been estranged from can be worse than if you were close. There's more to mourn—the loss of the relationship long before the person died, the guilt for not trying harder, the wish that things had been different.

It occurs to me that I didn't check the mailbox when I returned from the city last night. I've been expecting a telephone message all along. Is it possible Jack would write? It's an odd notion, but I'm desperate. I throw back the covers, pull on my robe and take the stairs two at a time. At the back door, I step into Jack's work boots, left under the coat rack.

Outside, a ghost-like mist hovers over the pond and drapes itself casually over one end of the barn, like a comforter sliding off the foot of a bed. A thin, metallic scent of rain holds sway as the sun's scouts blaze the undersides of leaden clouds. An invigorating chill sweeps up under my robe. How extraordinary is this retreat of mine, every aspect, in every direction I look. Would it be the same if Jack never returned? Yes, I consider that possibility, but immediately dismiss the idea. His boot laces, wet with dew, tap the pebbles of the driveway, threatening to trip me. And yet, I am so happy to be, literally, in his shoes.

The mailbox is stuffed with magazines, bills and flyers. Nothing from Jack.

Turning back toward the house, I notice George, my neighbor, walking along the road toward our driveway. He's wearing a expensive-looking hunting jacket, all wool plaid and leather with tortoise-shell buttons. We meet at the end of the driveway. He smiles. "You guys are up early," he says.

I consider a couple of improbable explanations, but abandon them in favor of the truth. "Just me, I'm afraid."

"Where's Jack?"

"He's in Nebraska. His mother died."

"Oh, I'm sorry."

"He left last Sunday, and I haven't heard from him."

"I see," George says, looking down at the work boots and flagging laces. "Is he okay, do you think? Have you tried calling him?"

"I've sort of been waiting for him to call me. I mean, he knows how to reach me, right? And he probably knows I'm worried as hell." This explanation sounds petty, as if not speaking to Jack all week were some sort of power play between us. "I must look ridiculous," I say, glancing at my knobby knees and the blond hairs of my shins, standing on end in the damp chill.

"Sexy."

"Depends what you're into, I guess." We chuckle.

"Are you alone, then, for the weekend? David and I have a bunch of friends coming up from the city tomorrow morning. Why don't you join us for dinner?"

"I'd like that," I say, turning toward the house. I imagine George telling David there's trouble next door, and a nasty competitive feeling rises in me. I don't want Jack and me to look like we're failing. It's the least of my worries right now, but still, there it is. "Shall I let you know definitely in the morning?"

"That would be fine. Why don't you try reaching Jack? I'm sure he'd like to hear from you."

"Maybe I will."

Halfway down the driveway, George turns back. "You all right, Corey?"

I wave.

Inside, I sort the mail at my desk in Jack's old room, discarding flyers, opening bills. As part of our arrangement for sharing expenses, Jack took responsibility for the oil, electricity and phone bills. But paying bills has always been a kind of therapy for me, a restoration of order, a fleeting sense of control, so I pull out my checkbook.

My sympathy for Jack, from before, evaporates as I stare at the telephone bill. He has called Chadron, Nebraska five times during the last month, all on days when I was working in New York. It has to be the professor. I wonder how long this has been going on and mount a half-hearted search of the desk drawers for past phone bills, to no avail. Sleuth, I'm not, and I hate checking up on Jack. The professor. How ridiculous that I don't even know the man's name! I'm tempted to call the number on the bill right now. But what would I say?

A sickening sensation rises in my chest as I picture the two of them talking on the telephone, Jack with his feet up on my desk. It strikes me, suddenly, that things with Jack will not end well. The thought sends a painful constriction into my throat, that tender precursor to tears. I recall Gina saying, the day we fought and she left here for good, that a shared past, a history, is what keeps people together, not passion. With Jack, there is no sense of past, though we've been together long enough now to have created one. Even the mix of Jack's things in this room—the tattered pillows, the worn kilim; and mine—the antique desk, the oak filing cabinet; seem less to blend than to coexist uneasily, each item somehow reflecting Jack's reserve or my diffidence. I fear that I have stepped beyond the strict set of safety parameters I set for myself when I was sixteen. I've loved and trusted in ways I promised myself I never would, and now, as if in spiteful compensation, I feel the bottom falling out from under me, just as it did then.

I pick up the phone and dial information. The brother Jack mentioned, Jeb, must live around North Platte, since he had driven over to his mother's to find her dead. He would know where Jack is. The operator gives me a number. I dial it, and Jeb himself answers. I tell him I'm Jack's friend, which sounds insufficient, but I doubt that Jeb Krakouski knows much about his brother, and I'm not about to make any revelations. I just want to find Jack. He tells me Jack had stayed at his mother's house until after the funeral, when he went to Chadron to see a friend who is a teacher there. Jeb didn't know the teacher's name. I decide, while talking to Jack's brother, to go to Nebraska. I'll find Jack and we'll talk. Maybe I'll even meet the professor, finally, and put an end to this mystery. Jeb gives me directions to his mother's house, tells me the place is never locked, if I get there and Jack isn't around.

I hang up and step to the bookcase, where I pull out the road atlas. The most striking thing about western Nebraska is how blank it is on the map, how few red and blue lines cross its vacant expanse. I find North Platte on the Platte River, right in the middle of the state. It takes me a while to find Chadron, a remote outpost in the northwest corner amid the Nebraska National Forest and the Ogallala National Grassland. I feel jittery. I hope Jack won't find my arrival in Nebraska intrusive. But I'm his lover, for Christ's sake. I want to be there with him, whether he needs me or not. I want to hold onto him, figure out later on whether we're right for each other.

I take the atlas upstairs with me and throw it in the bottom of my suitcase.

The flight is quick and uneventful, and it's shortly after noon when I rent a car at Eppley Airfield in Omaha and head west on Interstate 80. I'd expected the flat, open terrain, but not its imposing austerity. The Great Plain, all divided into immense cultivated squares, as clearly delineated as if they'd been cut from construction paper and pasted on matte board. Corn, wheat, barley—amber, green, brown. Quiet, ordered, with a sense of underlying restlessness you get from the relentless wind—Jack's internal nature laid out on the surface of the land.

The miles pass quickly, and the enduring landscape inspires me to hope that my link with Jack, despite how it's felt this last week, is as solid and durable as the fields flashing past the windshield. I am eager to see him, while nervous about discovering some possible new side of Jack, revealed here among the dusty grasslands. After exactly four hours of turnpike driving, I take the exit for North Platte, and inquire at a gas station how to find Route 83 north to Gandy. The attendant, with a smirk, points out the window to the road in front. "I'm looking for the Krakouski place," I say, setting a pack of gum and a carton of orange juice on the counter. The man only shrugs, rings up the purchases and hands me my change. I thought mid westerners were supposed to be friendly. If he's heard of Jack's mother, he isn't saying. I get back into my rented Ford Escort and head north on Route 83.

My own mother called just before I left Connecticut to invite Jack and me to their place in Florida for Thanksgiving. The tentativeness in her voice is probably my fault. Since the incident with my teacher, over twenty-five years ago, I've kept both my parents at a distance. A very long time to hold a grudge, I think now, if that's what I'm doing. It seems more complicated than resentment, though, more that I don't really expect to be understood, to be able to explain something that still feels so raw. The rift that spring of my sophmore year in high school had been so painful, so complete, that I hadn't wanted to mend it. But since being with Jack, I've softened somewhat toward my parents. Maybe being happier, in general, helps one forgive. Still, I continued to avoid any awkward discussion with my father about me being with a man.

The particular question I had wanted to avert came, finally, on a visit to their home in Sarasota two years ago. We'd been cleaning up, my dad washing the pots and pans from dinner and me drying. I was telling him about my practice in New York. He had asked what sort of patients I saw, and I suspected the real question was whether or not they were all gay. "Do you think it's because of what happened with that Dean character? You being homosexual, I mean?" he asked, finally.

I remember wishing my father would use the word "gay." Homosexual sounded so clinical, so disease-like. Despite having anticipated the question, I was taken aback by it, and even wondered if my father might be feeling guilty—that he should have suspected Dean's conspicuous attention and been more protective of his son.

I didn't think Bill Dean had made me gay. No one possesses that sort of power. The damage had been more profound. What happened with Bill Dean had made it impossible for me to trust anyone, man or woman, gay or straight. With Dean, I came to believe that sex—and by extension, love—was some sort of powerplay you either had to control or surrender to. Later, I learned, intellectually at least, that giving up some measure of control was essential to a relationship. But the actual surrender had always made me feel as if I were jumping off a cliff. I just couldn't do it.

Jack had been in the next room, talking with my mother, sharing the easy sort of confidence that for years had seemed impossible for me with either of my parents. I wondered if Jack had one ear trained on my conversation with my dad in the kitchen.

"No, he didn't make me gay," I answered, accepting a dripping pot, wishing questions about sexuality could be put away as easily as cooking utensils.

A silence had ensued, in which I thought about the power I had developed over Bill Dean when I was just twelve years old, how I had learned to manipulate him in order to get the attention I craved, and how I had used that power, ultimately, in a jealous rage, to destroy him. The shame of that had followed me for years. Whatever people say about victims and perpetrators of sexual abuse, I behaved badly, too.

I despaired, standing there at the sink, of being able to explain all that to my father. And I was reluctant, believing it was the aftermath—the part he had orchestrated—that had been the most destructive. For sure, I hadn't been ready for sex with a grown man, but I was even less prepared for the violence that came of it. My father's worst suspicion, that my teacher had made me gay, seemed almost irrelevant to all the damage inflicted back then.

"Sexual orientation is likely determined early on," I said, hearing how pedantic I sounded. "It's probably mostly chemical, or genetic."

I was lying. I had little doubt that there were psychological factors in sexual preferences—gay, straight or otherwise. But might not my experience with Bill Dean have sent me running as far away from men as I could get? Certainly, for a while—too long—it had.

The conversation left me unsettled. I wanted my father to be less concerned about why I was gay and more interested in how it had all been for me back then, how I had managed to keep things a secret for so long, how lonely and confused I had felt. I wanted to tell him that all along I had been seeking the attention I wasn't getting from him. Of course, my dad would never ask such questions. And I probably would have retreated from hurting him with the answers.

He could never really understand, but someone loved me who *could* understand—Jack. Yet that night, sharing one of the twin beds in my parents' guest room, I had lain next to him, mute, all that I might say locked in my chest.

I check the Ford's odometer now. I've driven twelve miles down a road as straight and narrow as a yardstick, then four miles on another road no different from the first, except that it runs perpendicular to it. I wonder what would happen if the car broke down out here. I've encountered only one other car in the last twenty minutes. I can almost feel the slow pace, the limitless landscape stretching out on all sides, the aloneness Jack grew up in.

On the phone with my mother this morning, I told her that Jack was in Nebraska at his mother's funeral, and that I hadn't heard from him. I sometimes think there is a lot I could learn from my mother about living with a laconic, emotionally-closed man, if I wanted to ask. She has mellowed over the years, and I am more appreciative of her intelligence, her irreverent wit, her liberal politics. She's taken a part-time job in a library in Sarasota. Why she married my father, I don't know. Security, I suppose, and to flee the motherless home she grew up in. Over the years, she seems to have come to terms with her marriage and made a life of her own, alongside, yet quite apart from, her husband.

"I'm so sorry about Jack's mother," she said, this morning. "What happened?"

"She was just old, I guess."

"Is Jack okay?"

"I don't know. They weren't close." Raising the issue of mother-son closeness made me uneasy. I suspected my mother was thinking how close she and I had been once, or at least that was how it had seemed.

"Is it harder, Corey?" she asked me.

"Is what harder?"

"Being with a man?"

My grip on the telephone tightened. We so rarely spoke this way. "Well," I said, "there aren't the usual conventions of marriage and joint property and kids to keep you together. And there's always the question of how someone is going to respond at a cocktail party or in the checkout line at the grocery store. Not a scene or anything. Something more subtle, a curtness, an averting of the eyes that could be homophobia or just that they're having a bad day."

Then it had occurred to me that my mother wasn't asking what it was like being gay as much as what it was like being with a man versus a woman, since I had done both. "Men are more competitive," I told her. "And the roles aren't clearly defined, so it's freer, but it's also harder. You have to find what works for each of you, and it may be quite different from the conventional." At that point, I gave up, wondering, finally, what my mother was really driving at and realizing how hard it is, still, for me to be open with her.

"That sounds good to me," she said, "not having all the conventions and expectations, having that freedom."

"I guess."

"But you and Jack do have joint property, don't you?"

"Not really. I own the house."

"But he's worked so hard on it."

Did my mother think that that entitled Jack to half the house? "I miss him," I said, changing the subject.

After eight miles on this second road, I start watching for names on occasional mailboxes at the ends of driveways that disappear behind arid brush with no sign of a house. I slow, finally, in front of a battered green mailbox on which someone—Jack? When he was six?—had painted Krakouski in bold, childlike letters. A plastic pot of skeletal geraniums leans against the post.

The house, which sits at the end of a rutted approach you couldn't really label a driveway, looks as if it might have been a bunkhouse fifty years ago. Faded blue, with a tarpaper roof, it appears to tilt slightly to one side, as if it had been dropped there and forgotten like the pot of geraniums. A derelict car seat sits out front, facing away from the road and away from the house, away from everything but the endless expanse of plain that stretches, desolate, in every direction. The house is obviously empty. No car. Not a sound. To me, it explains so much about Jack, about his love for our place in Connecticut, about his humility, and perhaps also his bitterness.

I pull ahead and back in, so the Ford is facing out, for ready escape. Of course, I'm not leaving. I'm waiting for Jack, however long it takes. I get out and stand on the uneven ground. So this is where Jack grew up. The barrenness makes sense, I suppose, but not the dereliction. Jack is nothing if not neat. But, of course, he left years ago. He had been confined here, alone with his mother. This is where he would have caught the school bus, I think, glancing back toward the road. I walk to the barn he mentioned once, more of a lean-to. Weathered holes gape where its windows used to be. Spools of rusted barbed wire lie alongside the remains of a tractor and a pile of warped lumber with a bicycle leaning against it. The tires on the bicycle are flat, of course, the handlebars rusted, the seat rotted away by the sun. Jack's bike. I grip the handlebars and look around again. Nothing. Nothing but emptiness, beginning to lose the light.

The blemished door rattles as I push it open. The kitchen is surprisingly cheerful, with a yellow-and-white gingham table cloth spread over an oak table. The linoleum floor is scrubbed, as are the gleaming white appliances. No doubt, Jack got right to work when he arrived. Physical work relaxes him, something we have in common. A plastic TV sits on the counter. A kettle on the stove stands ready to boil water. The room smells aged and closed-in, with an overlay of lemon-scented cleanser.

I feel like an intruder, neither invited nor escorted by Jack. Before going back outside, I check a small bedroom off the kitchen to see if his things are still here, and they are. The hope that he'll return soon is more desperate than is called for. I feel suddenly exhausted, stooping under the water-stained ceiling. But I resist lying on the bed.

Back outside, I sit behind the wheel of the Ford. What if Jack doesn't show up? Could I find my way back to the highway in the dark that will envelop this place in an hour or so, or do I spend the night here in his mother's empty house? Maybe I should drive up to Chadron State College, I'm thinking, when the ring of a telephone jars the silence. Instinctively, I look at my watch—3:10. Whoever is calling is persistent. I wait for the ringing to stop. Then I change my mind, fling open the car door and dash across the pock-marked yard to the porch. As I reach for the telephone on the wall by the door, the ringing stops. I walk back onto the rickety porch. The ringing starts again, and I pick up.

"Hey, it's me."

"Jack? How did you. . . ."

"I called my brother."

"I came out," I say.

"You came out three years ago, pal."

Jack's joke makes me smile, a little of the Jack I love coming to me at the end of a phone wire in the middle of nowhere. I am so happy to hear his voice, I could cry.

"Not much, is it?" he says.

"What?"

"The Krakouski ranch."

"I've been crazed, worrying about you."

"It's a long story. I'm sorry."

"You're in Chadron now?"

"Yeah."

"With the professor?"

"I have stuff I need to tell you, Corey."

I look across the porch at the lean-to, my rental car, the mailbox. "I can't believe how far apart everything is around here," I say.

"I'm leaving now, okay?" Jack says. "I should be to my mother's place in a few hours, four at the most. We can talk, then."

Jack's tone is more confident, the way he had sounded when he first came to the house four summers ago. "I'll wait," I say.

"Good. I'll be there soon as I can."

"I love you, Jack."

The dial tone clicks on. The withering light leaves a residue of long, pointed shadows across the porch floor. I cross them and step to the border of the wheat field. Whatever Jack needs to say, whatever he still has going on with his professor friend, I vow to hear him out.

The wheat, stretching into the distance, is tall and bends under its own weight. A fiery gold pulsates in low-strung clouds. I glance back at the house with its faded blue siding, then enter the field.

Chapter Fourteen
1965

The morning after I blabbed to my parents about Mr. Dean, the lawyer who had handled my father's purchase of the Ford agency back in 1963 arrived at our house. Apparently, relationship closings, like real estate closings, required a lawyer's seal. If we were going to press charges, he needed to know the details of what had happened with this Mr. William Dean. Uneasiness must have registered in my face, because the lawyer suggested, for confidentiality, that we talk in his Lincoln parked in the driveway outside our house.

Curly black hairs reached out of his collar when he swallowed. Springing late into puberty had left me overly focused on the standard symbols of male maturity—hirsuteness, for example. Or maybe it was those first months with Mr. Dean, always wanting to be more like him. I imagined smatterings of hair on the lawyer's shoulders and back, matted against the warm leather seat of the Lincoln.

"How long have you known this William Dean?" he asked me.

"Since seventh grade. Four years, I guess."

"Since you were twelve?"

"Eleven. I'm young for my grade."

"And when did he start . . . touching you."

"Then."

"In seventh grade?"

"That fall."

"Exactly what did he do to you?"

"You mean. . . ." I made a vague gesture toward my lap.

"It's the only way I can defend you. With details."

"I need defending?" Mr. Dean was my enemy now.

"It'll be your word against his. He'll deny it." The lawyer peered at me over horn-rimmed glasses and forced a smile that was probably intended to be reassuring, like a dentist grinning as he reaches for the drill. "I need to know what he did to you."

"He touched me," I said. Would I be arrested, too? I wondered. Everything we'd done, we'd done together.

"Where did he touch you?"

Did this guy think I was going to send Mr. Dean to jail with some pathetic confession? "Mr. Dean was my friend," I said. But if he was been my friend, why had I betrayed him? Yes, petty as it sounds, I suppose I'd wanted to get back at him for taking up with Jimmy Harkness. But I never thought things would go this far. Now, this lawyer and my dad seemed more like the enemy than Mr. Dean.

"Friends don't make you have sex."

How could I tell the lawyer that Mr. Dean hadn't made me do anything? Did my willingness mean I was queer, too? "He touched my dick," I said.

The lawyer wrote a single word on his pad—penis. Then, in the silence that followed, I watched him shade the holes in the p and the e with his pencil. Everything reduced to that one word.

"Where else did he touch you?" he asked, without looking up from his doodling.

In my mind, I counted the empty spaces he could shade in ass—one, in balls—two. Sex had ruined things with Mr. Dean. Same with Gina and me. I'd always suspected that sex was dangerous, but I'd had no idea how much damage it could actually do. I stared out the window of the Lincoln. Pink and white dogwood bloomed in the dappled light of the woods beyond our swimming pool.

"Oral sex?" he said. "Did he put his mouth on you?"

Sex was the only thing that mattered to this lawyer, too. "You think that was all it was?" I asked him.

"What do you mean?"

"Sex?"

The lawyer started penciling lines that angled out from the base of the letters in penis, shadows, as if some radiance had risen behind the lonely word. I imagined this simple, adorned note in a manila file labeled 'Corey Moore.'

"What did you think was going on?" he asked me.

He loved me, I wanted to say. He thought I could have a career in music. He was my friend. All of which sounded absurd now.

"Well, that's all the law is interested in," the lawyer said. He had completed his shading operation and stuck his pencil into the ringed binding of his notebook. Apparently, we were finished.

The lawyer seemed the picture of unhappiness to me, as he stared ahead out the windshield of his Lincoln Continental. Perhaps he had a son. Perhaps he was imagining his own boy sitting across the seat from him. Would he be asking him these questions? Would he want to hear the answers?

"Did he penetrate you?" he said now, turning to me.

My stomach clenched. Fucking? It had never occurred to me that Mr. Dean might do something like that. The idea repulsed me. "No," I said. "Like I said, he was my friend."

"As you go through life, you'll learn to choose friends who are not going to take advantage of you. What this man did was wrong, and we have laws to protect kids from predators like him."

"What if I don't want to press charges?"

"It's not up to you. It's up to your father. The law doesn't consider you competent until you're eighteen."

The law was never going to understand about Mr. Dean and me. Nobody would.

"Is there anything else you want to tell me, Corey?"

I thought about the trips Mr. Dean and I had taken to Pittsfield. I thought about how my work at the keyboard had improved the four years I had studied with him, about the long rides home in his shiny convertible. I shook my head.

"Look," he said, "I know this must be hard for you. But just because this happened, it doesn't necessarily make you homosexual. All kids want attention. That's what makes them vulnerable. Your dad says you have a girlfriend. Everything's going to be okay."

I guess he was trying to be helpful. I didn't know how to tell this lawyer that a much larger and scarier question plagued me. Love, it seemed, could destroy people. How was I going to avoid it in the future? Was being alone the only answer?

"There's one more thing," the lawyer said. "Is there anyone else you think this William Dean might have done this sort of thing to? Another boy, maybe?"

I pictured Jimmy Harkness, leaving school with Mr. Dean. "Why?" I asked.

"Because right now, like I said, it's your word against Dean's. We would have a stronger case with another victim."

I was a victim, allied with my dad and his lawyer against Mr. Dean, the perpetrator. Adults had the ability to boil things down to their essence. Or so they thought. It seemed to me that Mr. Dean and I were each a victim and a perpetrator, but I could see there wasn't much hope of getting this lawyer to see that. "And if I tell?"

"They'll have to testify, too. You'll be brought in together, so no one will know who initiated this action against Dean."

I told him.

The lawyer withdrew his pencil from the spiral binding. He wrote James Harkness on his yellow pad and drew a circle around it. "I guess that's it," he said, snapping the notebook shut and slipping it into his briefcase. "At least you don't have to worry about the windows."

I gave him a questioning look.

"Down the road. Your dad paid for them. The owners aren't going to make a fuss. He didn't tell you?"

I shook my head.

"A healthy sum of cash."

"I'll pay him back."

"I don't think he's expecting that. Maybe just. . . . Maybe you could tell your folks when something's bothering you, from now on. They're good people. They'll understand."

Telling them anything, from that point on, seemed extremely unlikely. I reached for the door handle.

"I'm sorry you had to go through this," the lawyer said. "I'll do what I can to make the rest as painless as possible."

"Will he be arrested?"

"I imagine so."

"Do we have to go through with this?"

"He deserves to be punished. And we don't want him molesting any more kids. You're protecting other kids. Look at it that way."

Could I sneak out of the house this afternoon and warn Mr. Dean? What would he do to me when I told him what I'd done? I opened the door and slipped off the seat of the Lincoln.

Upstairs, I lay on my bed, staring at the ceiling. I pictured Gina, alone, recovering from an abortion in White Plains, New York, a place I'd never even heard of until a week ago. Had she told Jane Brenner why she was there? Knowing Gina, probably not. Was she in pain? Was she frightened? And I thought about Mr. Dean who would soon be getting a knock on his door from the police. I imagined him getting up from his chair by the window to answer the door, seeing the uniformed men and knowing right away why they had come.

So much damage, all of it my fault.

Chapter Fifteen
1988

My walk among the wheat stalks behind Jack's childhood home starts out leisurely. I imagine Jack as a boy, riding a neighbor's huge grinding combine, squinting through clouds of aromatic wheat dust as a ten-yard width falls beneath its giant blades. This land reared Jack and taught him his basic good sense. Had it also made him restless, sullen, impetuous? Soon, I'm moving faster through the quivering dryness, the long grass stinging my shins through my chinos. The sun has nearly descended to the flat line of the horizon, which seems to vibrate with its fireball proximity. Suddenly, I realize I've been running for some time, and, breathless, I stop. Bent wheat caresses my calves now like a neglected cat. The vast openness has a weird effect on my mind. I have the urge to curl up and sleep, with only the immense darkening sky for a roof. So what if I never find my way back to the house? Would anyone care? This landscape alienates with a silent and haunting abandonment.

Fatigue, listlessness, a lack of concern for what happens to me—these are feelings I've been fighting off since I was fifteen, the ones I've kept myself too busy to consider, the ones I've outrun up to now.

I turn back in the direction I came, indicated only by the path I've pressed into the wheat. High clouds are stretched sheets in the darkening sky. The simple task of setting one foot in front of the other is an effort. My whole body aches. The thought of Jack appearing here is all that keeps me moving back toward his childhood house. We'll talk. All the reasons we've stayed together will be obvious again. We'll sleep entwined in his childhood bed.

Soon, I sit back inside the Ford in a gathering blackness already more complete than I'd ever imagined existed. No moon, no stars, no glow of a street lamp. Only a pale, leftover sun-blush at the horizon. A chill wafts through the car's open window. I recall Jack saying once how, living with me, he often felt small by comparison, and unimportant. Walking in that vast field beyond the house, I can see that feelings of smallness and irrelevance invaded Jack's blood long before he met me. I wish I'd been more empathetic. I've felt small, myself, at times. It's clearer to me now than it's ever been that I have maintained my own distance from Jack, and from Gina before that. I'd been so determined, at fifteen, never to be weak or defenseless again.

I must have dozed off. My back is stiff and throbbing as I awaken and switch on the ignition. Squinting into the orange dashboard lights, I watch the gas gauge rise reassuringly to Full. In the rearview mirror, I can see my own face in the eerie light—drawn, hollow-eyed, worn out. My watch reads 7:40. I turn off the ignition. The last thing I need out here is a dead battery. I lock the doors, then run my fingers through my hair, massaging my scalp and my neck. I lean my head against the seat, trying to remember when I ate last, when a pair of headlights sweeps over the rutted yard and beams directly into my eyes. I lift my hand to block the blinding glare, just as it vanishes, throwing me back into blackness. A car door slams and I hear footsteps in the parched dirt.

"Sorry, it took forever," Jack says. I unlock the car door and he pulls it open. "What are you doing out here? Why didn't you go inside?"

"I did. It didn't feel right, being in there without you." I think I detect the smell of liquor on Jack, but that seems impossible because he so rarely drinks. "I must have fallen asleep," I say. "Is it always this dark around here?"

"Except when the stars are out. Dark nights like this are just a set-up for the light show that follows. Come on. Let's go inside."

"Should I get my bag?" I ask, stepping out of the car, shivering in the cold that has descended with the black curtain.

"Leave it," Jack says. "We'll get it later. Let's just go get warm."

We walk together toward the house, our breath misty clouds. I feel Jack's hand on my arm, turning me, and then the muscles in his shoulders as he hugs me. "I missed you," he says.

"Me too."

He kisses me, and the stale taste of liquor is unmistakable. He leads me onto the porch and into the kitchen, where he switches on the overhead light. He moves as if he'd never left this house, the exact location of door handles and switches and drawer pulls as familiar to him as are, no doubt, the constant whispering winds I hear as I close the door behind us.

I steady myself against the counter. If we're ever really going to be a couple, I'm going to have to tell Jack all that happened with Bill Dean and with Gina, years ago. My secrets are clear now. It's not just Jack. I can't seem to get warm. I rub my hands and move instinctively toward the oven, which is cold, of course, but it's near Jack.

He pulls a bottle of cheap bourbon out of a cupboard and two small glasses. "This'll warm us up," he says.

I'm ruffled by this unfamiliar Jack—the liquor breath, the quick movements, the assertive voice. We sit at the table by the window, where I notice our reflections in the dusty black glass—two men, drinking, cowboys in a saloon.

"You never drink," I say.

"It's been a tough couple of days."

That's no explanation, but I let it go. "How are you doing?" I ask him.

He swirls the bourbon in his class, staring into it. Jack told me once that he'd stopped drinking before we met because he suspected he had a problem, or would if he kept it up. He didn't want to turn out like his mother. My own family had been so straight-laced, at least when it came to alcohol. Taken individually, our differences seemed insignificant, yet they had mounted up over three years until it got so they were all I could see.

None of that matters now. I want to be with this man, whatever it takes. I want to understand him and have him understand me.

"That's a complicated question," Jack replies. "There's so much I have to tell you."

I feel a tightening around my eyes. Maybe our mutual reticence is what has sustained us all along. "About your mother?" I ask. "Has it been difficult?"

"I hardly knew my mother. I left this house when I was seventeen. She'd been lost in her own past for years, anyway. She probably didn't even notice I'd left." Jack looks around the kitchen, as if his mother might have appeared at the stove or the sink.

"Still, she was your mother. You must feel something."

Jack sets his glass down hard. "You always want me to talk, Corey, but when I do, you don't accept what I say."

"I'm sorry."

"You question everything, and I end up wondering if you're right and I'm wrong. About my own feelings. Stop playing the goddamned shrink with me!"

"I'm sorry. I didn't mean to. . . ."

"I know you don't mean to."

We pick up our glasses. The bourbon burns my throat, then spreads its heat into my chest. I vow to shut up and let Jack talk.

"I need to tell you about the professor," he says.

The ache around my eyes swells into my temples. I'm scared. Finally, I will hear about the man who has always lurked in the shadowy borders of our life together.

"It's such a complicated story. I don't know where to start. But the professor I told you about. . . ." Jack pauses, picks up the tacky Hansel and Gretel salt and pepper shakers next to the napkin holder, still stacked with napkins. He fingers them, then sets them back on the table, facing one another, their wooden clogs and pink lips touching.

"I've always said we were lovers, the professor and me, but I'm not sure we really were. We loved each other in different ways, I guess. He never really desired me—sexually, I mean. Funny, we were the opposite of what people would have guessed, looking at us. We helped each other sort out a lot of past stuff. More like best friends."

I wrap my feet around the legs of my chair, swallowing questions. The last of my bourbon ignites my throat and I suppress a cough. I'm determined to hear Jack out.

"I was so young," he's saying. "It's not the sort of connection you just let go of."

How ironic, I think, feeling a little light-headed from the liquor. Jack has had the sort of relationship with the professor that I always wanted with Jack. I shove my glass into the center of the table.

"Do you want more of that?"

I shake my head no.

Jack pores himself more. "He was good to me, at school," he says. "I know it's a cliché, but he was the father I never had. I mean he really wanted me to have an acting career, whatever it took. And he knew it would mean my leaving Chadron, leaving him."

Jack's relationship with the professor sounds a lot like mine with Bill Dean, back in high school—the mentoring, supportive part. With a major difference, of course. Why had Jack let his relationship with this teacher fade? Would I have remained close to Bill Dean, after high school, if things had worked out differently?

"Then, he met my mother and they hit it off," Jack is saying. "We visited here." He gestures to the oddly cozy kitchen, which spins around me now. Alcohol goes right to my head. "He made me appreciate my mother a little, because he did."

Jack downs half his second bourbon. The drinking is making me nervous. If ever there were a time when we should be sober, it's now. But I don't interrupt. "He came out to New York to see me in plays, but he didn't really fit there, you know? I felt like he was holding me back. I needed to be free of him, but I owed everything to him."

So Jack had, in fact, lied about seeing the professor after college. Why? The question adds to my uneasiness, but I let it go, at least for now.

The lines around Jack's eyes are deeper than I remember them. I have the urge to reach out and touch his face, he's so obviously stressed to the breaking point.

"He was the only person I ever told about myself—all the craziness growing up, I mean. I just couldn't give that up, you know? Whether we were right for each other or not."

Jack's voice has an imploring quality, as if, more than anything, he needs me to understand about the professor. And I think I do. When I reestablished contact with Gina, a year and a half after she left, it was painful for Jack because she would speak to me and not him. Still, I started seeing her occasionally in New York. The person you live with every day isn't necessarily your primary confidante. Other things bind you—the mundane tasks of making a life together, sex, the little things you can't even put into words.

"I don't see why you felt like you had to let that friendship go, Jack."

"I could never love you and him, too."

"Why not? I love you, and I still love Gina, in a whole different way. When someone is that important. . . ."

"Corey, the professor. . . ." Jack gets up and goes to the sink, where he dumps the rest of his bourbon and runs water into the glass. He turns back to me, though he doesn't quite look me in the eye. "Jesus, I didn't mean to let it go this far. I really didn't." Jack's chin vibrates, as if he's about to cry.

A chill descends my back. I want to put my hand over his mouth. Suddenly, I don't want to hear whatever it is he has to tell me. I'm just too tired and too afraid to be thrown into some new mayhem. I want to let my dizziness overwhelm me, have Jack hold me, go to sleep together in his old bedroom. I know this would probably only delay matters, but even that would provide a much-needed sense of control. I've always believed that stalling can tease fate, toy with inevitability, even allow one to disrupt the future in some small way. But then, of course, you take responsibility for the future's altered course.

"The professor, Corey. It's Bill Dean." Jack's eyes dart to the floor. He seems to lurch slightly, off balance. "Your teacher back in Massachusetts."

My initial response is to laugh. Then I feel as if I've been punched. I try to make the connection—Jack and Bill Dean—but my mind refuses. I feel a scream making its way up into my throat.

"Nebraska is a good place to hide," I hear Jack say. "This is where he came, after what happened."

"Jesus Christ, Jack. You? You know Bill Dean?"

Jack comes to the table. He sits and reaches to take my hand.

I jerk it away and stand up. My chair screeches across the linoleum floor and falls over backward. I move across the kitchen, shaking, getting as far away from Jack as I can. "How did you ? . . ."

"Corey, please sit down. Let me explain."

I picture myself getting back into the rental car and . . . what? All those straight two-lane roads to nowhere.

"Bill never really loved anyone after you, not in the same way. When I got to know you, I was afraid to tell you for a lot of reasons—you'd be angry, you'd think the whole thing was some sort of weird ruse. I even thought you might want Bill again, and I would lose you both. It got pretty crazy, keeping it all a secret. And then so much time passed. It got to be too late."

For a moment, I imagine Jack feeling guilty—the longer the lie lasted, the more impossible to set it straight. I want to give him some benefit of the doubt, but I'm outraged—Jack knowing the whole time and never saying. "How the hell can I ever trust you now?" I say, looking back at the table where Bill Dean probably sat just two days ago, having a meal with Jack.

"Dean didn't love me. He abused me. There's a difference."

"Corey. . . ."

"Did he know?" I ask. "About you and me?"

"Yes."

"When?"

"Not long after I met you."

I cannot believe the level of deception. "And?"

"He stopped calling for a while. He thought that would be best."

"Good of him! And Gina? Did she know?"

"No."

I rub my eyes, trying to think. The man who abused me as a kid was Jack's ex-lover. "How did you ? . . . When did you know that I ? . . ."

"From Gina." Tears glisten in Jack's bloodshot eyes. He presses his hands to his temples. "The day she announced she was getting married. I recognized your name right away as the kid Bill had talked about being in love with, back east."

He knew, I'm thinking. He knew the whole fucking time! I feel like throwing up.

"I flipped out," Jack is saying. "I couldn't believe the coincidence. It was so weird. The kid I felt like I was always competing with was right there, about to marry my best friend."

"Was it, Jack? Was it really a fluke?"

"What do you mean?"

"It's a pretty extreme coincidence."

"I knew Gina before you came back into her life. How could I have arranged such a thing? It seemed like some sort of strange . . . I don't know, fate or something."

I recall standing in the hallway of my school the first day of seventh grade—small, young for my grade, wearing my favorite blue-and-green striped shirt, my new sneakers. Bill Dean said something to me that day about fate, about things happening that we have no control over. It had been in reference to my name. Yes, that was it. That we don't always get to choose things in life. Had he been thinking, even in those first moments, of what was in store for me?

"If this happened in a book," I say, "you'd be the first to say it was unrealistic."

"Actually, I wouldn't. What is fiction, but artifice? The coincidence of stumbling upon you like that, the storybook drama of it, was a big part of what made me want to meet you."

I hold Jack's eyes with mine. Why the hell hadn't he told me?

"I was curious, Corey. I'll admit that. But I never pushed meeting you. Months passed before she invited me up to Connecticut. Most of our friends had met you, but not me. I was curious, but I never had anything else in mind, believe me."

"Like what else?" I say. I still can't believe that Jack lived with me for over three years, knowing everything and not saying.

"Corey. . . ."

"I want to know, Jack. Jesus Christ! You've been lying to me since we met. Don't you think there was something besides curiosity going on?"

"You mean did I want to make Bill Dean jealous? Did I want to hurt him for not loving me like he did you?"

"For starters."

"No, I don't think I'm that fucked up."

I open the kitchen door and peer outside into blackness. I hear the faint buzz of the overhead light on the porch, smell dew dampening the dry wheat beyond the yard. I turn back into the kitchen. "Fucked up, Jack? Showing up by my bed in the middle of the night, secret phone calls to the professor whose name is never mentioned in three years? That kind of fucked up?"

"You've always been disappointed in me," Jack says. "I was never smart enough or successful enough for you. Now you have a real reason, right? Don't you think I knew all along that you'd probably dump me some day?" Jack links his fingers, cracks them. His chin quivers. "It doesn't change anything, Corey, me knowing Bill Dean. We're still the same two guys, you and me. We still have three years together."

"If it doesn't change anything, then why the hell did you keep it from me all this time? And you more than knew Bill Dean, Jack. Come on! You were in love with him."

"We both were, weren't we?"

"I was eleven when I met him, Jack. That fucker abused me!" I can feel the heat rising in my face. All the years I had repressed memories of Bill Dean, the years of anxiety about being sexual with anyone, much less a man. Where do I start trying to explain this to Jack? Why should I have to? "It was different, Jack," I say.

I turn away and step out onto the porch, bombarded with renewed rage. Looking out over the empty landscape, I recall that morning, three years ago, when blackbirds had covered every inch of the yard in Connecticut, how intensely I'd loved Jack at that moment, how I had interpreted the birds as the evil we would encounter, being together, how ready I had felt for that challenge. Now I see that I wasn't so far wrong, about the evil, anyway, but naïve as hell about our ability to overcome it.

All I want right now is to be away from Jack. I step down onto the rutted ground, where I kick a stone, bend, pick it up and toss it into that damned silent blackness. I pick up another, and another, flinging them as far into nothingness as I can. A breeze off the field smells moist and hollow, as if to confirm how unfazed the landscape is by my antics. Winded, I sit on the porch step and bury my face in my hands. Jack and Bill Dean—I still can't believe it. I try to picture them together, but the Jack in my mind is the Jack I know now, not a nineteen-year-old, and the Bill Dean I picture is a man in his twenties, driving an Impala convertible on the back roads of Williston. I can't put it all together. Nor do I want to. I can't think here. Jack is too close. So is Bill Dean.

I can feel Jack's presence in the doorway behind me. "Please come inside, Corey," he says.

Deception is the one thing I had thought Jack incapable of. Sure, he had his secrets, and I had mine. How ironic that they'd been the same secret—Bill Dean. But a deliberate lie? I reach into my pocket for the car keys. I step off the porch.

"Corey!"

Jack's hand grazes my shoulder. I speed up. He catches me and grabs my arm. I turn, yanking free, and the back of my hand strikes him hard in the face. Jack's fist catches me in the temple. Stunned, I thrust both fists into his chest and he reels back, barely keeping his balance. He drops his head and drives forward, butting me in the stomach. I clutch Jack's ribs and we fall. We roll across the rutted ground, still warm from the day's sun, coming to rest near the front tire of my rental car. I stare up at him. His eyes are dark disks in the half-light pouring off the porch. "Get off me," I hiss.

He doesn't move, just stares down at me, blinking as if he's waking from a nightmare.

"Get the fuck off me." I heave as hard as I can, throwing Jack to one side. I manage to get to my feet and start around to the driver's side of the car. He reaches and grabs my foot. I kick free.

I find the door handle, pull it open and fall behind the wheel. The engine roars to life.

"Corey!" Jack is on his feet, off to my right. I jam the gearshift into drive and floor the accelerator. The Ford lurches ahead, skids around Jack's mother's car, rights itself and bounces onto the road.

In the rearview mirror, I make out Jack's hunched silhouette, his arms hanging at his sides.

Chapter Sixteen
1965

My father parked behind Williston's only police cruiser, under the marquee at the Williston Inn. He turned off the ignition. It was nearly midnight. The heat wave had relented somewhat, but passing thunderheads had yet to unleash their fury, leaving the night of the Williston High senior prom thick and threatening. A Friday night, exactly a week after Gina left and a week after I had watched Mr. Dean drive slowly up South Street with Jimmy Harkness sitting next to him on the front seat.

I could hear the muffled strains of the orchestra winding down inside. Gina hadn't returned to school on Monday, after her weekend in White Plains, and I'd been beside myself all week, wondering if she was okay. I left her books on a table outside the principal's office. I tried calling the Daleys, but there was no answer, and my father said I should wait to hear from them. My parents asked if I knew where Gina was and they let it go when I said no. I guess they figured we had enough going on with Mr. Dean right then.

It wasn't until much later that it occurred to me why the police chief, and apparently my father, had chosen the night of the Williston senior prom to apprehend Mr. Dean. It had provided the greatest drama, of course, with half the faculty as chaperones and just about every senior in the school at the Inn that night—the most potent humiliation for Mr. Dean, the most perverse satisfaction, perhaps, for my father.

The four doors of the cruiser in front of us opened and four policemen emerged. The chief, whom I had seen at parades and other small-town functions, climbed the wide wooden steps with the sergeant, and together they disappeared inside. The other two officers took up sentry positions by the potted palms on either side of the pillared entrance. One was Rick Ferraro, Gina's first boyfriend and the man who had sold Mr. Dean the Impala. His volunteer's uniform hung on him like a costume, his same heavy work boots peeking from under rolled cuffs. It all seemed alarmingly backward—these buffoons exercising such power over one of Williston's most esteemed teachers. How quickly things could turn, I thought, as I sat with my father staring into the eerie yellow light under the marquee.

The music died, suddenly. I looked across the seat at my father, who stared straight ahead. Then I glanced toward the steps where Mr. Dean appeared in his white dinner jacket, a red carnation like a splash of blood on his lapel. When I saw him, I realized once again just how serious telling my parents had been. The events I had set in motion one week ago were to end with Mr. Dean being arrested and probably put in jail. His career would be ruined. It hit me then that nothing would be the same now—school, my relationships with my parents, my friends, even Gina. Everyone would know that I had sex with Mr. Dean. Why else was he being arrested? And that I had betrayed him.

I sank down into the seat.

The chief and sergeant each took one of Mr. Dean's elbows and escorted him down the steps. The two sentries fell in behind them. Rick Ferraro scurried to open the back door of the cruiser. Mr. Dean looked back at our car, his expression grave. Fear was unmistakable in the pinched lines between his brows and maybe shame in the straight line of his mouth. I don't know whether he saw me, but of course he recognized my father's station wagon. He ducked his long frame into the back seat, the soft, creamy jacket straining across his back. Rick Ferraro closed the cruiser door with a dull thud, ran around the back of the cruiser and jumped in next to Mr. Dean. The other sentry walked off toward the parking lot.

What seemed like a hundred chaperones and couples in gowns and tuxedoes had gathered at the entrance and spilled out onto the steps. Others gawked from the tall windows that overlooked the drive. The marquee lights reflected off the rear window of the cruiser, obscuring the back of Mr. Dean's head. Corey, I imagined him saying to himself.

Of course, it was Corey. He would hate even the sound of my name now, the sight of the director's baton I gave him, the memories of everything we'd done together over the last four years.

The cruiser's engine rumbled, its brake lights glared and the car seemed to groan as it crept from under the marquee. The smell of exhaust wafted through the open windows of my father's car as he followed the cruiser down the tree-lined driveway to the street, our headlights flashing wraithlike off the solid gray trunks of the elms bordering the lawn. Mr. Dean was in custody.

At the end of the driveway, the second sentry appeared, driving Mr. Dean's Impala. My father waited as he pulled ahead of us, behind the cruiser. All three cars turned onto South Street, driving slowly past Saint Francis Church, past Williston High School, and past Gina's house where all the windows were dark. A three-quarter moon cast a pale unnatural glow onto that row of Victorian houses, so familiar to everyone, symbols of the town's permanence, its rightness. I glanced again at my father, whose lips were pressed together in what seemed to me a grim sort of satisfaction. He was probably doing what any father would have done. But I hated him, anyway.

I imagined Mr. Dean being questioned at the station under the glare of a bare bulb, like in some 1940s gangster movie, his hands tied behind a chair, those hands that had wamred my shoulders and played alongside mine on the piano.

The cruiser turned onto Route 20 and headed south, away from town, away from the police station. Mr. Dean's Impala followed, and so did my father. "What's going on? I asked.

My father only stared straight ahead to the cars in front.

"I thought Mr. Dean was going to be arrested," I said.

"We changed our minds."

"So what happens now?"

"He gets off."

Heavy air, smelling of exhaust and impending rain, filled the car. A tentative, hopeful feeling seeped into my chest. They were going to put Mr. Dean in his car and let him drive off. He would be free. But why was my father following them? I dreaded some sort of scene with Mr. Dean. Nothing I could say would make up for what I had done.

We continued traveling south on Route 20 as my mother and I had done on our way to the Yale campus ten days before. But the two cars up ahead pulled to the side of the road, a few hundred feet from the highway sign that read Entering Pittsfield. "What's going to happen, now?" I asked my father.

The three engines died, as if on cue, and we all sat in an eerie silence broken only by the rustling of leaves in the woods along the road. Clotted clouds hung at the horizon. Sprinkles of rain dotted the windshield. My heart pummeled my ribs. I wanted all this to be over. I wanted to watch Mr. Dean step out of the cruiser, slip behind the wheel of his Impala and drive away. I wanted to go home and start a life I couldn't yet imagine, without him.

Then I had a fantasy that Mr. Dean got out of the cruiser and started walking toward our car. I get out and stand by the side of the road, watching him. "Are you okay, Corey?" he asks me.

"Mr. Dean, I'm sorry . . ."

"It's okay."

It seemed so real, him standing there, his big hands hanging at his sides, the light rain swirling around his face.

"I didn't mean to. . . ."

"I know. Things don't always work out like their supposed to." His shoulders are stooped, his eyes edged with tears. How easy it had been to hurt him—the wrong words to my parents, the mere mention of sex. "We don't have much time," he says, "and there's something I want you to know." He wipes his lips with the back of his hand. "I loved you. Remember that. Whatever anybody else says, I loved you."

Of course, that didn't happen. Instead, when the cruiser's doors did open, four men got out. Mr. Dean had taken off his jacket and tie. The sentry who drove Mr. Dean's Impala got out, too. They all walked to the rear of the convertible, where the sergeant tossed Mr. Dean's white jacket, glowing in the dim light, on top of the rain-spotted trunk. They were less than thirty feet away. I could see Mr. Dean's car keys in the sentry's hand, a pebble pressed into the tire tread of the Impala, my father's parking lights glinting off the buttons of Mr. Dean's formal shirt.

My father reached behind me and locked my door.

Mr. Dean glanced back at our car, just as the sergeant swung his fist to the side of his head. I heard it connect to bone, as Mr. Dean's head snapped back and he staggered to one side. The chief grabbed his arm. Rick Ferraro, that slime-ball, stepped up and took Mr. Dean by the collar of his shirt. He punched him in the stomach. Mr. Dean slumped forward. I gripped the dashboard and looked over at my father. How could he be letting this happen? But I could see from his look that he knew all along. He had planned this scene. I imagined him having agreed with the police chief—no trial, too embarrassing, too public. But the guy has to be punished, right? Make him think twice about ever touching another kid.

Rick Ferraro kicked Mr. Dean in the crotch, and he doubled over, falling against the trunk of the Impala. Blood gushed from his nose.

My father had wanted me to watch. Why?

Mr. Dean slumped to the ground. The chief kicked him this time. I pulled on the door handle, but it didn't release. I opened my mouth. Nothing came out. They picked Mr. Dean up and heaved him onto the trunk of his car. His head bounced off the metal with a dull thud. The rain had picked up and soaked Mr. Dean's shirt and his hair. My father started our car and turned on the windshield wipers. Watered-down blood pooled and dripped off the lid of the Impala's trunk. I turned away, but it was too late. I had probably killed my best friend.

My father shifted our car into gear. "No! No, please," I pleaded, pulling at the door lock. Our car shot out onto the highway. The tires squealed as he turned back toward Williston. "Please, Dad, let me out." I got the door open, but his sudden acceleration threw me back against the seat and the door slammed shut. The car swerved. I reached again for the door, but his hand yanked me back, tearing my shirt. I pictured the police pulling away too, leaving Mr. Dean lying motionless, his arms and legs splayed on the trunk of his car, blood trickling onto the ground.

As we sped north, I stuck my head out the window. Blacktop raced by under the wheels. Rain soaked my face. I squinted into the wind, retched, and turned as vomit splashed against the rear fender. Back inside, I wiped my face on my sleeve and huddled tight against the seat, my back to my father. I was responsible, as surely as if I'd smashed Mr. Dean's head against the trunk of the Impala myself.

My father parked in front of our house and turned off the engine. We sat in silence as a steady rain peppered the windshield of the Country Squire and heartened the thin, earthy smell of the new grass along the driveway. It was almost summer, just three days until the end of school.

I imagined my father wondering, as I did, how we would ever return to a normal life now. How could we even look at each other and not think about that scene at the side of Route 20? How could he hug me as he had just days before, on this very same car seat? I never wanted him to touch me again. Had watching the beating been intended to toughen me? To show me what becomes of homosexuals? Whatever it was, he would never say, and I wouldn't want to hear. I knew very well what it had accomplished. I would never trust my father again.

He opened his door and got out. "Come inside, Corey," he said, standing by the open door, rain dripping down his forehead.

I ignored him. He waited another moment, then closed the car door and walked to the house.

I sank against the seat, trying to blink away the scene I had just witnessed, trying to think how to avoid ever entering our house again. Had my father left his keys, I'd have pulled that car back onto the road and driven to Mr. Dean. I would have helped him, if he was still alive. I would have driven away with him, leaving Williston forever.

But instead, my mother yanked open the passenger door and leaned inside. She lifted my head up. "Oh my God," she said, putting her arm around me. "What did he do to you?" She folded the torn flap of my shirt back into position and pushed my hair back off my forehead. She pulled my head onto her shoulder and held it there. "Come inside," she said.

Rain, heavy now, blew in the car's open door, soaking us. I didn't move, certain my legs wouldn't keep me upright.

She took my arm and pulled it around her shoulder, lifting me up and out. She was remarkably strong. I don't know whether I couldn't, or wouldn't, walk into that house. Somehow, she managed to drag me across the rain-slicked driveway and into the hallway, where I stood, my hands covering my face.

My father appeared at the foot of the stairs and reached to help her. "Don't touch him," she said. "Don't come near him."

Taking my arm again, she hoisted me forward. He moved toward us. "Don't!" she said. Together, we reeled past him to the stairs. I was aware of his eyes on us the whole way to the top. In my room, she lowered me onto my bed and closed the door. She lay beside me and pulled me to her. Her breath was rapid and quivering, her hair damp against my cheek.

She stayed with me that night. Between long silences, she talked of the happy times we'd all had together—trips to Cape Cod, birthday parties at the pool—as if to drown out the memory of that night, or perhaps to reassure herself that we were still a family, that we could go on. In the morning, she went to the kitchen and brought back crackers and soup and ice cream.

The next evening, when my father returned from work, she left my room. It was time to move on, she seemed to be saying. The Pittsfield Gazette he brought home had a small article on an inside page. "Morals Charge" was the headline under Mr. Dean's picture. No names were mentioned or the genders of the minors involved.

I remember feeling, during the last three days of school, as if I were encased in a glass jar, bright and visible to everybody, but silent and completely isolated from the world. Kids avoided me, turning away in embarrassment, disdain, blame. Though there had been no arrest or trial, Mr. Dean was gone for good. So, it seemed, was Gina. I longed to talk to them both. But what would I say, even if I could find them? They would want nothing to do with me.

The rest of that June, I hid, sitting at the side of the swimming pool in our back yard, an open book in my lap. I stared into the numbing, disconsolate surface of the water, aware that the world around me was moving on and leaving me behind. Schoolmates had summer jobs, went on family trips, took college prep courses, picnicked by waterfalls, made out in their parents' cars. They laughed and shouldered their way into their futures. The clear pictures they had of themselves, framed in a solid predictability, grounded them and gave them purpose. My own picture had derived its meager distinction from being with Mr. Dean, and with Gina. Now, that picture faded like a Polaroid snapshot abandoned to the gleaming refraction of the pool.

The whole episode with Mr. Dean was never mentioned again by either of my parents. Never. And just as well. I had nothing to say. Conversation with Mr. Dean had consisted of nuance, hints and traces of meaning, replete with anticipation. The words of my parents and their lawyer had made everything sordid, explicit, and of course, illegal. The silence that enveloped us that summer was a relief, and I sank into it like a stone dropped into a swamp.

Time passed slowly. Dinners were particularly long, pushing parcels of meat and vegetables around my plate like a slacker looking busy. Afterward, I watched angles of fading sunlight color the walls of my room a bloody maroon, then purple, then gray. Any sort of movement required a summoning of absent will. I had a vague sense of waiting, but for what? I imagined my potential for love as an ugly wound in my belly that would never heal, would only grow gray and sinewy and hard. Alone, I might be ambushed by tears, my mouth gaping in a silent, aching scream. More than anything, I wanted never again to care. Guilt and shame would be my partners in a profound hopelessness for who I would become.

The week before the Fourth of July, my father announced that he'd arranged a summer job for me, replacing some kid who had quit doing lawn work in the middle of the season. I learned to knock myself out each day so I could sleep at night. My body tanned and firmed. I imagined Gina living a new life in White Plains as I mowed around walkways and pulled weeds from flower beds. I imagined Mr. Dean wandering from town to town in the Impala, working his way west, waiting for his wounds to heal before finding a job perhaps not so different from mine—hard physical work to still grief.

One evening, at home alone, I packed all my music into boxes, much of it containing Mr. Dean's scrawled notations in the margins, and carried it to the basement. I never played the piano again.

Some nights, I slipped out of my parents' sleeping house and walked to the end of our road, where the new house, with its new windows reflecting silver light, loomed behind leafy maples. I made my way south on Route 20, walking all the way to the spot where I'd last seen Mr. Dean. The occasional car whooshed past. Arriving there lacked the emotional punch I anticipated, and eventually I stopped going there. Mr. Dean was gone.

When I did sleep, I dreamed of him, always the same dream, that he returned to Williston for me and I was elated until I saw the knife and realized he had come back to kill me. Lying awake, I sensed that I would never know pleasure again without feeling afraid. Love, that astonishing and inexplicable bliss I had stumbled upon, first with Mr. Dean and then with Gina, would forever be lashed to remorse and dread. Love was illicit and devastating. I promised myself to steer clear of it, which turned out to be a very difficult promise to break.

Chapter Seventeen
1988

I manage to retrace the narrow roads from Jack's mother's house, bisecting the black October night, back to the gas station at the North Platte exit of Interstate 80. The adrenalin rush of the first few miles is wearing off. Still, I am alert, entirely sober and as determined as I have ever been to be in the only place I feel safe, alone in my home in Connecticut.

I pull onto the highway toward Omaha. Driving straight through, I should get to the airport by four in the morning. I'll check into a hotel, book the first flight back to New York, shower and rest an hour or two. By the end of the day, I should be in Connecticut, which feels like the exit of the chilling cave I've been wandering in for the past week. I want only to be alone now, to think, to decide where the hell I go from here.

I line up the left front fender of the Ford with the dotted line of the highway, and keep it there. There is no other grounding point, no horizon, no tail lights to follow, only the occasional dim glow of a town in the distance and its hazy reflection in curdled clouds, like the dying embers of a fire. I'm exhausted, yet wide awake, an unpleasant, wired sensation that could easily short-circuit, leaving me nonfunctional. I tune in some unidentifiable music on the radio, using the jarring beat and incomprehensible lyrics to keep me awake. My urgency to get home is matched only by the relief I feel to be away from Jack. I can't get the last hour clear in my mind—so hopeful, so elated to see him, and then stunned by the realization that he's been deceiving me the entire time I've known him. And the fight, of course. Tears sting my eyes as I recall my fists sinking into his chest. This is not me. The whole episode is unreal, as if it never happened, though I know it did.

Across the center divide, the occasional huge semi passes in the opposite direction, a hundred tiny orange and yellow lights defining its hulking, speeding silhouette. I recall a similar truck parked next to mine the day Jack painted the first mural panel. My anxiety then seems only a prelude to the upheaval I feel now. How fragile is a relationship that it can shatter like crystal?

The Ford's speedometer reads eighty-eight miles per hour. The little car vibrates. Miles pass. My eyelids descend slowly until I blink them aloft. You're almost home, I whisper to myself over and over, like a mantra.

Several times I cross the dotted line of my lane, correct my course and slap my face awake. Twice I am jarred by the realization that my right tire is only inches from the soft gravel shoulder of the highway. I should pull into a rest stop. I have hours to spare before any flight to New York. Yet I don't pull over. I have to keep moving. I can't rest in this alien land, Jack's land.

I pull out the gum I bought that afternoon, which seems like days ago now. Chewing will keep me awake. I take two sticks, and then a third, until my mouth is half full of the fragrant sweet wad. I sing around it, tap my fingers on the steering wheel to the steady, deafening beat of the music. I'm a tiny earsplitting space vehicle, careening through the cosmos, creating a ruckus no one can hear. I roll down my window, allowing the cold night air to batter my face.

Still, I nod off.

When I blink awake, my chest blasts adrenalin. I grip the steering wheel. The car is half off the highway's gravel shoulder, half on grass, at a thirty-degree angle to the road, going at least sixty. I yank the wheel back in the direction of the highway. The car swerves the other way, spitting gravel onto its undercarriage. It's about to roll. I reverse the steering wheel again, correcting the spin, and the car rights itself, shudders and bounces down a steep grade into grass and who knows what else. My mind races, responds instinctively, accepts that the only viable action is to ride out the next few seconds and let the car take its course off the highway. I hold the wheel and brace myself as it surges and rebounds, heaves and plummets, and comes to rest, finally, in a dream-like quiet, amid clouds of dust, swirling across the headlights' beaming glare.

I let my forehead fall against the steering wheel. I turn off the ignition, though the engine is already dead. My thighs quiver. Gratitude that I'm alive rises in me like a sweet scent, slowly draining the stiffness in my jaw. When I lift my head, the dust has begun to clear and the Ford's headlights ignite a dazzling silver grid, stretching uninterrupted for as far as I can see. The car has come to rest not twenty feet from a chain-link fence that separates the Interstate from the miles of open grassland it spans.

I lean back against the seat, thinking how erratic and absurd life is. Just a few days ago, I'd taken Metro North to Grand Central with a million other commuters, seen my patients, returned phone calls and had a friendly, civilized dinner with my ex-wife. Now, I'm alone at the side of a highway in some Godforsaken, deserted corner of reality. Security is an illusion. It doesn't exist.

I need to get this car back onto the highway, I think, turning to look behind me, before some trooper comes along with a lot of questions and a breath test, though all I had was one bourbon. I can't afford the time. I need to be on that first flight back to New York. That's the only goal that makes any sense right now. I open the car door and step into the silent, black night. I walk around the car, checking its condition. All I can make out in the dim light are clumps of grass and dirt crammed around the front bumper. The same with the frame underneath, though I can only see a bit of it, in silhouette. Who knows about the rocker panels or the muffler system or the axles? I don't smell gasoline, so presumably the gas tank isn't punctured. I sit back inside and turn the key. Miraculously, the engine starts. I back slowly away from the fence, turn toward the highway and bump along over ruts and mounds of grass, back up the grade to its edge. I stop there, get out and shinny on my back underneath the car. I run my fingers over its dirt-clad belly, feeling for dripping oil or any protrusion that doesn't feel as if it belongs. Fuck it, I think, sliding back out, the insurance will cover it if I run the thing dry.

Soon, I'm back on my way to Omaha, alert, both weakened and invigorated by the mishap.

The night attendant at Avis is young and sleepy. He raises an eyebrow at the bedraggled look of the Ford. "We got SUV's, you know," he says, yawning, "if you want to go off-road."

"Sometimes things happen you don't plan," I say, forcing a smile as I paraphrase Bill Dean's first words to me, back in seventh grade. The attendant grins and holds my eyes just a little longer than seems necessary. Christ, he's flirting with me.

He accepts the car and doesn't penalize me for handing in half a Nebraska hayfield along with it. "Can you hang out a while?" he asks me.

"Maybe some other time," I say, though I'm flattered, despite my state. "But could I use your telephone?"

After booking an eight a.m. flight back to New York, I rent a room at the Radisson, where I shower and eat two granola bars from a machine in the lobby. I ask the clerk at the front desk to wake me at six-thirty. That leaves me an hour and a half to sleep.

But sleep won't come as I lie on stiff sheets in a room that smells of cigarette smoke on the sixth floor of the hotel. I imagine Jack in his old bedroom at his mother's house, maybe also unable to sleep. I picture Gina, waking up in New York and getting ready to go to work, even though it's Sunday. I think about my parents, who seem to have negotiated the rough spots of their relationship, accepted the disappointments and made some sort of peace with one another. What would they think if they knew Bill Dean had resurfaced in my life this way?

And what about that man? Had I just been the sexual obsession of a pedophile? A victim or an obsessed, young co-conspirator? Jack claimed that Bill Dean had loved me. Do I believe that? How much had Dean distorted things in his own mind in order to go on with his life after Williston? What is love between a grown man and a twelve-year-old boy, anyway, other than rationalization? And how had I distorted that relationship, wanting to believe I was loved? Bill Dean was a man who preyed on children. That's reality. Yet I still find it impossible to accept that I was just a kid in the wrong place at the wrong time.

Suddenly, it doesn't feel right to be running away like this. I stand and walk to the window overlooking the Radisson parking lot, and in the distance, a turmoil of signs and exit ramps, vast airline terminals and a surrounding network of runways. In the black, invisible expanse beyond that, I imagine the rolling plains of Nebraska and Bill Dean, asleep out there. I bang my fist into my palm. I will drive to Chadron. How difficult could it be to find him? Jack had said once that Chadron is a small town, not much more than the college, itself. Bill Dean's address would be in the phone book. I'll figure out what to say to him while I drive there.

I pull on my clothes, excitement and dread vying for prominence in my chest, another pairing I learned from Bill Dean. My fingers quiver as I tie my laces. I call United and cancel my reservation back to New York, call Avis and request the maroon Ford Escort I'd returned a couple of hours ago, the one with the hayfield crammed into the bumper. It has to be that one, I tell the same sleepy attendant, the one that saved my life by not rolling over on the Interstate, though I don't mention that part.

Less than twenty-four hours after my first trip on Interstate 80 to find Jack, I retrace my route west, this time to Chadron, Nebraska, to find yet another missing person, my former school teacher. The open landscape is familiar now, as is the confined interior of the Escort. A yellow sun rises in the sky behind me. What will I say to Bill Dean? What makes me think anything useful can come of such a meeting? Sure, I'm curious about the man I can only picture as he looked twenty-five years ago. I wonder what our relationship had meant to him, if anything. Maybe I only want to know that I can face this man I had admired and feared and finally betrayed all those years ago.

It's almost noon when I reach the exit for North Platte, imagining Jack making lunch for himself at his mother's house. Or maybe he's on a flight back to New York by now. Who knows? I stop at what is becoming my favorite gas station in Nebraska, refuel and buy chips and coffee from the same laconic clerk. I pull back onto the Interstate and drive another forty-five minutes to the Ogallala exit, where I pick up Route 26, heading northwest around Lake McConaughy and along the Platte River as far as Bridgeport, where I take Route 385 north. The distance between small towns—Angora, Alliance, Berea—is essentially straight highway, long and boring enough to make the villages themselves a welcome respite. Chadron is tucked into the northwest corner of Nebraska, perhaps thirty miles from the South Dakota border. The ground begins to heave and roll a bit as I near Chadron, like the dented bottom of a skillet. And there are trees suddenly, thousands of them, the Nebraska National Forest.

It's nearly four in the afternoon when I pass a line of truck dealerships and a shopping mall on the outskirts of the town. I pull in at a Best Western hotel and park the Ford out front. I'll find Bill Dean's address, but then what? I still don't know what to say to the man. Will we go to dinner and have a stilted conversation, circumscribed by surrounding tables of families? Will Dean apologize? Will I? Will I forgive him? The whole enterprise makes my stomach churn.

I get out of the Ford and make my way across the dismal parking lot to the entrance of the hotel. The brown-carpeted lobby smells of disinfectant. A bouquet of silk flowers adorns a faux-marble table in the center of the room. There's a public telephone near a pair of tan house phones. In the directory, I find a William Dean on Prospect Street in Chadron, tangible proof that he is actually here, in this very town, walking-distance away. My mind struggles to reinsert him into a reality he'd been banished from all those years ago. I write down the number. I go to the men's room, where I hardly recognize my face in the mirror, dark circles, a two-day growth of beard. Exhaustion would have collapsed me by now if I weren't so tense. I pee, then splash water on my face and towel off. I walk out of the hotel.

A right turn off of Route 385 takes you down the main street of Chadron, where I park, get out and lock the car. I walk past stores that Bill Dean and Jack would likely know. Chadron is a pretty town, oddly familiar. It might be a village in western Massachusetts. It makes some sort of weird sense that Bill Dean would settle here.

Without realizing it, I've made my way to the entrance to the Chadron State campus, not hard, I suppose, since it is Chadron's reason for being. A gust of wind bends the branches and rustles dry oak leaves clumped along the walkway. It's growing dark. I pass a number of low, brick buildings—classrooms, administration, dormitories, generic architecture of the 1950s, clustered around a green. I hear some young men laughing in the hallway of one building. I'm hoping the relaxed feeling of the campus will relieve some of the stiffness of my body before I call him. It occurs to me that he could be down in Gandy with Jack by now, but I dismiss that thought.

A man approaches, carrying a stuffed, old-fashioned briefcase, bent slightly from the weight of it. My stomach tightens. He's tall, with a familiar, slightly awkward gait. He's wearing gray pants, as he had been that first day of seventh grade, and a turtleneck sweater under a zippered jacket. His hair is parted the same way, only as he draws near, I can see that it's shorter, and gray now.

Mr. Dean smiles as he passes, not his old conspiratorial grin, something more formal, a greeting to a stranger. I turn and watch as he continues down the sidewalk, then stops, perhaps twenty feet away, where he turns around.

Neither of us moves. "Mr. Dean?" I say.

Another gust of wind yanks the collar of Dean's jacket. With his free hand, he pushes the collar back in place. "Yes?"

"It's Corey Moore."

Dean's puzzled expression disappears as something like fear or pain narrows his eyes. "Yes," he says, leaning forward slightly. "What are you doing here, Corey?"

"I was on my way back to New York," I say, stuffing my hands into my jacket pockets. The keys to the rental car jangle against some loose change, reminding me of the storage room keys clanking into Dean's pants pocket, years ago.

"Is Jack with you?" Dean asks, glancing into the shrubs to my right, as if Jack might be about to spring out onto the path.

A couple of young women, toting heavy-looking backpacks, approach, greet Mr. Dean and pass by.

"What do you want?" he asks.

A simple question, yet I haven't been able to come up with a solid answer the whole day's drive across Nebraska. "I don't know," I say. "I guess I thought we might talk."

"What about?"

"I just found out you know Jack." Face to face like this, I'm unable to think clearly. It's not Jack I want to talk about, obviously. But what is it?

"Yes," Dean says, taking a step backward. "I know Jack."

I can see that Dean wants only to get away from me. Behind the irritation in his manner, he's probably scared. "I used to imagine running into you somewhere," I say. "Now, it's hard to know what to say."

"Maybe because there isn't anything." Dean looks away, his eyes narrowing again.

I watch him, waiting to feel all that I had felt in this man's presence as a teenager, or for some flood of new feelings—aversion, hostility, forgiveness. But I'm numb. I feel nothing.

"I should be getting home," Dean says. "I have work to do."

Suddenly, I have a picture of what Dean's life must be like in this quiet, remote place, and I have a moment of pity for what I suspect is a very lonely man. Yet I am also the boy I was years ago, wanting something from him but not knowing what it is, and therefore not likely to get it. Or perhaps this is just not the person who is ever going to provide the responses I need. A heaviness takes over my shoulders as I recall the incurable longing of the boy I was, the impossibility of any satisfaction, then or now. "I was too young," I say, more to myself than to Bill Dean. "Way too young."

A light goes on in the second floor window of a nearby building. We both look at it, then back at each other. "I was twelve."

Dean steps further away. I move into the distance between us. "I was trying to help you," he says. "You were a sad kid. You were this little waif."

"And you found me, all right. Do you have any idea what chaos you created in me? Just the word 'love' still scares the shit out of me. That was your doing."

"I was trying to help you."

"But you didn't. You hurt me."

"Look, it's been a very long time, Corey. We both have other lives now. What's the sense?" He turns to go.

I step after him, take his shoulder and turn him back to me. Touching him sends the same shock into my chest, the same tingling down my back that it did twenty-five years ago. Only the electric impulse isn't that elixir of fear and excitement it was then. It's anger, the anger I'd buried as his accomplice. "You molested me. I hardly knew what sex was, for Christ's sake! I wasn't even. . . ."

Dean's eyes dart from left to right. He's afraid of this scene, another humiliation at yet another school. "I'm just on my way home," he says, brushing my hand off his shoulder. "You can walk with me, if you like." The apprehension in his eyes grips my chest as it had that night he stepped out of the police cruiser, his white formal shirt glowing in the headlights of my father's car. "But that's as far as it goes," he says. "I paid my dues for what happened."

I can't hold onto my anger. It melds to pity and slips from me the way my resolve never to go back to the storage closet had dwindled back then. Where else was I to go for comfort then but back to him? I realize that I have come to him now, after all this time, still seeking comfort, that that's all I have ever wanted. How stupid of me to think I could find it here!

I fall in beside him, and we walk along in silence. Why am I even bothering with this man? Why don't I just leave?

We exit the campus and turn onto a sidewalk behind a young couple. The woman hangs on her boyfriend's arm, glancing up at him and giggling. I recall standing in the living room of my parents' home, that first year I knew Mr. Dean, cornered at one of my parents' cocktail parties by a woman I'd never met before. She's talking about a house she and her husband intend to build at the end of our road, a copy of a house in Williamsburg, Virginia, she is saying, a brick house with plenty of tall windows.

Two things stand out in this memory. Her breath has the chemical odor of cleaning fluid, how I imagined an embalmed body might smell if it possessed breath. And across the room, I'm aware of Bill Dean flirting with a woman whose bare back is to me. Dean is grinning that conspiratorial grin I had thought was reserved for me. He's handsome. He exudes charm. The woman rests her hand on his arm. He touches her shoulder, leans in and whispers something that makes her guffaw. The bare-backed dress gapes.

I recognized, even then, that my mother was only playing with Mr. Dean, getting him to want her. It was the casting she enjoyed, the lure, the reeling in, not the catch. But I was fascinated by this display of power, how she held Mr. Dean's attention, made him vulnerable in a way I had never seen him, made him want her. Hotly jealous, it had occurred to me that I might do the same, attract Mr. Dean's attention, have him entirely to myself like that. I eluded the lady with the daughter, but I couldn't stop watching my mother and Mr. Dean. Her antics were so familiar, yet I hadn't focused on them before. Her behavior had only vaguely embarrassed me in the past. Suddenly, I saw the merit in it.

In the months that followed the party, I learned to mimic the way she had behaved with Mr. Dean that night. I'd been surprised at how easy it was—flattering him, laughing at his jokes, making lingering eye contact during rehearsals. Each week, it had seemed that Mr. Dean was more drawn in, more taken with me. It had all worked so well. I'd even arranged special practice sessions for fabricated difficulties with the piano score, and made them run late so that the janitor would have left school and we'd be alone, with the storage room door only a few nervous steps away.

It had all gone too far, though. I hadn't known how to turn back, until finally, I was no longer appalled by his touch. In fact, I grew to need that remarkable proof of the hold I had on him. He had become my major ally, my confidante, and, ironically, the only person I believed I could trust. It would be years before I figured out that our closeness had merely been his desire, attired in a colorful costume of affectionate yellow, attentive green, affirming red.

Walking silently beside Mr. Dean now, I can accept that yes, I'd been seductive. But whatever length I had gone to to hold his attention wasn't the point. He should have known better than to take advantage of a boy's willingness. That's what adults, particularly teachers entrusted with the responsibility of children, are supposed to do—look after their charges, protect them.

Dean's violent exit from Williston had not been my fault.

The sky darkens as we turn down a narrow street. An elderly couple passes in the opposite direction. A car moves past. Mr. Dean stops in front of a white clapboard house that is divided in half, with two front doors. His half is freshly painted, the door a somber, deep green. Two windows look out onto the street. There is an uneasy moment during which he searches his briefcase for his keys. I watch him, noticing the long white fingers, the slackness of his mouth, the lines spreading from his eyes. The numbness I had felt earlier is replaced by something close to pity, compassion perhaps, but not forgiveness.

"Here they are," Dean says, finally, withdrawing the keys.

I imagine how we must look, standing together, the difference in our ages no longer significant. We could be colleagues, parting after an afternoon in the library. But we aren't colleagues. We aren't anything, really, other than ghosts from each other's pasts. I smile. Perhaps I have gotten what I came here for, after all. I can put behind me whatever guilt I have carried all these years. And maybe some of the anxiety I've had about trusting someone. I have a whole rich life ahead of me, whether it includes Jack or not, a life full of the sort of promise I could never have imagined in that stuffy closet at the rear of the music room at Williston High School.

I extend my hand. "I have to be getting back," I say. The fear, the affection, all the feelings I'd once had toward this man are gone. "But I'm really glad I saw you."

Apparently relieved, Dean puts his hand meekly into mine, then turns toward his door.

I can't resist saying more. "I know I'll always think about you, Bill."

He stops at the base of his front step, but doesn't turn to face me.

"I wish I'd never known you, but that's silly. How can I wish myself a different past?"

Bill drops the hand holding his keys to his side, but still remains facing away from me.

"If it had only been frightening, being with you, I would have forgotten you long ago. But love got thrown into it, whether it was real or not. And that's what caused all the damage. It helps to see you now for who you are, and for who you probably were back then—as needy and confused as me."

Finally, my old teacher turns to face me.

"I used you as much as you used me. Did you ever wonder why I told my parents about us? I didn't have to, you know. I could have made up any reason for the sudden slide in my grades. You were my way to get to them, to smack them so hard they would have to pay attention. We seduced each other, Bill, and we hurt each other more than we ever could have anticipated."

Dean takes a breath and parts his lips, as if he's about to say something. But he remains mute, all that old charm gone now. It's fine. There really is no more that I need, at least not from him.

He turns, fits his key into the lock and opens his door. In the small vestibule, I glimpse a coat rack on which hangs a hat, a scarf and an overcoat. An umbrella leans in the corner. One of each.

I turn and start down the street, back toward my car. Behind me, I hear Bill Dean's door click closed, and then only the sound of my own footsteps on the sidewalk.

Chapter Eighteen
1988

My eyes spring open, as they do every morning at four, still startled that Jack is not lying beside me, though it's been over two months since I left him at his mother's house in Nebraska. I hunch my shoulders against the December chill of the bedroom.

Jack used to remind me, when he first moved upstairs in this house, that he didn't want to intrude on me, that I shouldn't feel confined or obligated. Perhaps he had sensed my initial reluctance, or perhaps he had feared he was just some transitional fling on my journey from heterosexuality, short trip that it was. (Or exceptionally long, depending on when I pinpoint its inception). Now, of course, I suspect that he'd been guilty about our love, beginning, as it had, with a deception.

I hadn't wanted freedom then. Just the reverse, I'd wanted to merge with Jack. Perhaps he had feared losing his own freedom, just as Gina had feared losing hers when we were fifteen and she'd been pregnant. Jack and I argued a lot during that first year—trivial quarrels that seemed like some sort of inverse function of our frenzied attraction, dampers that kept us from being consumed by one another. Now, I can see that those arguments had to do, at least in part, with Jack's ongoing dishonesty. I still try to imagine what it must have been like for him, a coincidence that became a lie and finally a gaping obstruction.

Through all our quarrels and stony silences, I never stopped loving Jack, my commitment oddly fortified, not by the successful resolution of our fights, because that rarely happened, but by our coming together afterward, physically, sometimes tearfully, always passionately.

A slat of crimson clears the top of the window and begins expanding down the plaster wall. Rising sun, symbol of hope. I hear the furnace rattle on as it has much of the night.

Long lost memories have surfaced since seeing Bill Dean in October—the old Steinway's sticking legato pedal back at Williston High School, the dry chalky smell of the music room, rides in the Impala over sun-dappled dirt roads arched with sugar maples. But lying here now, taking in similar refractions of sunlight through the frosted window, those memories are tempered by images of the lonely, ordinary man Bill Dean is today, a man who had been important to both Jack and me, two similarly lost boys, once.

On a bright morning, not unlike this one, back in early November, I had given up on sleep and slipped out of this bed, pulled on a pair of jeans and a sweatshirt and pushed up the thermostat at the foot of the stairs. The embers of the previous night's fire still smoldered in the dining room fireplace. George and David, the guys from next door, had been over for dinner. I had tried to explain to them about Jack and me, touching on highlights of our somewhat convoluted and ultimately incredible story. I wanted to let them know that they would probably not be seeing Jack here anymore. The evening had been a sad one, and I'd been relieved when they finally left and I could sit alone in front of the fire and finish up the wine from dinner. For better or worse, I remember thinking, I'm on my own now.

The next morning, I stirred the ashes and dropped on some kindling, staying to watch it crackle into flame. I took in the mural, thinking maybe I'd paint some sort of addition to it. But what? Maybe Jack's mother's house, off in the distance, though there didn't seem to be enough wall space for the surrounding landscape. Or maybe Gina. There certainly needed to be a record of her presence in this house. Maybe she should be peeking out from behind one of Jack's stalwart trees. A number of times since returning from Nebraska, I had had this same urge to paint something, but that's as far as it had gone. With Jack no longer living here, the mural had taken on a melancholy I wasn't yet ready to face.

All that went through my slightly hung-over mind that Sunday morning as the cedar remnants caught and I dropped on a couple of logs. When I turned to the window, I noticed a car parked next to the barn, a new compact. My heart clenched. Had it been there all along, all night? A pang of anxiety pressed into my throat as I walked to the kitchen and pulled on my down parka. I opened the back door, the blinds clanging against the window. But then I noticed that the car, an obvious rental, was empty. I eased the door closed again.

I knew then that Jack had come home, a moment I had been anticipating, without really admitting it, for weeks. I paused, standing in the middle of the kitchen, taking in the silence of the house. Was he here to say he wanted to try again? Did I want that?

I stepped into the ell, aware of the hallway's creaking floor and its soapy scent, spilling from the bathroom. I pushed open the door to Jack's old room.

He sat in the easy chair he'd acquired years ago, from who knows where, staring out the window toward the barn, alight in the morning sun. I stood by the door and held myself still. "You scared me," I said. "How long have you been here?"

He didn't turn to me. "You think I'm the scary one?" he asked.

"Maybe we both are." We'd hardly said hello, and already it felt like a standoff.

"How are you?" he said, turning to me, finally.

The room felt suddenly cold in the morning chill. What should I say, after I left Nebraska the way I did? "It's good to see you," sounded flimsy compared to the jumble of feelings in my chest. Yet, it was certainly true.

A crow landed in the driveway outside, and we both turned to it, watching it peck in the dirt and then hop into the frozen grass alongside. "I didn't know when I'd see you again," I said, keeping my voice empty, noncommittal.

"If I'd only understood earlier how stupid I was not to tell you about Bill Dean," he said in his inimitable way of getting right to the point.

He seemed different, but I couldn't put my finger on just how. Perhaps it was that same sense I'd had in Nebraska of some sort of confidence I hadn't known in Jack as long as we lived together. Did his confidence only emerge when he was away from me?

"There were a lot of things I couldn't tell you," he said. "I was so intimidated. You were so attractive, successful, so perfect. Look at this place." He gestured toward the window. "How could I tell you I spent my childhood in a shack?"

I looked around the room and I understood some of what Jack must have felt living here, with everything except the futon and his chair by the window belonging to me. I'd never considered those differences important. We had so much going for us, I had always thought.

I felt angry, again, a bolt to the stomach that hadn't lost a whole lot of intensity in the three weeks since I had last seen him. I had gone to my office in New York right from the airport that Monday morning, gone through the motions of my day. That whole week I'd been dazed and agitated, sleepless at night, exhausted during the day. The second week was better, and the third better than that. Each day I had said to myself—so this is what it's like, without Jack.

And I was irritated suddenly that Jack could show up earlier this morning, in the half-dark, just as he had appeared by my bed three years ago. Did he expect me to embrace him and have everything be fine? How many times in the last three weeks had I imagined how I would feel, seeing him again? But appearing the way he did made me resentful and sad and yet so pleased to have him back I could hardly breathe. From the day Jack moved upstairs in this house, I had always known what I wanted, despite all the tense times. Now, seeing him again, I had no idea.

Jack ran his palm back and forth across the arm of the chair, as if he were rediscovering it, making it his own again. "I was so happy when I first came here," he said, "Gina, you, the place itself, working to bring it back to life. I never felt so at home anywhere. When I was a kid, my mother would drag these guys back from the bar and bed them on the couch downstairs. I'd hear them come in and I'd try to stay asleep, though I was already awake, of course. I'd try counting or reciting passages from books, anything to drown out the sounds. I hated her. And I was so ashamed of myself for having a mother like that, for our ugly life, for not being able to fix it."

I thought how, as kids, we blame ourselves for everything that goes wrong, and then, as adults, we blame everyone else. The need is the same, though, some sense of control in a world where we have so little.

The crow appeared at the edge of the driveway again, extended its wings and rose to the barn roof, cawing raucously. Jack turned to it. "We had crows roosting in the shed, in Nebraska. They were so loud and aggressive. I loved that when I was a kid, as if they were screaming all the things I couldn't."

He got out of the chair, stood and ran his palms along his thighs, as he always did when he was nervous. He was wearing jeans and a plaid shirt I had given him. "God, I've missed you," he said.

"Why didn't you tell me about Bill Dean a long time ago, Jack? Why couldn't you have said . . .?"

A familiar flash of anger darted from his eyes. How many times had I watched as that silent resentment filled the space between us? He hadn't told me because he couldn't, just as I hadn't told him things that might have helped him understand me. The same thing, really, my story of Bill Dean.

He took a step toward me. "I'm sorry, Corey. It's an awful thing, lying to someone you love. And if you hide one thing, it's not such a big deal to hide something else. After a while, the only truth is that you hate yourself." He took another small step, as if he were struggling against the weight of that accumulation of deceptions. "There was nowhere to go, finally, but away from you. I took my mother's death as an opportunity to leave. But I realized, when we were burying her, that it was me I was trying to escape, not you."

Secrets, I thought, the seductive sense of possibility through control, the futile known in a sea of unknowables.

Jack ran his hands down his thighs again. "You know I'm not much for speeches," he said.

We both chuckled, because there he was—silent, laconic Jack—in the midst of one.

"I just came to tell you that I know I was wrong. But you can be sure of one thing, I will never lie to you again."

I held out my arms, and we hugged. Jack's shoulders quivered. He groaned and heaved, an erupting violence that broke off almost as abruptly as it had begun. We muttered words to each other that I don't recall exactly, about love, about truth. I took in the familiar smell of his hair, the reassuring heft of his shoulders, while behind him, a solid golden line of December sun spread across the pond we swam in and the field of wildflowers we planted, finally igniting the barn's stone foundation. "Look," I said.

Jack turned, and together we watched the barn kindle orange as the morning light climbed its wind-battered siding. "Remember the gay Noah's ark?" I asked him. He laughed as he wiped his cheek with his palm. I took his hand and we walked, two by two, into the kitchen.

Over coffee, Jack told me that he'd taken a sublet in the East Village, ironically not far from where Gina lives. And he'd taken a job tending bar. He'd even been to a couple of auditions and enrolled in an acting class. He sounded excited to be doing all the things he'd done before I met him. I pictured him serving up drinks and then running off to an audition the next day, and it seemed right. He said he needed to make a life of his own, and, of course, that was true.

There was a moment—I can't remember when it was, only that it was an instant in time—when I had realized that I loved Jack. Not the initial attraction, not the infatuation, not even that morning the blackbirds arrived, when I'd first used that word in my own mind. Something later, and far more profound and inexplicable, subtle yet baffling in its suddenness, though actually it had been building for a long time. Love had arrived quietly, taking me unawares. I'd been nearly forty, a long time to wait.

What would become of us now was anybody's guess. I felt certain, however, that we would know each other for a long time. Like Gina, I wasn't one to let go. And neither was Jack.

Together, that sunny November day, we loaded some of his things into his rental car. I poured coffee in a cup to go, and watched him head down the driveway, away from me and this house that had meant so much to him.

Since then, winter has arrived. Jack and I have had three "dates" in the city. My feelings for him, like the reliable rhythm of the seasons, have a life of their own, a momentous life, not in my control, and not at all predictable.

On our last date, a week ago, we saw a movie, and had a snack at Elephant and Castle in the West Village. Jack sat back in his chair afterward, thrusting those long, blue-jeaned legs into the empty space next to our table. "So," he said, "have you forgiven me?"

A snow-laced rain pelted the window overlooking Eleventh Street, and I watched the icy flakes glide down the warm glass and die away. "I've come to understand how it happened, I guess."

"But?"

"Look at my love life, Jack—Bill Dean, Gina, you."

"Three strikes and you're out?"

An ember of anger glowed in my gut. "I just keep wondering if I could trust you again."

Jack tapped the tines of his fork against the wooden table top in an irregular pattern, a coded message? I'm sorry. I love you. You hurt me, too. "Seems to me it's always a risk, loving somebody. You know you're going to get disappointed, or hurt or pissed off, right? The question is whether it's worth it."

"There are different kinds of disappointments."

Jack pushed the fork away. "This one's on me," he said, and I thought he meant the hurt, but he had signaled for the check.

I stand at the mailbox by the road now, returning from the grocery store in town, my truck idling alongside. I sort through Christmas cards, bills and some last-of-the-season advertising circulars. It's Thursday, the 22nd of December. My parents arrive from Florida tomorrow afternoon, for the holiday. Low, lumpy clouds obscure the late-afternoon sun, threatening snow. A white Christmas.

Jack is coming, too. So is Gina. Yes, they're in touch now, occasionally. They'll come up together on the train Saturday morning. I'll pick them up at the station. I smile at what my parents will think of the mix of characters. It'll be odd for all of us. I'm relying on the spirit of the holiday—love, forgiveness, good cheer—to get us through. My mother, her curiosity getting the better of her, will find an opportunity to ask me how things are going with Jack. But not with Gina. She'd never shown the least bit of jealousy toward Jack as she had with her ex daughter-in-law, with whom she had always maintained a cool reserve. I had confided in Gina when I was young, instead of her. Maybe that's the reason. Or perhaps it's only because Gina is a woman. Mothers of gay men are saved from having to share their sons with another woman. They just gain a son, and for my mother, who has always preferred the company of men, that was an obvious relief.

My father will leave any discussion of my personal life alone, though I vow to talk with both my parents before Gina and Jack arrive. I want to tell them what I know for certain—that I love Gina and I love Jack, each in very different ways, and that I can't really imagine my life without either one. Gina has been my haven for as long as I can remember—ironic, since she is so flighty and seemingly ungrounded, herself. And we have certainly had our thorny times, including a hiatus of almost twenty years. But we were best friends when we were thirteen years old, and we're best friends now. No matter how exasperated we might get with one another, that will never change.

And I have loved Jack for three and a half years now, an irrational, nonverbal link, oddly replete with disappointment, and yet passionate and more intense than any love I've ever known. I'll tell my parents that it's unclear what sort of relationship Jack and I can have now, that being together had hurt each of us in different ways, and only time would tell whether we will ever be a couple again. Perhaps this time apart is just a stage, or perhaps this is how things will be until one of us meets someone else, and we'll have some sort of ongoing friendship and our memories of being lovers.

This new feeling of flexibility gives me hope. I tell myself that relationships that can bend are less likely to break. I can't explain it any better, and even that seems positive—to admit there is something that means so much to me that I don't control and still haven't figured out.

I'll tell my parents as much of this as I can, after years of keeping them at bay. My long-standing anger toward them has not disappeared, but receded, helped along by knowing Jack, and perhaps even by my recent encounter with Bill Dean and some sense of resolution there, or perhaps just an enhanced awareness of my own fallibility and the relentless passage of time, itself. Right now, I'm eager to see them.

I set the mail on the seat next to me in the truck, taking a moment to look down the driveway toward the house, the surrounding oaks, bare and gangling, the fields dead-brown, the hulking stone walls gray as the snow-laden sky. The barn lists slightly, as it always has, its roof wavy yet solid. Two hundred years. How many husbands and wives and grandmothers and daughters and nephews and lovers had weathered some crisis here? I am only one more actor in a series of scenes in an ongoing drama, set on this property. The thought pleases me. I like to think of myself as a custodian, seeing the house through to its next occupation, filling its rooms with a quiet drama no more remarkable than those it has already witnessed and those yet to come.

Inside, I push up the thermostat and make a fire in the dining-room fireplace. I glance around at the unfinished mural and imagine describing its various scenes to my parents—what they all mean, their hidden significances. Or maybe Jack will do that. Yes, Jack's stories are more elaborate, more theatrical in their delivery, more fun. I will focus on getting the meal on the table. My mother will help. My dad will find something to fix. Gina will entertain us with descriptions of her escapades in New York. It's all going to work, I think, as the fire catches, producing a warm, yellow glow. This is going to be the best Christmas ever.

I pull an open bottle of Chardonnay out of the refrigerator and pour myself a glass, pick up this week's copy of The New Yorker and take it with me into the dining room. I can feel the heat radiating into the room already, smell the burning apple wood Jack and I cut last year. I sit, letting my legs stretch out before me, and begin thumbing through the magazine. But my gaze travels again to the mural. I imagine, one day, painting Bill Dean into that landscape. The right spot, the appropriate position and setting, remain to be determined. But he was there all along, of course, an invisible, lurking presence. There's no reason for him to be hidden anymore. He can't hurt us now. Painting him into the mural means acknowledging that he was the reason Jack and I met, that he will likely remain a friend to Jack, and that he is no longer a source of guilt or fear to me.

Does harm function just to set up the possibility of renewal? No doubt, some part of Bill Dean meant to be good. He had been a lost kid as much as I had. More, no doubt. And his interest and affection, in some ways, had helped me. Maybe he will even come here one day. It all seems possible, another of those unpredictable warps and zigzags in life that I have begun to accept, and even to appreciate, like the uneven and aging repairs made to this house over the last two hundred years. The forgiveness I feel toward Bill Dean right now is what I feel toward my parents, toward Gina and Jack, the realization that I have hurt them, too, that we are all victims and perpetrators, touching one another in at once painful and comforting ways.

I can't explain the warmth I feel any better than that. And explanations are a small part of a story, anyway. Truth is arrayed all around, haphazard and baffling, and often inexplicable.

I get up and go to the kitchen, where I start unpacking the groceries I bought for the weekend.

It's nearly Christmas, and my family is coming.

Biographical Note

Michael C. Quadland is a psychologist in private practice in New York City, where he has taught human sexuality to medical students and overseen research on AIDS prevention. He divides his time between New York City and Northwest Connecticut.